THE
FIGHTING
O'NEILS

THE FIGHTING O'NEILS

WILLIAM W. JOHNSTONE
AND J.A. JOHNSTONE

PINNACLE BOOKS
Kensington Publishing Corp.
www.kensingtonbooks.com

PINNACLE BOOKS are published by

Kensington Publishing Corp.
119 West 40th Street
New York, NY 10018

PUBLISHER'S NOTE
Following the death of William W. Johnstone, the Johnstone family is working with a carefully selected writer to organize and complete Mr. Johnstone's outlines and many unfinished manuscripts to create additional novels in all of his series like the Last Gunfighter, Mountain Man, and Eagles, among others. This novel was inspired by Mr. Johnstone's superb storytelling.

All Kensington titles, imprints, and distributed lines are available at special quantity discounts for bulk purchases for sales promotion, premiums, fund-raising, and educational or institutional use.

Special book excerpts or customized printings can also be created to fit specific needs. For details, write or phone the office of the Kensington Sales Manager: Kensington Publishing Corp., 119 West 40th Street, New York, NY 10018. Attn. Sales Department. Phone: 1-800-221-2647.

PINNACLE BOOKS, the Pinnacle logo, and the WWJ steer head logo are Reg. U.S Pat. & TM office.

First Printing: August 2022

ISBN-13: 978-0-7860-4900-4
ISBN-13: 978-0-7860-4901-1 (ebook)

10 9 8 7 6 5 4 3 2 1

Printed in the United States of America

Chapter 1

There was talk of a range war in the air, and the town of Mustang Flat, a long, single street of false-fronted buildings, lay still and silent under the blistering West Texas sun as though holding its breath. Fearful. Waiting to see what would happen next.

Only the Abe Patterson stage depot showed signs of life, two men and a woman sharing the meager shade of the ragged canvas awning that covered the timber porch.

The younger man, tall, lean and—according to the ladies at least, handsome—sported a large dragoon mustache, wore dusty range clothes and a walnut handled Colt holstered on his hip. By contrast, the big man with him looked smart in a city slicker ditto suit, tailor made to fit shoulders an axe handle wide, a bowler hat on his nail keg of a head. Unlike his younger brother Sean, Johnny O'Neil could lay no claim to good looks. Hard years as a bareknuckle prize fighter had battered and scarred his features, and he'd lost count of the times his nose had been broken. An opponent without mercy in the ring, he was nonetheless courteous to woman, kind to old people, and it was an inescapable fact of his existence that dogs and little children adored him.

Despite the shattering heat, the woman was cool and composed, a young, beautiful, blonde, dressed in the latest back-East fashion, her corseted green silk traveling dress complemented by a tiny, boat-shaped hat and veil and a huge bustle.

Sean put his hands on the girl's shoulders and kissed her affectionately. "Almost two years, Nora Ann. You've grown into quite a woman."

Pleased, the girl said, "A finishing school for young ladies and then travel will do that." She took Sean's hand and sighed dramatically. "Oh Sean, I've got so much to tell you about my travels. Boston is such a wonderful place, and New York at night is just too, too exciting for words."

Smiling, Sean laid his arm across his brother's shoulders. "I take it you met Johnny in Boston?"

"Unfortunately, not." Nora Ann shook her head, the golden waves of her hair moving like silk under the lacy froth of a hat. "We traveled on the same train, but in different carriages. It wasn't till we joined the Patterson stage in San Antonio that we became acquainted."

Recalling the jolting misery of the stage trip across seemingly endless miles of open grassland to Mustang Flat, Johnny groaned. "Believe me, it was a very fortunate meeting. It made bearable a journey that would otherwise have taxed the patience of Saint Patrick himself. In fact—" he winked at Sean—"I think this young lady's company would make a trip to hell bearable." The big man's face registered sudden shock and his hand flew to his mouth.

He turned quickly to Nora Ann. "Please forgive my use of that word, dear lady. It was thoughtlessly said."

The girl laughed. "There's no need to apologize, Mr. O'Neil. Believe me I've heard my father's hired hands say much worse. Besides, you've been a perfect gentleman and a most entertaining companion."

Johnny smiled and bowed graciously, but Nora Ann was already looking toward the southern end of town, in the direction of Oaktree, her father's ranch. "Speaking of Father, why isn't he here to meet me?"

"He'll arrive soon, I'm sure, Nora Ann," Sean said, his eyes suddenly hard. "I guess the colonel got held up for some reason."

"I suppose so," the girl sighed. "But really, this is quite unforgivable." There was a polite cough beside her, and she turned to see the little, pink-skinned man standing uncertainly in the middle of her piled trunks. "Oh, you poor man!" Nora Ann fussed over to him. "Have you been standing there all this time? I'm afraid I forgot all about you. How so very thoughtless of me."

The pink man gulped and stammered enthusiastically, "Oh, it's no problem, Miss Nora. I thought you might need some help with your luggage." The little man shot another worried glance at the huge and extremely heavy trunks scattered around his feet.

Nora Ann smiled prettily, knowing the effect that smile had on men. "Why, please don't bother, Mister . . . Mister . . ."

"Partridge, ma'am. Percival T. Partridge, but please call me Percival."

"Ah yes, quite . . . Mr. Partridge. But my father will

be here to meet me quite soon, and if not, I'm sure my stalwart O'Neils will give me all the assistance I require."

"Be assured of that, dear lady," Johnny said formally, ignoring his brother's sudden grin. He turned to Partridge. "I'm sure, sir, we can see the young lady safely home if need be."

Partridge, who had been dreading the job of lugging the trunks, and wasn't even sure he could lift them, beamed a grateful smile at the big man. He offered his hand to Nora Ann.

"I'll be in town for a few days. Perhaps—perhaps we can meet again?"

"Why of course, Mister . . ."

"Partridge, ma'am, but please . . . Percival. I'm a traveler, you know, in ladies' undergarm—I mean—in ladies' . . ."

"Yes, yes, of course, Mr. Partridge. I rather fancied that you are a traveling man of some sort."

"Ah yes, man and boy, since I took to the road when I was but sixteen. A Partridge by name and a partridge by nature, I always say."

Nora Ann smiled. "Do you always say that?"

"Yes, ma'am. Yes, I do, and so does my dear lady wife, ailing though she is."

"Ailing?" Nora Ann said, considering that.

"Oh, dear yes. Clara is a large lady who suffers from unstableness of the feet, and when she falls down, well, it's a chore for me to get her upright again."

"How, too, too awful for you," Nora Ann said.

The girl was obviously bored, her eyes searching the trail beyond the south end of town. She refocused briefly on the little man who searched her face with spaniel eyes.

"Come to my father's ranch one day, one day quite soon. We'll have coffee and chocolate cake."

Partridge allowed that it would be an inestimable pleasure, picked up his carpetbag and waved a friendly hand to the O'Neils.

Nora Ann watched the little man waddle off and her ripe mouth twisted in a scornful smile. "What a perfectly ridiculous little man. I'd rather have coffee with a hog. At least the hog would smell better."

Hearing her say that Sean felt a shock. Was this the Nora Ann Kincaid he'd known, the sweet, friendly girl who had left for the east just a year before? There had been a kindness, a gentleness in her then that seemed lost, replaced by something that Sean was not sure he liked.

If the girl saw the reproachful look on Sean's face, she chose to ignore it. She opened her white lace-edged parasol and irritably flipped it over her head. "Oh, where is Father? Really, this is dreadful!" Her eyes blazed green fire, her mouth set in a tight angry line.

"Like I said," Sean told her carefully, "the colonel is probably held up at Oaktree. In addition to everything else that's happening on the range, the Apaches are out. A score of them, all young bucks, quit the San Carlos a month ago and so far, they haven't been rounded up. Maybe they're causing him problems."

"Chiricahua?" Nora Ann said.

"Yes. At least that's what the army says."

The girl looked like she'd just tasted something sour. "Chiricahua. What a sorry bunch of filthy savages they are."

"They're not savages, Nora Ann." Sean felt a pang of

annoyance. "They don't have their women and children with them, so they're probably just hungry and hunting game."

The girl frowned. "Sean, I'd forgotten how naïve you can be at times. Even hunting Apaches carry war paint with them. I agree with my father that they're not to be trusted, not ever." She shook her beautiful head. "God knows, the colonel tangled with them often enough."

"The Chiricahua have never broken a treaty they made with white men," Sean said. "If an Apache gives you his word on a thing, you can trust him to never go back on it."

"Oh, for heaven's sake, and what white man in his right mind would even take a savage at his word?" Nora Ann said. "I know my father never did." She managed a wisp of a smile. "Sean, you're an intelligent man, but I swear, sometimes you don't make any sense."

Johnny looked quickly from his brother to the girl, not liking the sudden friction between them. He quickly jumped into the conversation. "May I suggest we walk to the hotel and take shelter in the waiting room? At least we'll be out of this hot sun."

Nora Ann smiled at the big man. "Why that's a perfectly capital idea, Mr. O'Neil. I think Sean needs to be out of the sunlight."

She watched as Johnny effortlessly hoisted up her two largest trunks and his own carpet bags. Then as Sean bent to pick up the others, she touched him on the shoulder. "Sean, when you were talking about the Apaches, you said, 'in addition to everything else.' What did you mean, 'everything else'?"

The tall man straightened. "You'll hear about it soon enough. We've had some trouble on the range, cattle shot, barns burned, and now a rancher has been killed. Murdered."

Nora Ann's hand flew to her mouth. "How awful, Sean. How perfectly awful. Who's doing these terrible things? Apaches?"

Sean hesitated before replying, then said without conviction, "We don't know who's doing it, but we're trying our best to find out. But I can guarantee it's not Apaches."

"Good. Then I hope you find the person responsible for all these awful things and bring him to justice."

Sean nodded. "Let's hope so, Nora Ann. Let's hope so." He picked up the girl's bags and followed his brother toward the Red Dust Inn.

The interior of the hotel was cool and shady after the hammering heat of the late summer sun, and the desk clerk was, of course, delighted to have Colonel Lance Kincaid's daughter wait there until her father arrived.

Nora Ann placed her parasol on the overstuffed sofa against the wall, then turned and put her arms around Sean's neck. "You can be so grim, Sean O'Neil. Are we still friends?"

The young man's face broke into a grin. "Of course, Nora Ann. We're still friends and we'll always be friends."

"That's wonderful to hear because I want you and your brother to join us for dinner tomorrow night. I've got so much to tell you about the east, Sean, the electric lamps on Broadway and Madison Square in New York that turn the night into day and the streetcars that run twenty-four hours a day. I swear the buildings are so high they scrape the sky."

Sean said something about not liking big cities, but Nora Ann spoke over him, shaking her head. "No, listen to me. Sean, you'd love the big eastern cities. The life, the noise, the fashionable people, the theaters, the restaurants, the . . . oh dear, just talking about it makes me quite breathless." The girl dropped her arms and turned to Johnny. "Now, I could tell you about Boston, but let Mr. O'Neil here do that . . . and besides"—she playfully nudged Sean in the ribs—"why did you never tell me your brother was a famous prizefighter?"

The girl laughed as Johnny made a polite reply about being famous only because he was soundly beaten twice over fifteen rounds by Gypsy Jem Mace, the great English heavyweight. Sean studied his brother's battered features and was suddenly glad that the big man's fighting days were over. His face was wide across the cheekbones, with a high Irish color, and the blue eyes were twinkling and kindly, but the nose had been broken beyond repair and the thin tissue above and under the eyes showed a tracery of cruel scars. Even the fine, intelligent forehead under the derby hat was scarred and knotted by healed tissue.

In his mind's eye, Sean caught a glimpse of the savage bareknuckle fights that had caused those scars. And he imagined his brother, battered and bleeding, pain and anger in his eyes, as the crowd roared for blood. He blinked once or twice, shutting out the image, and despite himself he shuddered. Slowly he became aware that Nora Ann was talking to him . . .

". . . so you will come, won't you, Sean? Oh please, say you will."

The young man turned to her, shook his head and smiled. "I'm sorry, Nora Ann, I missed what you said."

The girl frowned in pretended annoyance. "I swear, Sean O'Neil, you're trying my patience today. I said you will come for dinner tomorrow, won't you?"

"Well, to tell the truth, I don't know." Sean caught the puzzled look his brother threw him and ignored it. "Truth is, my ranch needs so much work. The corral . . ."

"Oh, nonsense. You'll be there at seven sharp, and that's final." The girl smiled her coy little smile again. "Besides, I do want to tell you much about my travels, about the east I mean. Oh, Sean, that's where I'm going to live one day, back east where life is so, well, just so wonderful. It's not like West Texas. Not like here. Not this sun-blasted wilderness of grass."

Again, Sean felt a pinprick of irritation. "You loved it here, Nora Ann, you loved the West. I don't understand it because that was only a year ago."

"Eighteen months." This time the girl's annoyance was real. "Oh Sean, don't be so pigheaded. What's the West but cattle and dust and flies and the smell of sweaty cowboys? Grow up, man, grow up like I've grown up."

"I'm sure we can talk about this at dinner tomorrow, Nora Ann." Johnny, his good-natured face concerned, tried to ease the tension in the air. "Perhaps we can educate my stubborn little brother on the civilized ways of Boston and all points east."

The two younger people still faced each other truculently, but slowly they relaxed, then smiled, then the tension dissolved into laughter. "I'm sorry, Sean," Nora Ann whispered. "I . . . I get carried away sometimes."

Sean pecked her on the cheek. "I guess we both do. Let's still be friends."

Nora Ann threw her arms around his neck. "Oh, yes, Sean, that more than anything else. We had something once, something clean and fresh and good. I . . . I don't want to lose it."

"Nor do I . . . but people change, I guess. Times change."

"You haven't changed."

"No, Nora Ann, I haven't changed."

Their eyes clashed, and finally the girl sighed and dropped her arms. "You're right, Sean, people change. And maybe . . . I don't know . . . maybe sometimes there's just no going back. I know everyone has a hard life out here and I appreciate that."

Sean smiled. "I reckon a couple of months from now you'll fall in love with Texas all over again and wonder why in God's name you ever left."

"That won't happen. I know why I left."

"Just give it time."

"No, I'll never get used to Texas again, not in a month, not in a twelvemonth, not in a hundred years."

"I guess I'm butting my head against a stone wall. This conversation is going nowhere."

"Yes, nowhere so long as you talk nonsense."

"All right, then let's call a truce," Sean said. "Tell me how you feel six months from now, and we'll go from there."

The girl shook her beautiful head. "Sean, you're

such a chucklehead. My mind is made up, and I won't change it."

"My guess is that you will. Just wait and see, Texas will work its magic on you."

"The East has already done that and there's no going back from it, and I don't want to speak of this any longer."

Nora Ann abruptly sat on the sofa and looked at the railroad clock on the depot wall. "Where can Father possibly have gotten to?" she said.

"I'm sure he's on his way, eager to reunite with his beautiful daughter," Johnny said and sat beside her. "As Sean told you, something probably held him up."

"I'll take a look outside. Maybe he's at the Patterson depot," Sean said.

His spurs chiming, he walked to the door and stepped out into the sunlight. Main Street was deserted except for a couple of horses standing hipshot outside the saloon and a black and white dog lifted a leg against a corner of the boot and saddle store. The sun had dropped lower in the sky, and the false-fronted hotel cast a rectangular shadow onto the dusty street. There was no sign of Colonel Kincaid. Sean wondered if the rancher would come to town in person or send his son, Billy. He secretly hoped the colonel would stay home. Sean didn't want a confrontation with the man. Not yet anyway, not until he got his ducks in a row and put his evidence together.

But the question of Colonel Kincaid's whereabouts was answered for him when he saw a buckboard appear around a bend in the trail from the direction of Oaktree. It was still too far to make out features, but the driver was a young towhead, and he recognized the outrider's paint horse as the mount of Dick Peterson, the colonel's ramrod.

Sean stepped back into the hotel. Nora Ann and Johnny were deep in talk about the finer points of Boston Brahmin society, but they stopped and turned when he entered.

The girl's face framed a question, and Sean nodded. "Buckboard coming. Looks like Dick Peterson riding guard and his young'un at the reins."

Nora Ann sighed deeply and rose from the sofa. "I suppose I was expecting too much of my father that he'd come to meet his daughter in person."

"Like I said . . ." Sean began.

"Yes, I know, he's a busy man." She turned and extended her hand to Johnny. "Thank you for your company, Mr. O'Neil. You made what would have been a tedious journey passing tolerable."

The big man bowed over her hand. "Believe me, ma'am, the pleasure was entirely mine."

"Now you won't forget dinner tomorrow night?" This to Sean.

Before he could reply, Johnny stepped in. "How could we ignore such a gracious invitation?"

Sean threw his brother an exasperated glance, then smiled his surrender. "We'll be there, Nora Ann. Seven sharp."

The girl's good humor was partly restored, and she smiled.

"We'll talk, Sean. We have so much to talk about, you and I."

A few minutes later the hotel door opened, and Peterson walked in with his son.

A tall, wide-shouldered man with a gun rep earned while he was a Texas Ranger, Peterson nodded briefly to Sean, then took off his hat and said, "Welcome home, Miss Nora Ann. The colonel sent me to bring you home to Oaktree." He smiled. "It's good to see you again."

The woman smiled in return and pointed to her luggage. "Load my baggage, Dick. I'll be out shortly. Be careful, the steamer is heavy."

The man beckoned to the boy and together they struggled outside with the luggage. The girl waited till they returned and took the remainder, then she turned to Sean. "Till tomorrow then."

Sean nodded. "Till tomorrow." Then as courtesy demanded, "I look forward to it."

Nora Ann tossed a dazzling smile to Johnny and then was gone in a soft rustle of silk, and her perfume lingered in the air long after the hotel doors had closed behind her.

Johnny waited for a while then gave a low whistle. "Now that's a beautiful woman, but a strong-willed one."

"Yes," his brother agreed, "she's all of that."

The big man gave a sly, sideways glance at Sean and went on in conversational tone, "Make a good wife for someone, some young feller who could break her to his saddle."

Sean slapped his brother on the back. "Nora Ann Kincaid will never let herself be broken to any man's saddle. Let's go, old matchmaker, we'll get a beer and talk."

"The best suggestion I've heard all day. But first"— the big man held Sean at arms' length—"let's take another look at you. Ah, Sean, my boy, you're still skinny as a rail, but as handsome as the devil himself."

The sentimental tears were again springing to the big man's eyes, and Sean, fearing another repetition of the depot scene, disengaged himself quickly. "Come on, brother, we've got talking to do."

Johnny scrubbed at his eyes and picked up his carpet-bags.

"Lead on, Sean, for it's myself who has questions in need of answers."

Chapter 2

The town was small, and could accommodate only one drinking establishment, the Crystal Palace. There was a Mexican cantina, tucked away behind the imposing bulk of the saloon, but white men seldom went there.

The Crystal Palace was the typical saloon of the frontier west. A narrow, false-fronted building, low ceilinged and floored in rough pine. A long, highly polished bar ran the full length of the room and the footrail, like the spittoons, were of gleaming brass. This late in the afternoon the lamps were lit, giving the place a warm, welcoming look. Behind the bar was the inevitable French mirror and steer horns. A notice attached to the mirror asked the question: *HAVE YOU WRITTEN TO MOTHER?* and informed the tardy that pen and paper could be had from the bartender for a nickel. A few gaming tables and some scattered chairs completed the furnishings, except for a small, raised stage guarded by a forlorn baby grand piano. A hand-colored daguerreotype of Robert E. Lee in a silver frame sat on a shelf behind the bar, and beside it, for reasons known only to the proprietor, a mourning photograph of scowling old Queen Vic.

When Johnny and Sean entered, the only other patrons were a couple of bored ranch hands playing brag for penny stakes and an ancient drunk, dozing over his whiskey glass at one of the tables.

The bartender, a lean, cadaverous man with black eyes and a yellowed goatee polished glasses before setting them on a shelf behind him.

"What'll it be, gents?" he asked.

The brothers ordered beer, took their foaming steins to a table near the door and sat down. The drunk continued to doze and the consumptive bartender went on polishing glasses, his fevered eyes blank and disinterested.

Johnny took a deep pull from his stein, wiped the foam from his top lip and said, "Busy place."

His brother smiled. "It gets busier later. But it won't really warm up till the drovers come in on Saturday." Sean's smile slipped and he added, "Of course with all the trouble brewing and the Chiricahua out, chances are they won't come in at all."

The big man nodded. "Okay, Sean, tell me what's going on here. Your letter said you needed help, and I heard what you said to Nora Ann Kincaid about the cattle being killed. Now there's murder done. What's happening, and how did you get involved?"

"I'll fill you in shortly," Sean said, "but first tell me about yourself. When did you retire?"

The big man stared at his beer on the table in front of him. "I quit the ring about seven, eight months ago. I woke up one morning, realized I was thirty-eight years old, and decided now was the time. In addition to which, I'd just taken a fearful bashing at the hands of a kid named

Beau Bowman, a man I could have whipped without breathing hard just a handful of years ago." Johnny sighed. "No, Sean, it was time to call a halt and go out gracefully before the few brains I have left were scrambled beyond all hope."

"Now what are you doing?"

"Why, what every self-respecting son of Ireland hopes to do one day—I bought myself a nice little tavern in Boston town to keep me in my old age."

"I'm glad, Johnny. Glad it's all over, with the fighting I mean."

The big man grinned. "It's all over. Boxing was good to me, but I'm done. Now, tell me about your troubles. Why did you send for me?"

"A refill first, then we'll talk."

"That first one went down fast, didn't it? Warm, but fairly good beer."

"I'm glad you like it. It's the only beer for miles around."

Sean walked to the bar. He was tall, a few inches over six feet. His body was narrow, but lean, hard, and enduring, the body of a horseman who's had all the lard melted out of him by long days in the saddle. His face was burned a deep brown, the corners of his eyes prematurely wrinkled by staring across great distances into bright skies. His hair was bleached blond by the sun, as was his fashionable sweeping cavalry mustache. He wore wide army suspenders over a faded blue shirt, canvas pants, good boots, and a wide-brimmed hat. High on his hip he carried a .45 caliber Colt with which he was fast and accurate, but he'd never drawn down on a man and had no gun rep. Withal, Sean O'Neil was tough, brave, and loyal to his friends, a typical product of his time and environment, and hidden deep within him his Irish blood had given him the soul of a poet.

The young rancher watched the consumptive bartender pull his beers. Without taking his eyes from the filling steins in his hand, the man said, "Show time on Saturday, Miss Corinda Mason all the way from Denver. She's in town already, got here sooner than she expected, I guess."

Sean was prepared to be friendly. "I've heard of her. One time I read in *The Texas Gazette* that a lawman by the name of Wyatt Earp in the Arizona Territory christened her the New York Nightingale, so I don't think she's from Denver. It's no matter, I won't be in town to see her."

"Wyatt Earp? Strange name. Wasn't he the ranny caused all the trouble in Tombstone that time? Seems folks still talk about it."

"I don't know," Sean said. "What kind of trouble?"

"The way I heard it, him and his brothers gunned a bunch of drovers in a street fight a year back. In them days they called Earp the Fighting Pimp, so I think it was a war about who'd run the local Tombstone whores."

"I can't say as I heard about that," Sean said. "Tombstone is a big silver-mining town, and I guess a lot goes on there."

The man pushed the beers across the counter. "Well, it's a pity about Miss Mason, you'll miss a good show." His smile was vaguely lecherous. "I hear she don't wear much and that she's a lady who knows how to fill out a corset."

"What brings a high-stepping filly like the New York Nightingale to a one-horse burg like Mustang Flat?"

"That I don't know. It's a mystery. But as near as I can

make out, she wrote a letter to Lucas Battles, he's the owner of the Crystal . . ."

"I know who he is," Sean said.

"Nice feller, Mr. Battles."

"You could say that."

"In the letter Miss Mason asked Mr. Battles if she could perform at the Crystal Palace to prepare for her new Western tour, and of course he said yes. Then she came in on the Patterson stage and went straight to her room at the hotel and she's been there ever since. I guess you could call her a mysterious woman."

Sean nodded his agreement. "I guess you could at that."

He carried the beers back to the table, watched Johnny sample his brew, then said, "All right, let me tell you how this range is in danger of being torn apart." Sean searched in his shirt pocket for the makings and was about to say more when the saloon's etched glass door slammed open, and three men walked inside.

The youngest of the trio was a stocky, freckled redhead dressed in dusty range clothes, but the two older men stood in marked contrast to their younger companion. They looked like prosperous city bankers in well-cut, high button suits of dark broadcloth. Both wore derby hats and sported gold watch chains as thick as a man's wrist. But above their full mustaches, their steel-hard gaze as they looked around the saloon gave the lie to their conservative appearance. Both men had piercing blue eyes, watchful and arrogant, and they moved with the relaxed, easy grace of natural athletes. One of them wore an ivory-handled Colt with confidence, as though he'd been born to it, the other had no gun showing, but the bulges in his coat suggested twin shoulder holsters. Sean realized instinctively that these were coldly dangerous men and probably for hire.

Johnny, born in Texas but new to the Frontier, did not recognize the men as typical examples of the up-and-coming draw fighter breed, and he nudged his brother with his elbow and said impatiently, "As you were saying, Sean?"

But the young rancher's eyes were on the men at the bar. His body was tense, pumping adrenaline already honing his reactions to a razor sharpness. Why was a pair of obviously prospering gunmen in a jerkwater town like Mustang Flat? Whatever the reason, it didn't bode well.

In the sudden quiet of the saloon the young redhead noisily demanded brandy. His two companions chose beer. The boy, who was obviously already very drunk, turned to one of the tall men beside him and asked in a conversational tone, but loud enough for Sean to hear, "What should a brother do to a man who's been seen trying to molest his sister?"

The tall man smiled but made no answer.

Sean moved his hand closer to his Colt.

"You're right first time!" the redhead snarled, his face vicious. "He takes a horsewhip to that man, then runs him the hell out of town."

The third man, the oldest of the three laughed loudly and punched the kid on the shoulder. "That's saying it like it is. You're a real charmer, Billy boy."

The redhead slapped the man's hand away. "I told you before, Lowery, don't call me a boy!"

For a split second something flashed in the eyes of the man named Lowery and Sean recognized it for what it was—an instant of anger. But, as soon as it appeared, it was gone. The man relaxed and smiled. "Sure, Billy, anything you say. No harm intended, no harm at all."

Billy Kincaid turned and leaned his back against the bar. His bloodshot eyes, truculent and full of fight. He met Sean's cool, steady gaze. "Is what I've heard about you and Nora Ann the truth, O'Neil?"

"I don't know. What have you heard?"

"Bad things. Maybe things low enough and dirty enough for me to kill a man."

"You've got a mind like a swamp, Billy. Nora Ann and I have been friends since she was just a slip of a girl."

The kid smiled. "You're a damned liar. Now think on this, O'Neil. Today might well be your last day on earth. How does that make you feel?" His smile twisted. "Scared?"

Sean rose slowly, the scrape of his chair very loud in the sudden quiet of the saloon. He was aware of Johnny getting up alongside him. The railroad clock on the wall ticked seconds into the silence like water from a leaky faucet. Sean sighed and said, "I don't want trouble with you, Billy. You're drunk. Go home and sleep it off."

The young redhead ignored that and motioned with his glass toward the men on either side of him. "I want you to meet a couple of friends of mine, O'Neil. This here"— the tall man on his right—"is Zachariah Elliot. This 'un here is John D. Lowery."

Sean saw a look of smug satisfaction settle on Billy's mean, schoolyard bully's face. The names were obviously meant to impress and intimidate, and with a lesser man than Sean O'Neil they might have. In common with most Texans who read a newspaper or listened to gun gossip, Sean knew about Zachariah Elliot. He was a hired shootist, a top professional who worked on either side of the law depending on who was paying the wages. He had killed at least seven men in as many gunfights, including the gambler Nairn St. John, a named fast-draw artist out of Wichita, Kansas, who'd gunned way more than his share. Zack Elliot was said to be a dangerous man in a fight, cool, deadly and quick as a striking rattler.

Sean had not heard of Lowery, but a gut feeling told him that this man would be the more dangerous of the two. Older than Elliot, Lowery was a watchful man who emitted the same cold threat as a saber blade. He had no weapons showing, but his coat was cut loose under the armpit suggesting a tailor who had compensated for the bulge of shoulder holsters.

Billy, Sean discounted. The young redhead was too far gone in drink to effectively use the pearl-handled Remington on his hip.

"Let it go, Billy," Sean said. "I've always treated your sister with respect, and you know it. You've never liked me, so it's between us, and keep Nora Ann out of it." He talked to Billy Kincaid, but his eyes were on the greater threat, the draw fighters who bookended him. A quick glance to his left told him that Johnny was breathing easy, relaxed, and watchful, and the sight of him brought the young rancher some comfort.

"You want to know what I heard?" Billy's speech was slurred, and he had trouble forming his words. "Why, I heard tell you was waiting for Nora Ann at the stage depot and then took her with you to the hotel. Everybody saw it, and I heard how you couldn't drag her off the goddam street fast enough."

"Billy, you're a piece of dirt and you were always a

piece of dirt and now on top of that you're a damned liar," Sean said.

A tense, uneasy silence filled the saloon. The bartender's labored breathing hissed in the silence.

Then Billy Kincaid's words dropped one by one, like rocks into a tin bucket. "I'm-going-to-kill-you-for-that-O'Neil."

It was that sudden, that shocking.

Billy grinned, knowing his father's hired guns would back his play. He was confident and eager and wanted to kill and watch a man he despised with a white-hot jealous hatred die with his bullet in him.

Sean watched the draw fighters put their beer glasses on the bar, then turn to face him. Both men were relaxed but ready, and Billy's hand was clawed over the handle of his gun. Sean's hand moved nearer his Colt. He would try to take Lowery first, then Elliot and lastly Billy. But even as he planned his move, he knew he'd never make it, not against three men, two of them professionals who'd been up this road many times. A few seconds ticked past after Billy smirked his challenge, but for Sean time had slowed to a snail's pace. He saw with unreal clarity the ashen-faced bartender move down the bar, away from the gun action. The old drunk was still asleep at the table, and the two cowboys had plastered themselves against the far wall, trying vainly to blend in with the furniture.

Unbidden, a thought came crowding into Sean's head. *I'm going to die here today*. And he prayed briefly for the courage to buy the farm with dignity. Then he heard a voice, hollow-sounding in the quiet of the room, say, "Anytime you're ready to try it, Billy." And he realized with sudden surprise that the voice was his own.

But it was Johnny O'Neil who opened the ball.

He exploded into action with surprising speed for so big a man, a sudden blur of movement as he crossed five feet of floor to where Billy Kincaid stood. The boy's gun was already in his hand as Johnny reached him, but the big prizefighter wrenched the Remington away and threw it into a corner. He grabbed the smaller man by the shirtfront and smashed a hard right into his mouth. Billy screamed, spurting blood, and Johnny backhanded him jarringly across the face, sending the young man's hat flying. Johnny O'Neil saw this arrogant, rich man's kid try to destroy his brother, and his anger made him pitiless. He slapped Billy very hard, back and forth and the kid's head bounced around like a rubber ball, scarlet fans of blood erupting over him. Then Johnny spun him around and kicked him hard in the rump. Billy sprawled across the saloon floor like a cartwheeling drunk and slammed into the door, smashing its fancy glass panel into a shower of shattered shards. He dropped onto his belly, his breath coming in sobbing, bubbling gasps and then lay silent and still.

Sean's gun was drawn, covering Elliot and Lowery, but neither man had made a move.

Then Lowery said, his amused eyes on Johnny, "Hell, big feller, did you punch Billy's ticket?"

Johnny O'Neil crossed the floor and then leaned over Billy's prostrate form. "He'll be all right," he said. "He'll be hurting and as weak as a kittlin' for a few days, but he'll survive." He stared at Lowery. "Better he lost a couple of teeth than getting plugged."

"You done spoiled his good looks," Elliot said.

"What good looks?" Johnny said. "He's a damned sewer rat and he looks like one."

"I think you could've taken him, O'Neil," Lowery said to Sean.

"Maybe."

"A few times I watched Billy shoot. He would've fanned his iron, a showboat play I told him never to use, but he did it anyway, sprayed bullets in every direction but at the peach can." Lowery shrugged. "Hey, but who knows? At five feet a man makes a big target."

Elliot sighed, relaxing. "Billy is a jackass. There's no doubt about that." Then, "Put the gun away, O'Neil." He turned, picked up his beer. "It's over. At least for now." He motioned with his mug toward Billy who was whimpering softly through smashed lips. "We draw guns for Colonel Kincaid, not his whelp."

Sean did not holster his weapon. Johnny, his Irish blood up, stared belligerently at the gunmen, snorting like an enraged bull. Sean smiled inwardly. He knew he would only have to say the word and Johnny would charge . . . even into the guns of Elliot and Lowery. It would take a lot of lead to stop such a man, and the damage he could inflict with those trained boxer's hands before he finally went down would be terrible.

Perhaps the draw fighters knew this, because they drained their glasses and Elliot rang a coin on the bar. He lifted the semiconscious Billy to his feet and Lowery picked up the kid's gun from the corner. Lowery knew Sean had his Colt pointed at him, so he lifted the Remington slowly and shoved it into his waistband.

As Elliot helped Billy to the door, Lowery smiled, showing remarkably white and well-cared-for teeth, a rarity on the frontier.

"Some other time, O'Neil," he said softly. "When the troubles come down, I'll be looking for you."

Johnny nodded. "I'll be where you can find me."

The tall gunman bowed with old Southern courtesy and walked to the door.

Suddenly Billy turned, pulling free of Elliot. His crazed eyes found Johnny and he snarled through, bloody broken lips. "Next time I see you, O'Neil, I'll kill you."

The big man's voice was very quiet, very controlled. "Next time you'll be welcome to try."

The saloon door banged shut behind the three men and Sean shoved his gun into the leather. "Now, how about another beer?" he heard Johnny say. "You can get on with your story, so recently and impolitely interrupted."

Sean smiled and joined his brother at the bar. The consumptive bartender poured a beer, then broke off when fits of violent coughing wracked him.

"You should do something about that, my lad," Johnny said.

When the man had recovered enough to gasp, "I intend to go somewhere more healthful for the lungs very soon. The Arizona Territory perhaps, maybe up Tombstone way. I hear the town has snap."

Johnny nodded. "A pleasant enough clime, if you don't mind scorpions and snakes and the like."

"We have those right here in Mustang Flat," the bartender said.

"Apaches, too, I'm told, but I've never paid much heed to the stories I've heard about them."

"And we have Apaches out from the San Carlos."

"I've had no contact with them," Johnny said.

"Apache, Kiowa, and Comanche, they're all brothers under the skin, and all mean as curly wolves."

Johnny smiled. "I hear the Arizona Territory is so dry the trees chase the dogs. Anybody ever tell you that?"

"I can't recollect that they ever did."

"You've led a sheltered life, huh?"

The bartender finished pouring the beers. He had all too obviously a cutting retort on the tip of his tongue, but the big man's recent violence made him swallow it.

Johnny looked round the saloon with a jaundiced eye and motioned to Sean. "Let's drink these outside," he said. "This damned place is getting on my nerves."

He and Sean walked out the door and into the cool evening. Blue shadows angled across the street and inked the corners of the buildings and the alleys between. A strong breeze, crisp with the promise of fall, sighed from the north, and Sean thought he could detect the scent of distant timber. A single scouting star glittered in the darkening sky, clearing the way for millions more.

The brothers sat on a bench outside the saloon. Johnny took a long, black cigar from his vest pocket, thumbed a match into flame and lighted it. He sighed with contentment, pushed his derby to the back of his head and without turning, said, "All right, Sean, now we can talk. Why did you send for me? What kind of trouble are you in?"

"I sent for you, Johnny, because I need someone I can rely on, someone who'll stand by me in a fight."

The big man nodded slowly. "You have that, Sean. I'll give you that anytime."

Sean stretched his long legs out in front of him, sipped his beer and said, "Things started to go sour about three months ago. I wrote you in the past telling you about the little spread I have just south of town. It isn't much, yet. I have a cabin, enough grass to run a few head, but it's a start. I figure a man's got to start somewhere, no matter how modest the beginning."

Johnny nodded his agreement. "You have someone working for you out there, Red or somebody, a name like that."

"Rusty Chang." Sean grinned. "He's Chinese and getting kind of old and tough to live with, but he's still one of the best hands with horses in the county and a first-rate grub wrangler."

"How is he with a gun?"

"He carries a Greener scattergun that's both wife and child to him."

Johnny said, "I knew a Chinaman once, worked in my corner, and like your friend he was the best at what he did, a crackerjack cut man. His name was Li Jie, but everybody called him Stitch." The big man shook his head. "I never cottoned to him much. You can never look at a Chinaman and know what he's thinking."

Sean grinned. "Rusty will tell you what he's thinking right quick."

"Uppity, huh?"

"That's about the size of it. Now, getting back to three months ago, and to shorten a long story, Colonel Lance Kincaid, Nora Ann's father, made me an offer, a very handsome one I might add, to sell out. I refused. Then I heard he'd made similar offers to the other small ranchers and farmers in the area. A few sold, glad to pack up and head off somewheres, but most refused, just like I did."

Johnny was squinting at the moon through his glass of beer.

"This Colonel Kincaid, he has the land hunger?"

"He's land hungry all right. He has a lot of cattle, good stock, Herefords, not longhorns. He recently got a government contract, and he needs more range to graze an expanded herd. The land he has won't support a huge number of cattle, so the colonel badly needs more grass."

"Seems to me, all he has to do is cut back on his herds. That way, he won't need the grass so bad."

Sean laughed. "I told you he has a government contract to supply beef to the army. This is the West, Johnny, not Boston. Colonel Kincaid, a man like that, he wants more land and more cattle because out here land and cattle are wealth and power. He wants that power for his own reasons, the state governorship maybe, maybe even the White House, or just to be the biggest auger in Texas. Who knows?"

Johnny said, "Well, I guess that's one way of looking at things."

"It's Kincaid's way."

"I'd like to meet that gent."

"You will, depend on it."

"So, after you refused the colonel's money, then what?"

"After the buyout offers were turned down, mysterious things started to happen. Cattle were found shot to death on the open range, barns burned at night, horses and mules found dead in their stalls. Then I figure some of the little guys started to fight back, because some of the colonel's cattle started to die—including a blood Hereford bull, shot in its pasture not a hundred yards from the Kincaid ranch house. And worse was to come."

Sean stopped and slowly and methodically began to build a smoke. Johnny watched the strong brown hands busy with the ceremony of paper and tobacco. With a trace of irritation in his voice, he said, "Okay, then what happened?"

The younger man grinned. "For a fighter, you sure don't show a deal of patience." Sean licked the paper closed, put the cigarette in his mouth, fired it, and went on, "Kincaid denied he had anything to do with what was happening. He blamed the killing of his bull on the small ranchers, and swore there was a conspiracy against him. Then, to make his point, he imported draw fighters. The two you bumped into today make top-gun wages."

"This draw fighter business is new. I never heard of such a thing before I left Texas. I recollect men fought duels of course, but getting the pistol out fast never entered their thinking. They stood ten yards apart, raised their shooting iron and cut loose. Usually, the loser got only an honorable wound and wasn't killed. At least, that's what I heard."

"A draw fighter shoots to kill, and most can draw and fire before the other feller clears leather. At close range, draw fighters like Lowery and Elliot are capable of raising a hundred different kinds of hell with a Colt's gun."

"Men to be avoided," Johnny said.

"Too late for that, brother."

Johnny smiled. "Seems like."

"Anyway, the colonel let it be known he would protect his herds and his range against all comers and shoot on sight anyone who tried to wrong him." Sean lit his cigarette and from behind a pall of blue smoke said, "Then a man was killed. He was a rancher by the name of Tom Rose whose spread borders on my own to the east. Tom had fought at Gettysburg and earned a medal, and he'd always been outspoken about the colonel, said the whole conspiracy business was just an excuse to import gunmen and drive us off the range. He reckoned Kincaid had set the whole thing up, the cattle killing and the burnings, even the slaughter of his own bull, so he'd have an excuse to move against us. Well, Rose was shot in the back one night near his home. He left a pregnant wife and three kids."

Johnny's broken face showed genuine concern. "That's bad, kids left without a father like that. But surely the law . . ."

"Man makes his own law in this country," Sean said. "Besides, Colonel Kincaid is the law. He has the power. There's a sheriff here in town, but he's lazy and fat and useless. In fact, that's why I'm right in the middle of this mess. I guess you could call me an acting, unpaid investigator for the small ranchers. After Tom Rose was murdered, they asked me to help find his killer."

"Why did you accept? Let them do their own investigating. There's a lot of them and only one of you."

"No, there's not a lot of them, ranchers, I mean," Sean said. "Like me they run a few hundred head and can only afford to hire hands when they need them for the gather and trail drive."

"How many ranchers?"

"North and west of Colonel Kincaid's range, maybe an even dozen and a few sodbusters trying to make a living growing corn and cotton on a few hardscrabble acres."

"Should be enough men, I reckon," Johnny said.

"It's not. I accepted because I knew I was the only one who could fill the job, and I don't say that boastfully.

The others are good men, stubbornly brave men, but they're not gunslingers. Me, I can handle a revolver as good as any and better than most."

"So, you're a qualified detective, huh? Like one of them Pinkertons we all hear about."

"I'm not much of a detective, but I figured I owed it to the others and myself to take the job. It's just something I have to do."

"You were always one hell of a man at the volunteering," Johnny said. "Remember that farm in Denton County where we grew up? We were just a couple of orphan kids being overworked for a bait of grub and a straw mattress in the attic, but even then, you were always volunteering, extra chores, painting the barn . . . chopping wood . . . milking the cow . . ." The big man shook his head in wonderment. "Always volunteering for something."

Sean smiled. "It was one way of staying out of an orphanage."

"The War Between the States ended all that after you volunteered for the army when you were but fifteen. Young for a soldier."

"I joined General Nathan Bedford Forrest's cavalry and after a few brushes with Yankee infantry I decided there wasn't much of a future in any more volunteering. I guess that's the only reason me and the general each ended the war one horse ahead."

"I remember that. You came back to the farm, man grown, riding a big black horse with three stripes on your arm. I was so proud of you that day."

"I don't know why. In the end, the Yankees beat us like a redheaded stepchild."

"I missed the war," Johnny said. "I should have been with you."

"You stood by John Link after he was all stove up from the rheumatisms and he and his missus were getting old. Link was a mean old cuss, but he needed you on the farm. Think on the bright side, Johnny, your cornmeal helped feed the Confederacy."

"And now you've been and gone and done it again."

"Done what?"

"Volunteered."

"Right, I've done it again."

"I hope you're not fighting another lost cause."

"Win or lose, times are desperate, so I'll take my chances. I need to know if Tom Rose was right. Is Colonel Lance Kincaid staging the whole thing as an excuse to move against every small ranch and farm in the valley? Deep in my gut I think he'll move and move soon and try to force us off the range."

"Including you?"

"Especially me. The way things are now, he knows I'm just about all that stands in his way."

"I guess that explains why his son acted the way he did in the saloon," Johnny said. "But how do you feel about Nora Ann? I'm no expert on the female gender, but it seems to me the way she looked at you in the hotel lobby suggested a lot more than just friendship."

Sean nodded, his face solemn. "I know, but Nora Ann has changed. She's not the same innocent, sweet tomboy she used to be. Or maybe it's just me that's changed, getting older and more critical. But we've known each other for a long time, and I know she has no real quarrel with me or any of the other ranchers, so I guess we can't blame her for what her father is or does. I reckon it may be that Nora Ann is the one person who can help us end this whole sorry business."

"Her father sent her east to grow up and learn the social graces, little brother, and that's what she's done. If you can accept the new Nora Ann is now a lady maybe things will work out better between you."

"Maybe so." Sean smiled and tipped his brother's hat over his eyes. "You're a born matchmaker, Johnny O'Neil. I really think you missed your calling."

The big man grinned, tilted his head toward the sky and watched a thick cloud smudge a thumbprint on the bright face of the moon. From the open window of the hotel, a sweet, clear woman's voice started to sing "The Minstrel Boy" and Johnny closed his eyes, humming along with her the ancient Irish melody.

"Ah, that must be Miss Corinda Mason, all the way from New York City or Denver, take your choice," Sean said, adding innocently, "I wonder what that barbaric song is she's singing?"

But Johnny would not be drawn. When the song ended, he wiped a sentimental tear from his eye and said, "All right, Sean, I'm here and I'm ready to help. So where do we go from here?"

"Our first job is to find evidence linking Kincaid to the Rose murder. Then we can take our case to the federal marshal, or even to the governor's office if need be. So far, we don't have a scrap of evidence linking the colonel to the murder or even the cattle killing and barn burning. We can't call in the U.S. Marshal until we have something concrete to give him. It's a big job, brother, and we'll have to do it together."

The big prizefighter smiled and shook his head. "You know, maybe I shouldn't try to hitch you up with Nora Ann Kincaid. Seems to me, she's hardly going to take kindly to the man who puts her father away, maybe for life, or even sees him hang."

"I guess that's a decision she'll have to make for herself when the time comes." Sean's handsome face seemed carved out of rock. "I know what I have to do, and there's no going back."

He stood, adjusted the gun belt on his hip. "I figure we might as well head on out to my place. I brought a horse for you, and we can pick him up at the livery stable."

"I've never been keen on horse riding."

"Don't worry, she's a nice little buckskin mare with a smooth gait, and she'll make a believer out of you."

Johnny stretched and yawned hugely. "Ah well, that sounds good to me. It's been a long and very trying day."

"You don't go to bed until you've tasted Rusty's cooking first," Sean said. "That's an experience every man should have at least once in his lifetime."

Johnny looked suspicious. "What kind of experience?"

"A good one. Rusty Chang is an excellent cook."

The young rancher picked up Johnny's carpet bag, and together they headed toward the livery stable. Suddenly Sean stopped, and Johnny slowed down beside him.

"You know, there's one thing that bothers me about this whole business," he said. "Colonel Kincaid spent a small fortune on that Hereford bull of his, had it shipped by steamer all the way from England. He was mighty proud of the animal, so why would he kill him? A man backed up by wealth and fast guns had no need to do that."

Johnny's battered face was puzzled. "You know, you

may have a point there. I don't know much about cattle, but I've heard men talk of Herefords and the like. To destroy an animal like that, a man would have to be crazy. He'd . . ."

A shot racketed, shattering the still night into a million jagged fragments. Sean heard his brother's sudden, sharp intake of breath. Then they were running, running toward the sound . . .

Chapter 3

"The shot came from near the saloon," Sean yelled as he ran, his brother's abandoned carpetbag lying in the street behind them. "I hope to God one of our ranchers didn't tangle with Billy Kincaid and his gunmen!"

Johnny, running beside him, saw moonlight gleam on the barrel of the blue Colt in his brother's hand.

A rank, narrow alleyway separated the saloon from a combination hardware and drug store. When the brothers arrived, there were already six or seven people gathered at the mouth of the alley, peering timidly into the gloom.

"Where's Sheriff Beason?" Sean asked.

A thin man, dressed in pants and a collarless shirt grunted, "Dunno. Sleeping off a drunk somewhere, I reckon."

Somewhere back in the darkness of the street a man hooted a laugh.

Sean, his Colt up and ready, touched his brother on the arm. "Let's go," he said.

The alley was foul, smelling of years of accumulated garbage, stale puke, and piss. The O'Neils advanced slowly, cautiously stepping through crowding darkness. Suddenly Johnny grabbed Sean's arms and whispered, "Over there."

A shapeless form, darker than its surroundings, huddled against the wall of the hardware store. The gloom in the alley was impenetrable, the darkness suffocating like an entity malevolent and alive. Johnny reached down and felt the arm of a man, already cold in death. His hand came away wet and sticky. Just then the moon pushed aside a black, silver-edged cloud and cold white light gleamed on the contorted face of the man, his features wearing his death agony like a grotesque mask. As far as Sean could tell, the back of his head had been blown away.

"My God," Johnny whispered, "it's Billy Kincaid."

"Looks like someone snuck behind him and shot him."

"Whoever it was, followed him into the alley or hid in the dark and waited for him."

"The alley leads to the Mexican end of town. Billy had a sweetheart there," Sean said.

Johnny shook his head. "Then she was the death of him."

"All right, all right, what's going on here?" The voice was the wheezy, petulant whine of a grossly overweight man who has just been wakened from sleep and wanted the town to know it.

"It's Billy Kincaid, Sheriff," Sean told him. "He's dead."

In the moonlight, the slack-jawed, big-bellied man gaped like a stranded fish. "Dead," he said. "Dead." He repeated the word like a death knell, disbelief in his voice. "Oh my God, oh my God . . . this is terrible . . . just terrible."

"Nothing back there," Johnny jerked a thumb toward the end of the alley. "Whoever did this is long gone."

"And who are you?" the lawman said.

"I'm Sean O'Neil's brother."

"Here to stay?"

"Visiting."

"Then I'll tell you when you can leave."

Johnny would've argued the point, but Sean said, "He'll keep in touch with you, Sheriff."

"See he does," Beason said. "As of now, he's a suspect and so are you."

"Every last person in town is a suspect," Sean said.

"I know, but some are more suspected than others." He tapped on his nose with a forefinger. "I can smell out murderers, O'Neil. Don't forget that."

Beyond the alley, there was a rectangle of open ground, then the darkened cantina surrounded by a jumble of tents and tarpaper shacks. Those were the homes of the Mexican laborers who found occasional work on the surrounding farms and ranches.

"Cantina's closed so we figure the murderer had a horse waiting back there knowing it wouldn't be seen," Sean said. "We'll never catch him now, not in the dark."

"See any boot tracks or anything back there," the sheriff asked.

Sean shook his head. "Who am I? Dan'l Boone? Go look for yourself."

Bob Beason worked hard to regain his composure. He tried to inject a note of authority in his voice as he turned to Sean. "Sorry, O'Neil, you'd better come back to my office. Reckon you've got some questions to answer."

"What about Billy?" the young rancher asked. "You going to let him lie there?"

The sheriff's reply was stillborn when Clem Milk, a fat, jolly-faced man who didn't look like an undertaker, but was, plucked at his sleeve and said, "I heard the shot. Business for me, Sheriff?"

"I'm afraid so, Clem. It's young Billy Kincaid. Half his head blowed away."

The undertaker bent over the body, straightened up and clucked and tutted like a fussy chicken in a hen house. "Too bad, and him so young. As I said to Mrs. Milk just the other day, wealth and influence are no guards against the angel of death. Ah, yes, his dread shadow falls on all and . . ."

The sheriff cut short Clem's soliloquy, calling to the gaping bystanders, "A couple of you men, lend a hand here."

"Take him to the mortician's office. I'll attend to him," Milk said. He looked at Beason. "Bill to the city or to Colonel Kincaid?"

"Go to hell," the lawman said, scowling.

"Then it's the colonel," Milk said. He sniffed. "At least he'll pay me."

As Billy Kincaid's body was carried away, Sean and Johnny walked with the sheriff back to his office.

Sheriff Beason settled his huge bulk into the swivel chair behind his desk. He grunted uncomfortably, unbuckled his gun belt, pulled it free of his massive hips, and threw it into a corner. The .45 in its cracked leather clunked loudly in the tiny office.

"Hate that thing," he muttered. "Two and a half pounds of iron, and the only way I can hit something with it is if'n I throw it."

"What's on your mind, Sheriff," Sean said. "I didn't kill Billy Kincaid if that's what you're thinking."

"You don't know what I'm thinking," Beason said.

"You're right, I don't."

"I'm trying to understand what's happening here. Why was Billy Kincaid murdered?"

"Probably because of his father," Sean said. "There are folks who think the colonel is trying to start an all-out range war."

"Range war. Two words I hate. Folks die, the range is laid waste and a lawman stuck in the middle of the feuding parties gets shot. I don't want that to happen here."

The fat man opened a drawer in his desk and produced a pint of cheap whiskey. "Anyone care to join me?" Seeing no response, he poured three fingers into a cracked and dirty glass. "Then you won't mind if I help myself."

He tossed down his drink, poured another and studied Sean.

"I'm old, and I'm slow, and I'm fat, and I drink too much. But I still got a brain, and I can think. I heard this man"—he nodded in Johnny's direction—"got in a fight with Billy Kincaid in the saloon tonight."

"You have your ear to the ground," Sean said. "Billy drew down on me, but my brother stopped him from pulling the trigger."

"A couple of punchers stopped by and told me all about it. They say Billy lost teeth."

"I slapped him around some to teach him manners," Johnny said. "I had no reason, or desire, to want him dead."

"Could be, could be," Beason smiled. "What's your name, anyway? Sean here didn't think to introduce us proper."

"Johnny. Johnny O'Neil."

A glimmer of recognition appeared in the sheriff's dull brown eyes. "I guess a man with half an eye could tell you're a pugilist." A light went on in the lawman's face. "Wait a minute . . . wait a minute . . . could you be Boston Johnny O'Neil, the feller who beat that fancy Englishman a few years back, the one they was all toutin' as the greatest bare-knuckle fighter of all time? Let me see . . . let me see . . . what was his name . . . Lord somebody or other . . ."

"Lord Jim James," Johnny supplied, bowing ironically from the waist. "I had the honor of beating that aristocratic gentleman over twenty-one rounds in Philadelphia in the fall of seventy-two. My, he was game, and he could box, and he was a true gentleman. We got quite drunk together later, after our faces could be seen again in polite society."

Beason yelped delightedly. "Yes, I knew it was you! I'm honored to make your acquaintance, sir." He took Johnny's hand in his own pudgy paw and shook it heartily. "Now tell me, what brings you West? Not a prizefight, surely. I doubt if anyone around these parts would stand up to you for long."

Out of the corner of his eye, Johnny caught the warning

glance his brother threw him, and said easily, "Just came to visit, Sheriff. It's been a long time for my brother Sean and me. I'm sure you understand."

Beason nodded, smiling. "You're a very pleasant man, Mr. O'Neil, a cordial man. In fact, sir, you're gold dust. It's nice to be nice, I always say. Don't cost a man one thin dime to be nice."

"If you really want to be nice," Sean interrupted, "ask your questions and let us get out of here, Beason."

"Very well." Now the sheriff was firm and all business, a different man from the wobbling jelly he'd been in the alley. "You're here because the only suspects I have with any kind of motive are you and Mr. O'Neil, here. My sources tell me Billy Kincaid told you to stop molesting his sister . . ."

"That's enough, Sheriff," Sean said, his voice quiet but edged with a warning.

The fat man fluttered a placating hand in the air. "Repeating what I heard, Sean, only repeating what I heard."

"Then you heard wrong."

"Maybe so, maybe so. But you did have an argument with young Billy over his sister, and your brother did beat him up, quite badly from all accounts. And you do have a motive. I mean your feud with Colonel Kincaid, an' all."

Sean opened his mouth to speak, but Beason held up a hand to stop him. "Let me finish. I know all about the cattle killings and arson that's been going on around here. And now Tom Rose lies cold in the grave, and his poor widow is prostrate with grief and her young'uns hardly half-growed. I know the ranchers hold Lance Kincaid responsible and have appointed you to investigate him—

even though that's a job for the law. Could be you decided to take things into your own hands tonight and cut off a promising branch of the Kincaid family tree, so to speak. To be short, I mean you gunned down your enemy's son, blowed his brains out."

"Sheriff!" This time Johnny's voice was angry. "You know that's a load of horse dung. Sean didn't kill Billy Kincaid. We were clear to the livery stable when we heard the shot. When we arrived, the youngster was already dead. We were nowhere near the alley when he was killed."

"That's what you say, Mr. O'Neil. Pardon me for doubting you, but I have a job to do. You understand?"

"I understand that you don't have a shred of evidence against Sean and me."

The sheriff stared over his steepled fingers, as wise as an overweight owl. "Now, here's how I see it, the crux of the matter you might say. Now I ask you a question . . . could you or your brother have shot Billy, ran out the rear of the alley, doubled around the saloon and reappeared at the front—after the crowd had gathered? Answer please, honest and true."

Sean sighed. "Beason, I've never pulled this gun without it was for a good reason and then only to kill a gray wolf or a cougar skulking around my herd. But right now is a good enough reason to draw it again." He slipped his Colt out of the holster and offered it to the sheriff. "Smell it, Beason. It hasn't been fired."

The sheriff waved the revolver away. "Alas, you could have used another weapon and got rid of it after the killing. You had time, and there's plenty of places in this burg to hide a gun. Look at my brow, all wrinkled up, and that's because I'm thinking here, O'Neil, piece by piece putting my case together."

"Beason, you're an obstinate man," Sean said.

"Obstinate, that's the ticket. They say Bob Beason is so pigheaded he wouldn't move camp out of the way of a prairie fire. But when there's evil abroad in the dead of night, it pays a lawman to be obstinate, obstinate and vigilant. And if you think otherwise, you're singing off the wrong song sheet."

Sean tried to hold onto his always uncertain temper, and as evenly as he could, he said, "The question is, does Lance Kincaid have you in his pocket? Is that why you're trying to pin his son's murder on me, his worst enemy?"

"Ah, a good question, a crackerjack question. Am I crooked and open to any bribe? And the answer is yes, crooked as the devil's backbone, but not recently and only when times are hard."

"I'll take your word for that," Sean said.

"Please do, and thank you, thank you kindly. But I must say that you're very blunt in your dealings with people. You use a battering ram instead of a kind word."

"Then I'll be blunt again. How well do you know Colonel Kincaid?"

"How well? I don't really know."

"Why don't you know?"

"Why? I don't know why I don't know."

"That seems hard to believe."

"We don't run in the same social circles."

"Kincaid is an important man. Seems to me he'd want the town sheriff in his pocket."

"He's rich, very rich."

"What's that got to do with you not knowing him?"

"Wealthy, important men don't invite a forty-a-month hick lawman for cake and ice cream."

"How well did you know Billy Kincaid?"

"He was a troublemaker and a rich man's son. That's all I know."

"Ever have a run-in with him?"

"About a six-month ago he beat up a whore, a tall lass by the name of High Timber Hattie Wells. She worked out of the Crystal Palace, mostly Friday and Saturday nights when the punchers come in."

"Did you arrest him?"

"I put him in the cell overnight, but next day Hattie dropped all charges, said she got drunk and fell over and that's why she got all bruised up. Afterwards I was told the colonel paid her a hundred dollars to keep her mouth shut." *

"All right, Sheriff," Sean said, "if you think we killed Billy Kincaid, why don't you put the manacles on us?"

"O'Neil, you're a questioning man," Beason said. "I'm supposed to be the one asking the questions."

"And I'm the one looking for answers," Sean said.

"Got nothing to hold you on. No evidence, and the law needs evidence. I got a hunch, but I can't hold a man on a hunch. Hell, maybe it was the greasers. They have a cantina behind the saloon and no love for Billy and his bully boys. Every Friday and Saturday night they lock away their wives and daughters."

---

*Hattie Wells later quit the profession and moved to Philadelphia where she became an active Suffragette. She never married and died in 1920 of breast cancer, the year the Nineteenth Amendment was ratified.

"Mexicans didn't shoot Billy. I know that and so do you," Sean said.

Beason shook his head. "Don't tell me what I know or don't know. I know what I know and I know what I think." He waved a hand in the direction of the door. "You two are free to go. In the meantime, be friendly, keep in touch, come and see me now and then, bring cookies." Beason sighed. "There's been too much happening recently that I don't like, and I reckon this night's work is part of it. Depend on it, I'll find out what's going on around here and stamp it out."

Sean stepped to the door and hesitated, his hand on the handle. "So will I find out, Sheriff. I plan to get to the bottom of this, and if it's all on Kincaid I'll nail his hide to the wall."

Beason wheezed as he shifted his bulk in the chair. "Maybe you killed young Billy and maybe you didn't," he said, "but I'm giving you fair warning, O'Neil, steer well clear of this. It's now the law's business, not yours."

With some difficulty he rose to his feet and said, "Before you leave, Mr. O'Neil, let me shake your hand again, your right hand, the hand that shook the world."

Johnny, against his better judgment, stuck out his hand and Beason took it in his great paw, pumped, and said, "It's been a real honor. It is my sincere, no, my whole-hearted hope, that I don't have to hang you."

"That makes two of us," Johnny said.

As the door closed behind the O'Neil brothers, the fat man sighed. He waddled to the corner and picked up his gun belt. Beason returned to his desk and for the first time in years began to take his Colt apart for cleaning.

He poured himself a drink, tasted it, then intoned like a witch over a cauldron, "There's trouble brewing . . . bad trouble . . . it's in the air like electricity during a thunderstorm . . . old Bob Beason, he can smell her . . . strong and rank, not subtle like the scent of a pretty woman . . ."

The fat man sighed, shook the pretty woman image out of his head, and busied himself with the Colt. The clock on the office wall chimed eight times.

Chapter 4

Beason's office had been hot and muggy, full of the acrid sweat stink of the man himself. Once out in the cool night, Sean and Johnny gratefully breathed the pure, dustless air.

"What do you think, Sean?" Johnny asked. The moon was high in the sky, round as a silver coin, and the town was silent, cowed by the earlier gunfire. Small rectangles of dim light revealed the windows of scattered cabins, one or two adobe, the rest timber or tarpaper, the abodes of the citizens of Mustang Flat.

"I don't know what to think. All I know for sure is neither you nor I killed Billy Kincaid."

"All right, so we didn't kill him. The question is, who did?"

"The obvious answer is that one of the small ranchers or farmers got tired of being pushed around by Kincaid, took the law into his own hands, and laid for Billy in the alley. That's the obvious answer—maybe way too obvious."

Johnny pulled on his ear, thinking, and then said, "One thing for sure, Kincaid didn't order the death of his own son, but it certainly gives him the excuse he's been looking for. Who's going to blame him for getting rid of the nest of rattlesnakes that murdered his boy?"

"No one, I guess," Sean said. "But it still doesn't add up. There's something wrong, something I can't put my finger on, and it troubles me."

"But you said it yourself. The colonel's looking for an excuse."

"That's just it," Sean said. "Kincaid doesn't need an excuse. He has power, influence in the governor's office, maybe even in Washington. He doesn't have to justify his actions to anyone, maybe not even to himself. If he wanted to move against the rest of the range, his hired guns could do it now, today, this very minute. He knows there's nothing to stop him, and that includes the law. So why wait for an excuse? Who's he trying to justify his actions to unless it's his Maker?"

"Even from the little I've heard of the man, I doubt that," Johnny said. "He doesn't seem the God-fearing type. How about Nora Ann? Maybe she's stopping him."

"It's possible," Sean said, thinking aloud. "He's always doted on Nora Ann, even though he used to say his empire needed sons and grandsons. But when the girl's mother died about three years ago, Kincaid sent Nora Ann off to finishing school in Boston. If he wanted to spare her feelings, he could have made his move then, while she was gone." The young rancher sighed and rubbed the back of his neck. "No, he's not trying to justify his actions to Nora Ann. Maybe he's simply unwilling to risk an all-out range war. Could be he's trying to wear us down, bit by bit, until we're all glad to sell out and head somewhere a sight more peaceful. I guess that's as good an answer as any, but it still doesn't explain the Hereford bull shot dead in its pasture on the Kincaid ranch in the middle of the day. That troubles me."

"I reckon somebody on your side shot the beast?"

"None of the ranchers l know would keep a thing like that a secret. They're not boasting men, but they'd want Kincaid to realize that the shooting of his prize bull was a warning he should heed."

"They might keep quiet, if they wanted to go on living," Johnny said.

"That wouldn't even enter into their thinking. The timid ones all left in a hurry, and the men who stayed the course are tough. Most of them fought in the war. They're the ornery kind who cut their teeth on a rifle barrel and won't be railroaded." Sean's eyes were suddenly bleak. "If I can find the evidence to set all this on Kincaid's doorstep, I'll save a lot of good men's lives."

"Then, like I said, Kincaid shot the damn animal himself," Johnny said. "It's got to be the answer."

"He was right proud of that bull."

"Yes, as you've said."

"Proud enough that he wrote to New York and had *The Century Magazine* do an article on his bull, all about how it would help improve America's cattle herds." Sean turned his head, his eyes lost in shadow under the brim of his hat. "Do you know why he named the bull Wahkan?"

"No, but I'm pretty sure you'll tell me."

"It's a Sioux word that means sacred," Sean said. "Apparently Kincaid considered the Hereford some kind of spirit animal."

"So, then he goes and puts a bullet into its skull."

"Doesn't seem likely, does it?"

"Not to me."

"Nor me."

Johnny settled his derby firmly on his head, slanting it rakishly over one eye. "All right, little brother, where do we go from here?"

"We'll pick up your bag off the street and then head back to the saloon. Someone may have seen or heard something that could give us a clue to the killer. If it was one of my ranchers, I'd like to take the man to the law before Kincaid gets to him."

The saloon was still quiet. The cowboys had gone and only the ancient drunk still sat at his table, arguing with himself over an empty glass. The cadaverous bartender stood behind the bar polishing his inevitable glass.

"Evening again, gents," the man said. "What will it be this time?"

"Just some information," Sean replied. "I guess you've heard about Billy Kincaid being shot outside tonight."

"I heard."

"Did you see or hear anything, anything at all, that might give us a clue to the murderer?"

"Thought that was a job for the sheriff," the bartender said. Johnny leaned across the bar and gave him a hard look, and the skinny man added quickly, "Heard the shot, is all. Didn't think nothing of it. Hear shots all the time in this town. Them crazy greasers is always killing each other."

After a few more questions, but no answers, Sean and Johnny left.

Beason met them outside the saloon. "You boys still around?"

"Just leaving for home," Sean answered.

The sheriff made to walk past them into the bar, but

the young rancher held out a hand to stop him. "When did Lowery and Elliot leave Mustang Flat tonight?"

"I know what you're getting at, O'Neil, but they left a while back, well before the shooting. I've just sent a rider out to Oaktree to tell the colonel what happened. Maybe you boys shouldn't be around when he comes in."

Sean ignored that. "How come Billy didn't leave with his father's gunnies? He was beat up pretty bad."

Beason said, "Billy was mixed up with some little shantytown Mex girl, and I guess he wanted her to take care of him before he left."

"You know, Beason, you're full of guesses and no facts. Have you spoken to the girl?" Sean said.

"Not yet, but I will."

"Who is she?"

"Maria somebody or other, lives with her pa." Beason looked thoughtful. "Hell, maybe she shot Billy boy. Lovers' quarrel and all that."

"As a general rule, quarreling lovers don't shoot each other."

"Maybe in other towns. But that don't apply in Mustang Flat. Mexicans can be fiery folks and lose all self-control. You know how many I've hung since I became sheriff here?" He held up a pudgy hand and spread his fingers. "That number."

"You're a sweetheart, Beason," Sean said, his jaw flexing.

"Just doing my job."

"When Kincaid and his riders come in, don't tell him about the Mexican girl. He might shoot her out of spite."

"Don't tell me how to do my work, O'Neil. I'll handle the colonel in my own way."

"Or you won't handle him at all. I reckon you'll just lie down and roll over while he goes on a manhunt and destroys the range. Billy Kincaid was a piece of dirt."

"Good enough reason to kill a man, huh?" Beason said.

"Yeah, it is," Sean said, his gaze clashing with Beason's.

"I'll keep that in mind," the sheriff said.

"Let's go home, brother," Johnny said. "I'm tired and I'm hungry and I've had enough of Mustang Flat for one night. Here, let me take that bag."

Bob Beason, huge-gutted in the light of the saloon, watched them leave. "Keep in touch, Sean," he called. "You keep in touch, boy, you hear?" He smiled to himself as he bellied through the saloon door and into the sights and sounds and smells he knew so well and had come to love.

Chapter 5

Corinda Mason sat up in her narrow bed reading Jules Verne's latest novel *Around the World in Eighty Days* and smiled. Like herself, Phileas Fogg was a great traveler, though she conceded, not nearly as lethal. Fogg, to his joy, had just discovered that he had gained a day because he had constantly traveled eastward when she heard a gunshot. It seemed to have come from the direction of the saloon or the Patterson stage depot. Normally, she would've dismissed the firing as a reveler letting off steam or yet another murder in Little Mexico, as the owner of the Crystal Palace called it.

But, a careful lady, the shot disturbed Corinda. She had two contracts, one with Lucas Battles to sing in his dive, and another that was much more lucrative.

A dead cowboy . . . a dead Mexican . . . who cared? It was not of her concern.

But it was, and she knew it.

A few pages left. Did Mr. Fogg get his twenty-thousand pounds? She put the book down. She'd find out later.

Men's voices were loud in the street as Corinda Mason

threw a red silk robe over her nightdress, slipped her .44 Bulldog into a pocket, and stepped into the hallway. Two guttering wall lamps provided shadowy light as she made her way to the stairs. The night desk clerk, a sallow-faced youth with black hair parted in the middle and a small, trimmed mustache, shifted uncomfortably in his chair, his eyes fixed on the woman's unfettered breasts under the thin silk of her robe.

"Can I help you?" he said, words thick in his throat.

"Yes, I heard a shot . . ."

The clerk rose to his feet, his hands butterflying in front of him. "Please don't be alarmed, Miss Mason."

"I am of a somewhat timid nature," Corinda said, trying to look scared.

"I was just told that a man was killed, shot dead in the alley next to the Crystal Palace."

The woman's fingertips flew to the bottom of her throat. "Oh, how perfectly too awful."

"The killer is still at large, but you have nothing to fear, Miss Corinda." The clerk produced a small caliber, single-shot derringer from his coat pocket. "I have this, and I'll be standing guard all night."

"How positively gallant of you, Mister . . ."

"Green. Hadley Green."

"May I call you Hadley?"

"Yes, please do."

"Hadley, who was the unfortunate gentleman who was killed?"

"It's terrible, Miss Mason. I've no wish to frighten you."

"You're my protector, Hadley. Now I feel safe with you on the lookout."

"Then it was young Billy Kincaid. The rancher Colonel Kincaid's only son and heir."

The news hit Corinda like a blow. "Are you sure?" she said.

"Oh, dear lady, I'm sure. And I may have spoken out of turn. Was he a friend of yours?"

"No, he wasn't . . . but it's always such a shock when a young man dies so violently."

"You're very pale, Miss Mason. Perhaps you should lie down. May I assist you to your room?"

"No, I'll be fine. Good night to you . . . ah . . . Hadley."

"If you need anything . . . anything at all . . ."

"Yes. I'll let you know."

"Will you still sing at the Crystal Palace tomorrow, Miss Mason?"

"After what's happened, I doubt it."

"What a pity."

"Yes, it is . . . a real pity."

Corinda Mason returned to her room and laid her revolver on the table by the window. Beautiful though it was, a masterpiece of ivory and steel, she had no affection for the British Bulldog. It was a tool, no more than that, an instrument she needed for her line of work. In the past it had served her well. To date, she'd assassinated twelve men and one woman with the piece, but now her latest mark had gone and got himself killed. Damned fool!

Corinda looked out of the window. There were still men in the street. The murder of a white man always drew a crowd, especially if he was young and rich.

But who gunned him?

Probably some drunken cowboy during a fight over a two-dollar-a-trick whore.

Her eyes hard, Corinda sang to herself in a whisper . . .

Oh, where have you been all the day, Billy Boy,
*   Billy Boy?*
Oh, where have you been all the day charming
*   Billy?*
I've been to seek a wife, she's the joy of my whole
*   life*
But she's a young thing and cannot leave her
*   mother.*

Then, a bad taste in her mouth, "You son of a bitch, Billy Boy, you may have cost me five hundred dollars and expenses."

Corinda returned to her bed, plumped up her pillow and finished Mr. Verne's book. Phileas Fogg got the money and the girl, so it all ended happily.

But how would it end for Corinda Mason? Would her client still honor the contract now that some other man had triggered Billy Kincaid?

Her voice had always been a cover for her killings. Her shady theatrical agents in Houston, Greenlee & Greenlee, who then had offices all over the western states, arranged both singing and assassination venues so that they coincided. Before she'd landed in this west Texas hellhole, she'd been contracted to sing at the Birdcage Theater in Tombstone in the Arizona Territory. The mark was a gambling pimp named Wyatt Earp who attended the

Birdcage regularly. But two nights after she arrived, her client, a rancher named Ike Clanton, changed the target to Earp's brother Morgan. Corinda made the kill while the man played pool in the Campbell & Hatch Billiard Parlor. It had been a difficult shot, through the top pane of a four-paned door, the bottom two painted black. But at a range of ten feet the British Bulldog shot true, and her bullet shattered Morgan's spine, and he died shortly after. Like the Crystal Palace, the billiard parlor adjoined an alley and Corinda, dressed all in black, vanished into the darkness. She left Tombstone the next day after a delighted Clanton paid her fee in gold double eagles.*

Would her present client be as generous?

Corinda Mason did not kill for pleasure or out of any petty emotion. Murder was a business, cold, impersonal, its opportunities to be seized only when the odds of success had been meticulously calculated. It wasn't a game.

If her client didn't pay, she'd take the loss.

But it hurt.

*It's unlikely that Ike Clanton was aware of the services provided by the Greenlee brothers. But the more sophisticated Cochise County Sheriff, Johnny Behan, Wyatt Earp's mortal enemy, no doubt did, and whispered this information into Ike's willing ear.

Chapter 6

Sean and Johnny O'Neil were on open ground, about twenty-five yards from the door of the livery stable, when a sudden, muted scratching from the left corner of the wood-frame building stopped them in their tracks.

Sean drew his Colt, hammer back, and leveled it at the shadowed corner. "You better come out of there slow, with your hands in sight, or you're a dead man."

The scratching stopped, and there was silence. A long enough silence for Johnny to whisper, "Don't know about you, but I feel kinda naked out here in the open."

"Don't shoot, O'Neil, don't shoot!"

A shadow detached itself from the corner of the stable and shuffled warily toward the brothers. "It's only me, only poor old Sam Stolly, meanin' no harm . . . no harm . . ."

It was the ancient drunk from the saloon. He came closer, a matted, dirty old man dressed in a filthy army greatcoat. He carried no weapons, and Sean holstered his gun. "Why did you booger us like that, and what do you want, old-timer?" he said.

The old man cackled. "No need to be sceered of poor

old Sam. Old Sam, he don't mean nobody no harm." His eyes took on a sly, crafty look. "But Sam Stolly looks and Sam Stolly listens and he's got somethin' to tell you . . . somethin' you'll want to know."

Sean thought the old man was touched in the head but decided to humor him. "What have you got for us, Sam?" he said.

"Cost a dollar. If'n you want to know, cost you a dollar."

The young rancher flipped him a coin. The oldster caught it, bit it, salted the coin away in the pocket of his coat. He cackled again, grabbing both Sean and Johnny by a sleeve. "The bartender feller, can't recall the name . . ."

Sean supplied the name.

"Yeah, Tom Johnson. That's the feller. Well, he left the bar by the back door just a minute or so 'fore we heard the shot in the alley. Nobody seen him leave 'cept old Sam. Nobody seen him come back 'cept old Sam. Nobody wondered about that, 'cept old Sam. Them cowboys, they was too busy arguing over the cards to see what was happenin'. What's the bartender's name again?"

Sean told him.

"Yeah, that's right, Johnson. Well, he didn't pay no mind to old Sam, thought I was too drunk to see. But Sam sees, and Sam knows." Again the high-pitched, insane cackle and then, "I figure he went out the back door, killed young Billy, and come back in that way. Door leads out to the waste ground back of the alley and he must have arranged a secret meeting with Billy after the kid kissed goodbye to his little senorita. It figures, eh? Billy taps on the back door, Johnson hears it and goes out with a gun in his hand." The old man giggled. "Then bang!"

Sean couldn't see his brother's eyes in the gloom, but he could feel them asking him the same questions his racing brain was trying to answer . . . was the crazy old coot telling the truth or was he lying to earn a dollar?

Sean fished in his shirt pocket and gave the man another coin. "It might've happened that way, old-timer, but keep this to yourself. Tell no one, not even the sheriff."

The oldster hawked and spat. "I ain't about to tell nobody. Especially the sheriff. Now you know what I know, so put that in your pipe and smoke it."

Then he was gone, the darkness surrounding him like an old and valued friend.

Johnny waited till the man vanished from sight, then asked, "Okay, what now? I guess we go brace Johnson and beat the truth out of him."

His brother shook his head. "No. We wait. Johnson's already dying on his feet. Beat him up a little and you're likely to kill him. Besides, the sheriff is in the saloon and the less he knows, the better." Sean clapped the big man on the shoulder. "Let's get the horses. I want to study on this for a spell."

They rousted the livery stable hand out of his bunk and a few minutes later were headed out of town, Johnny's carpetbag on his saddle horn. The ride to Sean's Running-S would take better than an hour. They rode the first mile in silence under a bright moon horning aside a dazzle of stars. There was no wind, and the air smelled of grass and sagebrush and the delicate fragrance of night-blooming rain lilies.

"Thought it out yet?" Johnny asked finally. "I guess

I've taken one punch too many. My poor brain just can't figure it. Why would a bartender kill Billy Kincaid?"

"Nothing wrong with your brain," Sean replied.

"Glad to hear it. Consoles a man."

"Or if there is a kink in your thinking, then we're both buffaloed because I can't find an answer either. If it was Johnson, and we only have an old drunk's word for it, then someone must have paid him to kill the boy. It just doesn't figure. Hell, Johnson had nothing against Billy. The kid was a big tipper."

"If somebody did pay him, who would it be? One of your ranchers, maybe?"

"Again, that's the obvious answer. And, again, it's too obvious. None of the men I know has the kind of cash money to pay for a killing like that. You don't agree to kill Lance Kincaid's son without you ask for a pile of wampum. And, once you're paid off, you leave the country in a hurry, and for good. But we do know one thing, if Tom Johnson lights a shuck, then he's our man."

Johnny checked his horse, rose in the stirrups, easing his aching butt off the saddle. "If he runs, we can catch him."

"If he runs, we won't have to. Kincaid will trail him to hell and drag him back with the devil's own pitchfork."

"I know I sound fiddle-footed, but is it possible that Kincaid is crazy enough to have his own son murdered to get this range war of his started?"

Sean shook his head. "No, he doted on that boy. Men with only one son have a habit of doing that."

"Nora Ann doesn't enter into his thinking, huh?"

"He doesn't reckon a woman is capable of expanding

his cattle empire. In Colonel Kincaid's world it takes a man with a gun and a hemp rope to do that."

"Billy wasn't much of a choice."

"He was all Kincaid had, and he was determined to make the best of it."

"And now they've taken his son and heir."

"And his high hopes are dashed. And Billy wasn't murdered by *they* . . . he was shot by he, just one man."

"Then it all comes back to who paid Johnson."

"Maybe some other party wanted Billy dead."

Johnny smiled. "From what you've told me, that covers about half of west Texas."

"All the ranchers want is to be left alone. They'd nothing to gain and plenty to lose by Billy's death."

"Some other party . . . who? His senorita? A lover's quarrel." Johnny shifted uncomfortably. "Damn, I'd forgotten how hard saddles are. Are we almost home?"

"Not far now and your butt will harden up over time, like bois d'arc wood."

"I doubt that, and I don't plan on doing much riding. I'm missing the Boston streetcar cushions already."

"To answer your question, I don't think Billy's girl was involved. I think the killer could be someone who had much to gain from his death, and I'm talking money and power."

"Money and power? That doesn't seem to fit a lunger like Tom Johnson."

"He's worth considering as a paid killer. But the fact is, I'm beginning to wonder if Kincaid is innocent after all. Maybe somebody waiting in the wings hatched the whole terror campaign, including the deaths of Tom Rose and Billy Kincaid. If we all destroy ourselves in a range war, he can walk right in and take over. Question is, who would . . ."

A rifle report ripped a ragged hole in the fabric of the night.

Sean heard the *thunk* of a large caliber slug strike his horse. He relaxed instantly and pulled his feet free of the stirrups. The horse screamed and collapsed in a kicking heap on the ground. Sean rolled away from the animal as it fell, then rolled again, behind the bulk of his dying mount. He pulled his Colt as another shot racketed out of the darkness, and he saw Johnny slammed backward over his saddle by the impact of the heavy bullet. The big man lay winded for a while, then sprinted for the shelter of Sean's horse. A bullet spattered dust between his feet, and he dived the last few yards, dropping in a heap beside his brother.

"You hurt?" Sean whispered urgently.

"Only my feelings and a perfectly good carpetbag. The bag took the bullet, otherwise I'd be dead as this animal here." He shook a huge fist at the night. "If I get my hands on whoever's doing this, I swear on my sainted mother's grave I'll nail his hide to the outhouse door. I'll . . ."

As Johnny ranted, Sean took stock of the situation. It was bad. He had already spotted a jumble of glacier rock and scrub oak as the only possible lair of the hidden gunman. Between the rocks and themselves there was a series of shallow, undulating hills, without a scrap of cover.

The bushwhacker's gun roared again, and the bullet thudded harmlessly into the dead horse. Sean noted the muzzle flash, aimed slightly to the right, and triggered off two fast shots.

As if to show his contempt, the hidden gunman loosed off several rounds that whined dangerously close and sent the O'Neils to ground behind the animal's bulk.

"Range is way too much for a handgun," Sean whispered. "From this distance, I'd do better throwing rocks."

"What about the rifle?"

"Horse fell on top of it. It's jammed under him."

"I'll lift the horse. When I do, pull the rifle free."

Sean started to say that the horse was too heavy, but the big man had already bent over, pulling upward on the animal's saddle.

Johnny groaned in pain as the roped muscles of his shoulders and arms bunched like cordwood. Bullets started to kick up, perilously close, but he ignored them. A muffled groan escaped from between his teeth as the saddle rose two inches, then three . . .

"I've got it!" Sean yelled.

He pulled the .44-40 Winchester free and threw it to his shoulder.

Cursing his relief, Johnny let the saddle and horse drop back to the ground.

"You're even stronger than I thought," Sean said.

The big man snorted. "Remind me never to do it again. Now nail that no-good widowmaker before he's the death of all of us."

Sean nodded grimly, pushed the rifle over the barrel of his dead horse. "Now we wait till he fires again . . ."

The crescent moon was very bright. The clouds that had threatened earlier in the evening had disappeared and the sky was once again ablaze with stars. A soft breeze whispered over the buffalo grass and tugged at Sean's hat brim. A few yards away, Johnny's horse grazed steadily, seemingly oblivious to the firing and to the body of his dead companion.

A slow minute ticked past and then another. Sean was perfectly still, solemn as a cigar store Indian, but his brother groaned his displeasure. "Ah, I don't have the patience for this game. Maybe the bushwhacker's gone."

"Could be," Sean said. "But I'm not counting on it."

"I am. I reckon he missed us and now he's long gone."

A shot that hammered from the rocks and venomously split the air between the two men gave the lie to that statement.

Sean sprang to one knee, levered off three fast shots at the hidden marksman's gun flash. "Johnny, you want the Colt?" he said.

Johnny waved the pistol away. "No use to me. I never could hit anything with a gun. You know that. When we were younkers, I never shot a squirrel. Tried a bunch of times but could never hit one. Just as well, I like squirrels."

"I know, you ate enough of them," Sean said, his eyes probing the darkness. "Make a noise with the Colt."

"And give my position away?"

"I reckon the man already knows where you are."

"I'd just like to get close enough to use these." Johnny held up his gnarled fists. "I'd beat that prairie rat to a pulp!"

The hidden rifleman fired again, and Johnny's horse collapsed in a screaming heap.

Cursing, Sean returned the fire, jacking shells into the breech, squeezing them off fast as he could work the rifle. His last shot drew a yelp of surprise from the rocks . . .

Then silence.

Johnny stared in shocked disbelief at his downed horse.

"He's killed my horse," he groaned. "He's killed my animal and left me all afoot. Aaah, it's myself will rip out his black guts with my own bare hands!"

Then the big man was up and running, charging toward the rocks with a wild Celtic war cry on his lips and murder in his heart. Sean, his blood stirred, let rip with a rebel yell and charged after his brother, triggering off shots from the hip as he ran.

Later, neither of them would recall much about that wild charge across fifty yards of open ground in the face of an expert rifleman.

Sean remembered Johnny's screamed insults, swearing vengeance on the sewer rat that would leave a gentleman afoot far from home—and, worse, a gentleman descended from Irish high kings. And Johnny heard his brother yell like an angry Reb as he cranked off shot after shot from his Winchester, his bullets probing then caroming off the rocks.

Historians agree that it was the young rancher's skill with his rifle that saved him and his brother's lives that night because when they reached the bushwhacker's hiding place, the man was already gone. About two hundred yards away, flapping his chaps, they saw the bulky outline of a horseman, his face a white blur as he glanced over his shoulder as though the hounds of hell were snapping at his mount's tail.

Johnny sank onto a boulder and wiped his brow with his sleeve. He looked up, caught his brother's eye, and started to laugh. Sean looked at him in amazement. Then he, too, grinned. Slowly the grin grew to a great belly laugh the like of which he had not experienced for years, or ever thought to experience again. For long minutes they whooped and hollered in the night, tears in their eyes, slapping each other on the back, dancing a jig like boisterous schoolboys.

Then, as suddenly as it had begun, it was over. Sean wiped tears from his eyes and gasped, "Please, big brother, don't do anything like that again. If the rifleman, whoever he was, decided to stay and fight, we'd both be dead by now."

The big man slapped his thigh and grinned hugely. "Ah, but it was fun though, Sean. Wasn't it fun?"

"Sure, it was fun. But don't get my Rebel blood up like that again. A man doesn't live long out here if he charges headlong into a Winchester." Sean smiled. "I've charged into Yankee cannon and swore I'd never do the like again."

"And here you did."

"Yes, and here I did."

"Well, you played the man's part. I'm proud of you."

"All right, but don't let me play the man's part anytime soon. Now let's see if our friend left any clue to his identity."

Despite the bright moonlight, the rocks were shadowed by the few scrubby bur oaks, and the brothers decided to postpone their search till the next day.

After a struggle, the O'Neils gave up on freeing their saddles. They'd return in the morning with a buckboard and shovels.

Sean regretted the loss of two good cowponies. But he had dealt himself into a dangerous game and the price of taking cards came high and they'd probably go a heap higher. In fact, he'd been lucky. There were many horses, but he and Johnny had just one life.

As he fell in step beside his brother, Sean's brain raced, trying to find an answer to this latest mystery. Was the dry-gulcher one of Kincaid's men? Did the colonel really want a range war and know that Sean O'Neil stood in his way? Or was it the third person, the man who'd paid for the deaths of Tom Rose and Billy Kincaid and would profit mightily from a full-scale war between Oaktree and the other ranches? And had that person also arranged tonight's ambush?

Sean shook his head. No use thinking about it now, the answers would come—and probably sooner than he expected.

Chapter 7

As Sean and Johnny O'Neil made their way across a range made mysterious by the shadowy shapes of cattle, Corinda Mason's night was not over.

Her narrow hotel room contained only a bed, dresser and a small table and chair positioned at the window. Outside, Mustang Flat was in darkness, but for one pinprick of light in the distance, the home of a sleepless citizen or some regretful trencherman suffering from dyspepsia. A crescent moon hung in the night sky but did little to banish the shadows between the buildings where a pair of adventurous coyotes ventured under the hotel crawl space hunting rats.

Corinda sat at the table and, a fetish of hers when a contract was over, she unloaded her .44 caliber British Bulldog revolver and inserted fresh, stubby rounds from a U.S. Cartridge Company box. There had been fifty .44 Bulldog rounds in the box and half of them were gone. The engraved, ivory-handled revolver, a replacement for a plainer model, was a gift from an admirer, Jacob Greenlee, a lover very dear to her.

A beautifully shaped woman with thick, auburn hair,

full, sensuous lips that begged to be kissed, and slightly slanted hazel eyes that gave her an exotic, Eastern European look, she stared out the window with disinterest, but had no desire to seek her pillow. Though she'd taken no part in them, the exciting events of the night, violent and dramatic, had set her pulse pounding and robbed her of the desire to sleep.

Then Corinda Mason caught sight of the rider.

Cloaked in darkness as he was, the man was a dark silhouette, but she could make out that he was smallish, riding a cowpony, coming down the street at a plodding walk. She knew instinctively that he was in town to see her. Grown to caution by recent events, she pulled her clinging silk robe closer around her and stood, the British Bulldog hanging by her side. Then she waited . . .

A scratch at the door. No knock that could've been heard by other guests. At least the man, whoever he was, showed some common sense. Corinda crossed the tiny room, turned the door handle, and opened, the Bulldog coming up to her waist. A single oil lamp illuminated the hallway with dim, guttering light, enough for the woman to see the freckled, grinning face of a young puncher, a holstered revolver on his hip.

"Miz Mason?" the man said.

"You knew my hotel room. Who else would I be? Come in before someone sees you."

The youngster stepped inside, his eyes fixed on the swell of Corinda's breasts under the thin stuff of her robe, and his mouth hung slightly open.

"Well?" the woman said.

Like a man waking from a pleasant dream, the cowboy grinned and said, "This is for you." He passed over a heavy, manila envelope. "Sooner than you expected, Miz Mason, huh?" he said.

"Who sent this?" Corinda said.

"Mr. Peterson, the ramrod, gave it to me."

"What's in it?"

"I didn't look."

Corinda tossed the envelope on the bed. "I know what's in it, but I didn't earn it."

"I wouldn't know about that," the young puncher said.

"Do you know what happened here tonight?"

"I just rode into town, but the desk clerk told me Billy Kincaid had been murdered."

"Yes, Billy Kincaid was shot and killed."

The youngster's self-assurance fled. His mouth hung open and he said, "Billy . . . dead. It's hard to believe."

"Dead as he'll ever be. But I didn't eliminate him."

"El . . . el . . . what does that mean?"

"I didn't plug him."

"Why . . . why would a pretty lady like you want to kill him?"

"You don't know?"

"Nobody tells me anything. I'm just a drover."

"A common laborer on horseback. That's all you are. Do you know how to keep your mouth shut?"

"Yeah, I do. I know when to hobble my lip." The cowboy shook his head. "I can't believe Billy's dead. I need to tell the colonel."

"By this time, I think he already knows."

That seemed to satisfy the kid who didn't want to leave, captivated by the silk robe and the alluring woman who wore it.

"What did Peterson tell you?"

"He told me to give you the envelope, but he didn't give me a message to say."

"That's all?"

"Mr. Peterson doesn't talk much."

"I guess he yells a lot."

"Sometimes he sure does. Ma'am, who killed Billy?"

"I have no idea. Maybe he got in a gunfight over a woman. I heard the shot."

"One shot ain't a gunfight, ma'am."

"No, it isn't. Smart as a whip, ain't you?"

"Ma'am, I got to say, you're the prettiest woman I've ever seen in Mustang Flat."

Slightly bored, Corinda decided to tease.

"How many pretty women are in Mustang Flat?"

"Well, now you've asked me to study on it, some of the Mexican gals that ain't got fat yet are real lookers an' Bessie Gilmore, the pastor's daughter, ain't bad either."

"But I'm prettier?"

"Lady, I never in all my born days seen your like. Aren't you going to open the envelope?"

"I'll do it later."

"You know, you're a real nice lady."

"Thank you, and you're a peach. You can go now."

The cowboy's eyes moved to the bottle of bourbon on the dresser.

"I sure worked up a thirst on the ride from the Oaktree," he said. "I'm spittin' cotton here."

Corinda Mason smiled. "There's a horse trough in front of the hotel, help yourself. Now leave before I get cross. I wish to retire."

The young puncher said, "You're a lovely lady and a

famous singer an' all, so I guess I'm reaching for a star, ain't I?"

The woman opened the door and smiled. "Yes, you are and sometimes that's how the pickle squirts, cowboy."

"Nice meeting you, Miz Mason."

"You, too, whatever your name is."

Corinda shut the door and stood there until she heard the youngster's booted feet on the stairs. She laid her revolver on the table and got the envelope from the bed and shook out five hundred-dollar bills. Those and something else, a pressed wildflower, still retaining much of its original pink color. She smiled, delicately sniffed the dried bloom, and then pressed it to her lips, her eyes closed, long, black lashes lying on her cheekbones like Spanish fans.

Chapter 8

Neither Sean O'Neil's boots with their two-inch heels nor his brother's side-button, patent leather pumps were designed for long moonlit hikes across grassland. By the time they reached the Running-S, some two hours later, Sean's feet were hurting, and Johnny was in a thoroughly foul mood.

The ranch's timber, slat-roofed cabin, wood-frame horse barn, and large corral were designed for sturdiness and utility rather than beauty. But the two windows to the front glowed cheerfully, and a thin plume of smoke from the chimney tied gray bows in the star-scattered sky.

Johnny cursed loudly and endlessly as he and Sean approached the cabin . . . and then the light suddenly snuffed out.

A moment later, the door opened just wide enough to admit a gun barrel and a man's voice warned, "If'n I was you, folks, I wouldn't come no closer. I got me a scatter-gun here that's wife and child to me, and I kin use her."

Despite his weariness, Sean smiled. "Relax, Rusty. It's me, and my brother, all the way from Boston town."

A few seconds passed, and then the door opened and a small, wiry Chinaman stepped outside, a ten-gauge Greener in his hands. "Sean! What happened? Where are your horses? How come . . ."

"Enough!" The young rancher said, waving away the old man's questions. "I'll tell you everything later. For now, let me introduce you to my brother. Johnny, this is Rusty Chang, the best biscuit shooter in the west and a man to ride the trail with."

Johnny, in no mood for pleasantries, grudgingly stuck out his hand. "Pleased to meet you. How come Rusty? I expected a redhead with freckles."

The little cook shook the big man's hand, then answered sourly, "I surely haven't got freckles. Folks calls me Rusty on account of how stiff my joints are with the rheumatisms." He turned to Sean. "You boys et yet?"

"The hell we have," Johnny answered for his brother. "No, we ain't et. We've been shot at from hell to gone, we've crossed a hundred miles of prairie on foot, and I've lifted saddles that shouldn't be put on an elephant never mind a horse—but one thing we ain't done. We ain't et."

The big man's ill humor didn't faze Rusty Chang. The little man just shrugged and said, "Well, if'n you're in a mind to bite a biscuit you came to the right place." He turned again to Sean. "After you fill your bellies, you got to tell me about what happened. You understandee?"

The young rancher nodded. "I sure do, but it will take a spell to wring it out."

"Then wring it out you will. When my boss leaves on a hoss and comes back on foot, he's got a story to tell."

"You're so right about that, Rusty. I'll bend your ear into a bowknot."

The three men stepped into the cabin, and a few minutes later, the O'Neils were eating in dedicated silence. Johnny worked his way through beef and beans, a half dozen biscuits, a huge wedge of vinegar pie and a gallon of coffee before he leaned back, sighed, and loosened his belt and the top button of his pants.

"An elegant meal, Rusty. I've eaten better, but I can't for the life of me recall where or when."

The little man sniffed. "Well, at least you appreciate good vittles, unlike some I could mention"—his eyes slanted to Sean—"that eat like birds."

Sean looked up from building a smoke. "Come on, Rusty. I always said you were a crackerjack steak charmer. Why, the things you can do for beef and a sack of beans is just amazing. I always eat my fill."

The little man searched Sean's straight face trying to find the insult, decided there was none, and said, "You promised to tell me what happened, about how you were bushwhacked. You tell me everything now, you hear? Don't leave nothin' out."

Despite his tiredness, Sean recounted the events of the day, starting from when he met his brother at the stage depot and ending with the ambush after they left town. He told it, then retold it, then added to it again, humoring the little Chinese man's passion for news.

Finally, Rusty shook his head and tut-tutted. "It doesn't take a canister of fortune sticks to foresee trouble is brewing and heading our way. As we say in Texas, it's a natural fact."

"That it is, ol' hoss," Sean said. "The storm clouds gather, and I only hope we can head them off before more folks gets killed around here."

"And Colonel Kincaid's son murdered," Rusty said. "That's hard to credit. I only ran into Billy Kincaid a couple of times and didn't like him much, but it was a terrible thing, a young man getting shot like that."

"The colonel put Billy on a pedestal," Sean said. "No matter what the boy did, he forgave him."

"And covered up for him," Rusty said. "Remember Les Terrell?"

"Yeah, I recollect. When was that?"

"A twelve-month ago."

"So long? It seems like the day before yesterday. I remember folks in town called him Lonesome Les Terrell."

"Tell me about him," Johnny said, prepared to listen now he'd been fed.

"Les was a loner all right," Rusty said. "Kept to himself. The womenfolk in town said he was trying to mend a broken heart, but I didn't hold with that. I reckon he was just plumb mean and ornery. He was a cardsharp with a fast gun an' that's why everybody stepped wide of him. But Billy Kincaid sure ended his career in the Crystal Palace saloon. The way I was told it from a puncher who was there, Billy leaned across the card table and gut shot him. One bullet in the belly downed him."

"I never did hear the right of it," Sean said. "I always thought Terrel called out Billy for a cheat who knew both sides of the cards."

"Not hardly. Sheriff Beason said all Les had on him that night was a brass letter opener."

"A what?" Johnny said.

"You heard me, a letter opener."

"Why?"

"He must've opened a letter."

"And left his gun behind?"

"There's no accounting for folks," Rusty said. "Especially gambling men. Maybe he thought his gun was bad luck. Anyways, Beason called the letter opener a dagger and then he called the murder self-defense and Billy walked free."

"His daddy cleared it with Beason, huh?"

"I'm sure some of the colonel's money changed hands."

"Sean smiled. "Rusty, how do you know all this stuff?"

"Because when I'm in town I listen. Confucius says, 'A man has two ears and one mouth and should use them in those proportions.'"

"Wise man, that Confusion," Johnny said.

"Confucius," Rusty said, irritated.

Johnny said, "Whatever his name was, he was book learned and horse smart. Well, Billy Kincaid is gone, and it doesn't become us to speak ill of the dead."

"Billy was a skunk," Rusty said.

"Or skunks either."

"All right, so now tell me, have you any idea who your bushwhacker could have been?" Rusty said. "Another piece of pie, Mr. O'Neil?"

"I couldn't eat another bite . . . and call me Johnny."

Sean stifled a yawn. "Could've been one of Kincaid's

boys. Or it could be someone who's trying to get both me and the colonel. All I have is could be's . . . nothing else."

"I just can't figure it." The little Chinese man scratched his head. "The whole thing is shaping up to make no sense."

"That's for sure, Rusty. No sense at all. Now what you say we call it a night and bed down?"

"That's the best suggestion I've heard for hours," Johnny said. "After our trek through the wilderness, I could sleep for a week, maybe two. But I just thought of something—shouldn't we post a guard? Somebody tried to kill us, and he's bound to try again."

"I'll stand guard," Rusty said. "On account of how I hardly sleep anymore. Least hardly ever, less'n I'm likkered up an' that only happens on the Chinese New Year. Now I'm outta here."

The old man picked up his Greener, opened the door, and glided into the night.

"Where's he going?" Johnny asked.

Sean yawned. "He'll be around. Now I'm turning in. Johnny, your room is the door on the right."

Johnny rose to his feet. "Remember our room in the farmhouse attic?"

"I remember the corncob mattress was lumpy, and the place was full of cobwebs." Sean smiled. "During the war when I slept on rocks or mud or both, I often wished I was back lying on that pallet, lumps and all."

"Well, I hope your beds are softer."

"Swan's down, Johnny, swan's down. You'll sleep like a baby."

Minutes later, there was only the heavy breathing of two tired men in the cabin. But out in the night, an old man with stiff joints, keen eyes, and a scattergun was one with the shadows.

Chapter 9

The morning was already bright when Sean woke. He sat up in his bunk and saw through the open door of his bedroom Chang bending over the wood stove, a sizzling skillet of sliced bacon in his hand.

"Morning," the little man said. "Sleep good?"

Sean yawned and stretched. "Like a log. What time is it?"

"First light broke maybe two hours ago. Figgered after last night you'd want to sleep some."

"Not this long." Sean's voice was testy. "We all got work to do."

He rose, put on his hat and pulled on his pants, socks, and boots. Then he stepped into his brother's room and shook the big man awake. His prizefighter instincts aroused, Johnny roared and came up swinging, his huge fists beating the air as Sean quickly stepped out of range.

"Hey, ease up, brother!" the young rancher said.

Johnny rose to a sitting position and knuckled his eyes. "Sorry about that. I guess I should've warned you, never shake me awake when I'm on edge. It makes bad things happen . . . swing first and ask questions later."

"I'll remember, believe me, I'll remember," Sean said. "I'm glad you didn't have a gun."

Chang snorted and forked bacon from the skillet onto tin plates. "Glad to know that. Next time I'll waken you with a bucket of cold water."

Johnny eyed the little man with distaste. "You, I won't miss." Then, "Hold the bacon until I get back."

Rusty's jaw fell as the big man suddenly leaped out of his bunk in his long johns and went into a barbarous war dance. He leapt high in the air, then thudded to the pine floor in a deep knee bend, leapt again and once more performed the strange exercise. Sean and Rusty watched in amazement as this went on for fully several minutes, the big man snorting and grunting like a bull, breath whistling through his previously broken nose.

Suddenly the jumping and bending stopped. Johnny grabbed his derby, jammed it on his head, and ran outside in his bare feet, still in his bright red, long-handled underwear. Sean and Rusty followed him to the cabin door, their eyes huge. The big man ran in wide circles, throwing up spurts of dust, puffing like a locomotive, totally unconcerned over the strange figure he cut.

"Boss, you want me to shoot him?" Rusty said.

"No, not yet," Sean said. "Let him run a while longer."

After fifteen minutes, Johnny O'Neil sprinted around the windmill a few times and then stepped to the water pump. He took off his hat, cranked the handle and stuck his head under the rushing spout. Johnny gasped as water splashed over his shoulders and chest. Then he straightened, threw back his head, spraying like a wet hound dog and yelled toward the blue sky, "Top of the morning to you, Lord! It's Himself . . . greeting you on this fine day!"

"He's gone plumb loco," Rusty said.

"Seems like it," Sean said.

"Are you sure you don't want me to shoot him?"

Sean smiled. "No, old man. Just serve him breakfast. He looks like he's ready for it."

Sean and Rusty were already eating when Johnny sat at the table, dry in pants, shirt, and shoes. "And what's for breakfast, Rusty, my fine fellow?" he said, his ill humor of the night before obviously gone.

"Eggs, bacon, beans, and cornbread."

"Just what the doctor ordered. Well, don't just sit there man, bring it on."

Rusty turned to Sean, his face a mask of suffering. "You should've let me shoot him, boss, you know you should've."

Sean smiled, waited until a filled plate was before his brother and said, "Eat hearty, Johnny, we got a lot to do today."

"Such as?"

"I'll tell you after breakfast. I don't want to spoil your appetite."

"Nothing can spoil my appetite this morning, but I can wait."

The three men ate in silence. Then Johnny sighed, patted his belly and rose. He went to his coat, selected a slim cheroot, stepped back to the table, thumbed a lucifer alight and said through a cloud of smoke. "I recommend the exercise program you just saw me perform, Sean. It gets the body juices flowing, sets you up for the rest of the day. Of course, the salutation to the Good Lord can be included or left out, depending on your beliefs."

"I'll remember that the next time I run around in circles, but in the meantime, we've got things to discuss."

"Fire away, I'm listening. After the trials and tribulations of the night, Johnny O'Neil has risen a new man this day, more than ready to do your every bidding."

"Good. Well, here's my bidding, the first thing we do is ride back to where we were bushwhacked. There might be a sign that will give us a handle on who tried to kill us last night."

Johnny groaned. "Oh God, not another horse!"

"Yeah," Rusty said, "another horse. I served bacon this morning because I feared you'd eat the nag for breakfast."

The big man looked at the little man hard, then turned haughtily and asked his brother, "And after that?"

"Then we ride into town and have words with Tom Johnson at the Crystal Palace. I want to know where he was when Billy Kincaid was killed."

Johnny rubbed a hand over his stubbled chin. "Give me ten minutes to shave, then we can get started."

"No time. Get dressed while I go saddle the horses." Sean pulled on a gray wool shirt and turned to Rusty who was busily clearing the table. "Rusty, I want you to take a buckboard and a shovel and see if you can dig the saddles out from under the dead horses. But keep an eye on things and later ride out and check on my Herefords. The colonel's grief will probably keep him home today, but there are Apaches off the reservation, and I don't want them rustling my best beef."

The little man nodded. "I'll look after things."

Sean smiled. "I know you will, old-timer. Sorry to load you up like that."

"Hard work can end hard times," Rusty said.

"Confusion say that, Rusty?" Johnny said.

"No, I said it. And his name is Confucius."

"Oh, so it is," Johnny said, grinning. "A savvy gent for a Chinaman."

"A savvy gent for any man." Rusty said. He saw Sean walk to the door and said, "Watch out for your ownself, boss."

Sean turned and nodded. "I sure will."

He walked outside into the bright sunlight of the morning, buckling his Colt around his waist. There were a dozen horses in the corral. Sean looped a rangy, big-boned gray for himself and another buckskin mare for his brother.

He saddled the horses and brought them to the front of the cabin where Johnny was already waiting. He noted that the big man had found time to shave.

Anticipating the question, Johnny said, "I used to go days without shaving before a fight. Now I'm retired, I fully intend to shave every day."

Sean shook his head, smiling. "Mount up, brother."

The big man had made no concessions to western style. He wore his high-button ditto suit, elastic-sided boots, and derby hat. A clean white shirt and gray tie with a diamond stickpin completed his outfit. He swung into the saddle, groaning his distaste as the horse turned her head to look at him.

"We've got to buy you some clothes," Sean said mildly.

"What's wrong with my clothes?"

"Not a damn thing if you're going to a prayer meeting."

Johnny pulled his horse alongside his brother and sputtered, "Now listen here, Sean, for your information a gentleman always . . .

"Riders comin in!" Rusty's alarmed yell from the cabin door.

The little man ducked his head inside and vanished.

Sean looked to where Rusty had pointed and saw a group of horsemen in the distance. "Coming from the direction of Oaktree," he said. He adjusted the lie of his Colt and swung his horse to face the approaching riders, and Johnny drew rein alongside him.

There were seven men in the party, and at their head rode Colonel Lance Kincaid. Kincaid threw up a hand, and the men slowed to a ragged halt and spread out into a line some ten feet away from the O'Neil brothers. For long seconds no one spoke, hostile, distrustful men eyeing each other in the bright morning light. Sean saw that John Lowery and Zack Elliot reined up on either side of the colonel. His tall foreman, the handsome, muscular Dick Peterson and the rest of the men were punchers, not gun hands, but their rigid loyalty to the brand would make them dangerous.

Finally, Kincaid spoke. "My boy is dead, O'Neil."

"I know, Colonel," Sean said. "I was in town when it happened."

"Did you kill him?"

"No, I did not, but on our way back to my ranch my brother and I were bushwhacked. Was that any of your doing?"

"I have no knowledge of that. Bushwhacking a man never enters my thinking."

"And shooting a man when his back is turned never enters mine."

Kincaid read Sean O'Neil's eyes. Long experience had taught him that lies hatched like maggots in a guilty man's stare. He'd hanged or shot a dozen men with eyes like that and had spared others who had not, men like Sean O'Neil.

"I'm powerful sorry it happened," Sean said. "My sympathies are with you and Miss Nora Ann."

Kincaid's red rimmed eyes blazed. "I don't want your sympathy, O'Neil. I want the man who murdered my son."

Sean took time to compose what he would say next. He would have to play his hand carefully or there would be killing right here in front of his own cabin. He studied Kincaid, trying to fathom what the rancher was thinking.

The colonel was a tall, thick-bodied man, and his usually florid face was deathly pale. In his mid-fifties, he was still handsome, sporting a thick head of wavy, iron gray hair and a sweeping mustache of the same color. He looked comfortable, a man normally confident of his abilities, a man used to the finest whiskey, cigars, and women and figured he deserved them.

"I had no reason or desire to hurt Billy," Sean said. "He was young and sometimes foolish, was all."

"Damn right he was young!" Kincaid said. "And now he's dead, Billy's lying in the undertaker's embalming room and he's stiff and cold and half his head is gone. He'll never be young and foolish again."

Kincaid's head drooped and Sean saw the man's shoulders heave. There was a long, awkward silence, then the colonel looked up again, his grief terrible to see. Sean had seen grief like that only once before—on the face of a Northern Cheyenne war chief also mourning a son. That man's face had been painted black and Kincaid's was deathly white. But the aching sorrow was the same.

"Lowery says you picked an argument with Billy last night, and that your brother there beat him up." The colonel turned to Johnny. "Seems you were a little under-matched, bully-boy."

Sean heard his brother's sudden intake of breath and knew the big man's temper was stung. He interjected quickly, "Colonel, if Lowery told you that, he told you half the story. Billy was drunk and he pulled a gun. My brother made sure he didn't use it."

Kincaid said, "John Lowery, was that the how and why of the thing?"

Lowery's look at Sean was like a thrown dagger, but the man told the truth. "Billy drew down on O'Neil. The big feller stopped a killing."

"Postponed a killing, you mean," Zack Elliot said.

"Yes, as you say," Lowery said. "Billy was primed for a fight that night."

"Why didn't you stop him?" Kincaid said.

"Boss, you asked me that before," Lowery said. "Billy told us to ride back to the ranch. He said he would stay in town and visit his woman and there was no changing his mind."

Kincaid's head again bowed, as though it was suddenly too heavy for his shoulders, and he fell into silence. He looked like a Greek god who'd just received some mighty bad news.

Elliot and Lowery were watchful, tense, their eyes on Sean as though they half expected him to make a play.

But the young rancher placed both hands on the saddle horn and leaned forward, his eyes locking with Kincaid's. "Colonel, you've known me for a long time, before . . . before all this began," he said. "I know you don't believe I killed your son."

Kincaid slumped in his saddle. He looked tired, defeated, and Sean felt a pang of sympathy for him. This man's ambition might be plunging the entire valley into a range war, but it was impossible to witness his agonizing heartbreak and remain unaffected.

But suddenly Sean's sympathy died. Kincaid said, his words hissing like acid dropped on red hot iron. "Maybe you had a hand in Billy's death, maybe you didn't. I won't hang a man without proof, so tell me where you stand on this, O'Neil, because I want vengeance. The ranchers in this valley have tried for months to force me into a war. They've killed my cattle, killed my Hereford bull—and now they've murdered my son. Well, they've got their war, and I'll fight it to the end, until not a farmer or nester or a two-by-twice cattleman is left alive in this part of Texas."

The colonel swayed in his saddle. He raised an unsteady hand to his head and Lowery immediately put an arm around his shoulders. Kincaid roughly brushed the gunman aside and said, "Where do you stand, O'Neil? Do you ride with me or against me?"

Sean felt an icy hand twist in his gut. A range war would set the entire valley aflame. He'd heard of such a conflict before and knew what it did to cattle country. Both sides imported gunmen and after the shooting was over, there was little left but burned-out ranches, dead cattle, and the wail of widows.

As he looked into the terrible eyes of the colonel, it occurred to him there was something he could do, something he could do now—he could pull his Colt and kill Lance Kincaid.

Even as the thought entered Sean's mind, it appalled him.

If he succeeded, he would be a murderer, a dead murderer if Lowery and Elliot were as fast as they were said to be. Sean let his breath out slowly, willing himself to be calm. The whole idea was stupid, a marquee play. There had to be a better way.

"I'm still waiting for an answer," Kincaid said. Anger edged his voice. "And I'm not a patient man."

Sean nodded. He wondered briefly where Rusty was and looked around. But the little man was not in sight.

Johnny looked relaxed but ready, and that reassured him.

"Colonel," he began carefully, "other ranches lost cattle. Barns were burned by nightriders and one man was killed, leaving a wife and a passel of young'uns. The small ranchers and the farmers reckon you're the one responsible. Seems to them you want the whole valley for yourself and one way to get it is to start a range war and grab the land out from under them."

Kincaid jerked savagely on his horse's bit and kicked the animal closer to Sean. He looked murderously into the younger man's eyes and snarled. "Do you reckon I would kill my only son to satisfy my own ambitions, O'Neil? By God, don't tell me you think that."

Sean felt far from calm, and he was pleased when he

heard himself say steadily, "No, Colonel, I don't think that."

"Let me tell you something, young man." Kincaid seemed unaware that his two hired guns had edged forward on either side of him. "I fought for this land. Every square inch of it is fertilized by my blood and the blood of men I called friends. I've fought Kiowas, Comanches, Apaches, and some white men that were worse than any of them. I have a bullet in my lower back that a Chiricahua put there in the spring of sixty-seven, and my wife died here because the life was hard and dangerous, and she was raised a lady in a gentler place. I loved this land, and I was even willing to share it. I didn't complain when other ranchers, you among them, moved in and grazed on range that was mine by blood right. What did their small herds matter, wasn't the land big enough for everyone? But then came the nesters and their farms and their sheep and their hogs. Even when the cattle killing started and the farms were burned, for a while I was willing to let it happen. I saw that whoever was doing these things was ridding me of the scum ruining my range. But then my cattle started to die, and I realized it was a plot, an elaborate plot by the other ranchers to force me into a war that would destroy Oaktree and everything I've tried to build here. Sure, while it suited them, the cattlemen turned a blind eye to sheep and hogs and chickens because once I was driven out or dead, they'd move onto my range and then get rid of the sodbusters. I wasn't going to stand by and see Oaktree destroyed, so I hired guns and got ready for war."

Kincaid was obviously exhausted. He rubbed a tired hand over his stubbled jaw and said, "I didn't start this thing, O'Neil. Sure, I wanted the range, but given time I could have gotten it my own way. I could have bought them out, all of them, even you. Every man has his price, and I would've paid it. But now my son is dead, and it doesn't matter anymore. Now there's nothing left, only revenge, so I ask you once again. Where do you stand? With me or against me?"

Sean glanced at the sky, blue as far as the eye could see as the sun climbed higher. A small flock of white-tailed doves flew overhead then vanished into the distance of the warming morning. The colonel would not wait much longer for an answer, and what was said in the next few minutes could save the range from destruction.

"Colonel Kincaid, if you're leveling with me, it could be that you're not behind what's happening here," Sean said. "I know the farmers and ranchers are not behind it either. Maybe we're dealing with a third party, someone who wants the range for himself and hopes both sides will destroy themselves in an all-out war." Sean's horse tossed his head and its bit jangled. "Whoever it is overstepped himself when he killed your bull. I figure you were too proud of that animal to kill him as an excuse to start a war. Now he's taken a step too far again. This time much more seriously. He murdered your son."

"What are you trying to tell me, O'Neil?"

"I'm telling you if you move against the rest of the ranchers, you could play into the hands of a man who desires your death, Colonel, and probably Nora Ann's, too. He wants Oaktree and he'll stop at nothing to get it."

The colonel shook his head. "You're confusing me,

O'Neil. Anyway, what does it matter? Billy is dead and his soul is crying for revenge."

"Colonel, you still have Nora Ann."

"A girl? What does a girl want with a ranch, an empire? An empire is for a man, a man big enough to take it and hold it."

"Think about it, for heaven's sake . . . boys . . . grand-children . . ."

Kincaid looked up and incredibly there was a light, almost hope, in his eyes. "Grandchildren . . ."

Sean knew then he had him. "Right, Colonel. And the future could be theirs, just as it was Billy's."

"What are you saying, O'Neil?"

"Only that Nora Ann will want to wed one day, and the future of Oaktree will be hers and her children's."

"She could have sons, fine sons," Kincaid said. "Is that what you're saying."

Sean smiled. "Yeah, that's what I'm saying, a passel of boys with their grandpappy's sand."

"Damn you, O'Neil, you're a snake charmer. You're playing a tune on your flute you know I want to hear."

"I'm telling the truth."

"Or your version of it. Maybe Nora Ann will never wed."

"She'll wed, count on it."

"How the hell are you so sure? Did she tell you that?"

"No, not in so many words, but I'm sure that one day she'll want to get married."

"She wants to go back east to Philadelphia of all places."

Sean managed a smile. "Give her some time, Colonel. Texas will change her mind." Sean's eyes moved to John

Lowery. "You've been around, Lowery," he said. "How likely is it that Nora Ann will remain a spinster?"

The gunman was confused. "What kind of question is that to ask a man?"

"It's simple. Do you think Nora Ann Kincaid will marry some day?"

"Well . . . yeah. Of course, she will."

"Elliot, what about you?"

Colonel Kincaid said, "All right, O'Neil, I get your drift. What do you want from me, O'Neil?"

"Just this. Give me a week to find the man behind what's been happening around here. I'll bring you Billy's murderer. A week, Colonel. Just hold off for a week."

The older man might have agreed then, but Lowery stepped in, ruining Sean's attempt at compromise. "He's bluffing, Colonel," the man said, his eyes mean. "He's as guilty as all the rest. If he didn't pull the trigger on Billy, he sure as hell knew it was going to happen."

Kincaid waved a tired hand in the gunman's direction. "Don't rattle your spurs, Lowery. Let me think this through."

"I say, let's get it over with now!" Lowery opened his expensive coat, showing Sean two pearl-handled Smith and Wessons holstered high up under his armpits. "Let's open the ball, Colonel, and end this thing right here and now."

Sean took his hands from the saddle horn. He noticed Elliot was making no move toward his gun, so it was all Lowery's play. He knew with an awful certainty he was no match for the draw fighter but knew with equal certainty he was sure as hell going to try to be.

"Well, Texas, if 'n I was you, I wouldn't move a muscle. Fact is, I wouldn't even bat an eyelid."

Rusty stood in the cabin doorway, the 10-gauge steady as a rock in his hands. The black eyes of the Greener centered on Lowery's chest, but a man of caution, the gunman knew better than to turn his head. He marked Rusty's position by voice.

Lowery was railroaded and knew it, a twitch away from death, but Sean realized that man was not scared, not even slightly scared. He'd been up this road before many times, and nothing fazed him.

"Enough of this," Kincaid said suddenly. He had made up his mind. "O'Neil, you've got till noon Thursday to find my son's killer. If you don't produce him, I ride against his murderers." He looked hard at Johnny, then Sean. "All of them."

Sean knew protest was useless. He'd have to do his best in the time allowed, and his margin for success was a slim one.

Less than forty-eight hours . . .

"Let's get out of here," Kincaid said, swinging his horse away. The other riders followed, but Lowery remained. He stared hard at Sean and said, "Someday soon we're going to settle things between you and me."

"Hell, man. I hardly know you," Sean said. "There's nothing to settle."

"I don't like you. I kill men I don't like."

Johnny spoke up. "Mister, it will be the last time you'll pull a trigger because I'll take my hits and tear your fool head clean off."

"Call off your dog, O'Neil," Lowery said. "This isn't the time."

"Anytime, Lowery," Johnny said. "We'll be waiting."

"Boss, you want me to blow him right out of his saddle?" Rusty said. The little Chinese was primed, and his knuckles were white on the stock of the Greener.

"Not today, Rusty," Sean said. "Maybe some other day."

Lowery turned his head slowly. "Chinaman, I've marked you."

"You'll never put a tick against my name because I'll take you with me," Rusty said. He raised the muzzle of the scattergun. "All right, let's have at it. Eat some buckshot, draw fighter."

"No!" Sean said. "Rusty, let it go. Lowery, get out of here while you still can."

Lowery hesitated, not liking the odds, unnerved by the serene calmness and unwavering black eyes of the Chinaman. Finally, he said, "There will be another day."

He turned his horse and galloped after the others.

Rusty watched Lowery go, shook his head, and then said, "That man is a *yaojing.*"

"What's that?" Johnny asked. "Yao . . . yao . . . what you said."

"In Chinese it means monster."

Johnny nodded. "He's a monster all right, a monster with a fast draw and no conscience."

Chapter 10

The dead horses marked the spot on the trail where the O'Neils had been ambushed. Buzzards and coyotes had already found the carcasses, and the air was thick with fat black flies.

Johnny wrinkled his nose in disgust. "Sheesh, what a stink."

"Don't feel too bad," Sean said grimly, "it could have been us lying there."

The bushwhacker had picked his ambush site well. Measuring the distance with his eye, Sean reckoned only one hundred fifty yards of darkness had separated him and Johnny from their would-be killer.

The rocks themselves, massive granite boulders, were an unusual feature in this rolling cattle country. In ages past, the advancing glaciers had dragged them along, then as the ice retreated had abandoned them on the plains. They had stood for long centuries, silent monuments to a time long past. There was a flattened patch of grass between two of the boulders where the bushwhacker had lain. He had steadied his rifle in a V between two smaller rocks trying to make a hit more certain in the dim moonlight. That he had almost succeeded was a tribute to his keen eyesight and skill with a long gun.

Sean rooted around for a while, then bent to pick up a couple of empty shell cases. He studied them closely, and Johnny asked, "Tell you anything?"

The younger man nodded. "Yeah, they tell me the bushwhacker used a .44-40 rifle."

"And?"

"And that's it. There's maybe fifty men in this neck of the woods own Winchesters in that caliber, so it tells us nothing." Sean kneeled and studied the flattened grass. "I don't see any sign of blood, so I certainly didn't hit him." He sighed and straightened. "Know something, brother, we're lucky to be alive."

"Amen to that. Now what do we do?"

"We ride into town and have a talk with the Crystal Palace bartender. Maybe we'd better have a word with the sheriff, too, for what it's worth." Sean shook his head. "My time is running out."

"Tick, tock, tick, tock . . ." Johnny said.

"Brother, that's about the size of it."

Johnny looked at the dead horses, still saddled and bridled. "Maybe we should wait for a while and help Rusty."

"To dig out the saddles?"

"Yeah. It looks like it's going to be hard work."

"You've never seen Rusty dig a hole. I swear, there have been ofttimes when I figured he was trying to tunnel his way to China. He digs like a gopher."

Johnny smiled. "Is there anything that little runt of a Chinaman can't do?"

"There's something he can't do."

"What's that?"

"He's incapable of frying an egg without breaking the yolk."

"I saw that this morning. So, what else can't he do?"

"Nothing."

"Nothing?"

"Rusty can do anything he sets his mind to. One time I saw him carve a clipper ship, sails and all, out of cow bone. He sold it in town to Doc Grant for twenty dollars."

"Hell, how much do you pay such a paragon?"

"I don't pay Rusty anything. I give him room and board and he makes his living his own way."

"Making ships out of bone?"

"Among other things."

"I'll teach him how to fry an egg."

"Johnny, you're a daisy if you do."

Chapter 11

When the O'Neil brothers rode into town, Mustang Flat lay quiet under a noon sun. Ominously quiet. A killer was on the loose, and there was tension in the air. Even the prairie breeze was stilled. Two hipshot ponies stood at the Crystal Palace hitching rail, and a black and white dog lay on the Patterson stage depot porch, its pink tongue lolling in the heat.

Inside the saloon, a couple of punchers played poker, and a pile of nickels and dimes in front of each man showed that the stakes were not high.

"Want a beer, Johnny?" Sean asked.

The big man nodded. "Sure do, riding a horse on somebody's fourth best saddle always gives me a thirst."

"I thought it would be softer," Sean said.

"It wasn't," Johnny said.

The bartender was a different one from the night before, a magnificent creature in a fancy brocade vest, his thin hair parted in the middle and slicked down into kiss curls on either side of his forehead. Sean drank the foam off the top of his beer and motioned with his stein. "Where is the bartender who was here last night?"

"You mean Tommy Johnson? He was taken sick this morning. He won't be in till tomorrow, maybe the day after."

"Where does he live?"

The bartender shrugged. "I think he's got a cabin at the edge of town. Ask Clem Milk, the undertaker. He rents it out."

"We're obliged," Johnny said. He reached in his coat for a cheroot and put it in his mouth. The bartender scratched a match into flame and held it toward the big man's cigar.

Johnny nodded and puffed the stogie alight.

"Hey, do you smell something in here, Lefty. Like parfume or something?"

The O'Neils turned toward the man who had spoken, one of the poker-playing drovers. His companion, a rat-faced little man with green teeth grinned. "Sure do, Frenchy. Reminds me of a brothel I visited once upon a time in Denver."

"Well, if that don't beat all." The man called Frenchy grinned. "Some dude in here is wearing the same kinda parfume as them fancy Denver whores."

Rat Face giggled, nudging Frenchy with his elbow. "Bet it's the done-up dude in the derby hat, huh, huh?"

"Could be, could be, Lefty. 'Course he looks kinda beat up to be wearing fancy parfume and frillies an' all, but who can tell these days? Nothin' looks like it really is anymore."

Both men roared with laughter, as though Frenchy had cracked the funniest joke in the world.

Johnny set his beer carefully on the bar. "Know something, Sean"—he grinned—"I think I'm going to enjoy this."

The big man started toward the table, but his brother stopped him. "I know those two. They work for the colonel and they're trash, let them be. We've got other things to do, more important things." He pulled the big man back to the bar and said, "Important things like finding Billy Kincaid's killer?"

Johnny sighed, picked up his beer. "Whatever you say. I'm just a mite tired of being shot at, threatened, and pushed around, is all."

A chair scraped loudly as Frenchy stood up. The man's left eye was gone and a jagged scar angled from hairline to chin across the empty socket. He stood a little under six feet, but he was built like a gorilla. His chest was big as a beer keg and under his filthy shirt his arms were thick as a normal man's thighs. Big hairy hands dangling almost to his knees. Coupled with squat bowlegs, they gave him a powerful, simian look.

"Hey, fancy pants," Frenchy yelled, grinning. "You with the parfume."

Johnny turned, "Are you, fellow, by any chance alluding to my cologne?"

"Well, listen to that!" Frenchy turned to his buddy, sure of his audience. "What does allu . . . alluding . . . mean, Lefty?"

"Damned if'n I know," Lefty said. "It must be one o' them la-di-da words fancy-pant dudes use."

Frenchy roared with laughter. A false aggressive laughter

full of malice. He stopped abruptly and looked into Johnny's blazing eyes. "Listen, mister, next time you come here, if'n I decide to let you in, you better come smelling like a man or I'll take down your britches and whip your butt."

Lefty giggled.

"Smell like you, you mean?" Johnny said.

"Well, now you got it right."

"Then I'd have to stink like a wallowing hog."

The one-eyed man grinned. "You shouldn't have said that, fancy pants. Now I'm gonna cut your suspenders."

"Leave your gun on the table or I'll drop you where you stand, you sorry piece of trash," Sean said. His hand was near his Colt, and he was tense, ready.

Frenchy didn't want to die that day. He knew Sean O'Neil didn't have a gun rep, but the word around the barbershop from men that had seen him practice was that he was both fast and accurate. And Frenchy, who'd killed three men, was a craven, sure-thing bully who didn't take chances.

Without taking eyes off Johnny, Frenchy grinned, "Sure, O'Neil, anything you say." The man two-fingered his gun from the waistband and laid it on the table.

The little bartender, who until now had been silent, showed a surprising amount of sand by ducking under the bar and coming up with a sawed-off scattergun. "You gents want to fight, you do it outside."

"Suits me." Frenchy still grinned. "Suits me just fine."

The one-eyed man walked out the door, but Lefty paused as he passed Johnny. "Saw ol' Frenchy work on a fella in Wyoming one time." He giggled. "Tore off both that man's ears, bit off his nose and gouged out his eyes." Lefty put a thin, nervous hand to his mouth. "Found the dude a couple of hours later. He'd put a shotgun in his mouth and blowed his brains out. Didn't want to live no more. Can't say as I blame him."

"Get out of here, you little rat," Johnny growled. "Go out there and join your pardner."

"I feel sorry for you, mister," Lefty said. "When Frenchy's done with you, they'll have to pick you up with a mop."

"Git out of here," Johnny said. "Or I'll mop the floor with you."

Lefty grinned. "You poor chucklehead. God help you."

Johnny watched Lefty duck through the doors and said to Sean. "Don't go putting money on this one, brother. I'd say the odds are about even."

The young rancher's face was worried. "It doesn't have to happen."

"It does have to happen. You know that. If I walk away from this, I'll never again be able to hold up my head in the company of men."

Sean studied his brother's face, noted the stubborn determination, and said, "All right, let's go, brother," Sean said. He turned to the bartender. "Five dollars says my brother will win this fight."

"Ten says he won't."

"Then it's a bet," Sean said.

Frenchy was waiting in the middle of the street, Lefty off a little to his right. Across the way, on the other boardwalk, Luke Lawson, the hardware store owner, and a woman stood and looked across at the four men outside the saloon, their faces puzzled and apprehensive. No one else was in sight. And there was no sign of the sheriff.

"Thought you weren't coming," Frenchy grinned. "Figgered you might've snuck out by the back door."

"I'm here," Johnny said. He took off his coat and passed it to Sean. His hat, tie and stickpin followed. His huge hands came up in the classic bare-knuckle stance, and he said, "Right, boyo, let's have at it."

"Your funeral, fancy," Frenchy said, grinning.

He made a low animal sound deep in his chest and quickly stepped forward, hands low, fingers spread like claws. Johnny had anticipated this rush. He knew instinctively that a skull-and-boot fighter like Frenchy would try to grab him and then get close enough to where he could use a head butt followed by a fast knee to the crotch. Once his opponent was down, he'd go in hard with the boot and cave in his ribs.

Frenchy Laurent had it all planned out, but Johnny surprised him.

As he came in, Johnny's fist landed a straight left to Frenchy's face and followed up with two more that jolted the smaller man's head back and staggered him, making him step back out of reach of a wicked left. His face was already masked in blood. Johnny followed with grim, deadly purpose. Again, the left jab pumped like a piston, jolting Frenchy's head each time, followed by a beautiful right hook and then a series of clubbing punches that hurt Frenchy, who was now cut over his good eye. Johnny followed up with a roundhouse right, coming from his knee. The punch caught Frenchy flush on the side of the head. The man went down, then rose to a sitting position, spitting teeth and wiping blood from his face.

Johnny stood waiting. Two things bothered him. One, he was breathing a little too hard. He was out of condition, that was for sure, or maybe he was just getting too old for this kind of thing. The second, and even more disturbing, was that Frenchy had taken his best shot, the right hook that had devastated more than a few opponents, but it had not put the man away.

In fact, Frenchy was already on his feet. He'd been hurt and now he showed caution. He tried to close again, his hands down, splayed like massive talons, but this time he circled slowly, biding his time, more wrestler than boxer. Suddenly the shorter man came on at a rush, his bloody face bent into his chest, single eye keeping Johnny in view. Johnny tried to end it. He swung a right hard at Frenchy, aiming for the jaw. But Frenchy turned his head at the last split second, and Johnny's fist met a skull as hard as a cannonball. Johnny winced as the shock of the impact jolted up his arm. His right hand felt like it was shattered in pieces and his wrist, elbow, and shoulder were numb. He stepped back, jabbing with his left, but Frenchy moved with surprising speed. His arms circled Johnny's waist like a steel vice and he hugged the taller man to his chest. Frenchy's arms moved higher, squeezing the bigger man just under his rib cage. Johnny felt his breath cut off, and he laid his hands on Frenchy's shoulders, and flung his head back, gasping for air. He found none. The crushing power of Frenchy's massive arms totally closed off his lungs. Johnny heard the blood pound in his ears, felt his eyes pop. He opened his mouth in a silent scream of agony. The big man knew he was just seconds away from blacking out. Now he was fighting for his life. He tried to jab a thumb into Frenchy's remaining eye, but the man's

lowered head made it impossible. Frenchy was slowly
crushing the life out of him, and Johnny had to do something, and it had to be fast. He suddenly relaxed like a
puppet whose strings had just been cut and his arms
dropped to his sides. Surprised, Frenchy took his head
from between his shoulders for an instant and looked up.
It was all Johnny needed. He brought both palms up fast
and hard, slammed them with tremendous force into the
man's ears. Johnny almost passed out as a searing pain exploded in his right hand again, but Frenchy shrieked and
let go. Johnny stepped back, sobbing air into his tortured
lungs. The other man was moaning, holding his ears,
shaking his head like a confused hound dog. The damage
done by Johnny's muscular hands was devastating. He'd
ruptured Frenchy's right ear drum and the small bones in
both the man's ears shattered under the crushing impact.
Johnny O'Neil, weakening fast, knew he had to end it
right then. There was no pity in him as he worked on the
staggering Frenchy with lightning fast left jabs, smashing
the man's face into a pulp. Finally, Frenchy sank to his
knees, his bloody mouth gasping for air. Johnny stood
back breathing heavily, measured his opponent and then
flattened him with a vicious left hook that sounded like a
baseball bat hitting a two-by-four. Unbalanced by the
blow, Frenchy fell on his knees, spitting blood. But the
fight wasn't over. The man was not chawing the ground,
out of it, but Johnny stepped back and his tremendous kick
to Frenchy's face broke more bones, jolted the man's head,
and drew a hideous scream from his smashed mouth.
Frenchy, unconscious now, fell on his side, and Johnny, in
a murderous rage, went in with the boot. Vicious kicks
slammed, thudded, into the man's ribs.

"No! Johnny, no!" Sean yelled. "You're killing him." He ran to his brother, took his brother's raging face in both his hands and yelled, "It's over! You won!"

Luke Lawson, the hardware store owner, later said that Johnny O'Neil growled like a "wild animal" and pushed his brother's hands away, his eyes crazed.

"No!" Sean yelled, hanging on his brother's shoulders. "Johnny, it's over. Come back to me. Come back!"

It took a long minute before sanity returned to Johnny's eyes. He stared at his brother as though he was a stranger and then said, "Sean?"

"Yes, it's me, it's Sean, and it's over."

Johnny looked at Frenchy Laurent who was curled up in the dirt in a fetal position and said in a small voice, "I lost it, Sean. I lost my temper."

"Yes, you did. And now it's over."

"What about him?"

"He'll live."

The man called Lefty watched what had happened, was stunned and horrified and decided to make a play.

His real name was Cole Tandy and he'd killed before.

Raised an orphan, the only life Lefty had ever known was one of curses and blows, until he met Frenchy Laurent. For some reason Frenchy had taken a liking to the little runt, and they had been friends ever since. They worked as a team at Oaktree, and in the past they'd killed and robbed as a team. Now, seeing the only person who had ever given him a kind word lying in the dirt of the street, something snapped in Lefty's dim brain. He wanted to do one thing . . . kill the man who'd destroyed his partner.

But he made a fatal mistake. He called the play.

"Fancy pants, you're a dead man!"

The little runt's left hand streaked for his holstered Colt. He was fast, the kind of rattlesnake speed often found in smaller men. But Sean, from the steps of the saloon porch, was two shades faster. His Colt was out, firing, before Lefty got his revolver leveled. Sean's bullet crashed into the little man's shoulder, and the impact staggered him and his gun hand dropped. Lefty's shattered shoulder would not permit him to raise the Colt, so he tried to move the revolver to his right hand.*

A quiet warning from Sean stopped Lefty cold. "The next one goes through your head." Then harder, louder. "Drop it."

Lefty hesitated, the madness still in him. Sean saw him weigh the odds, the man's tight, mud brown eyes flickering to the Colt in his paralyzed left hand. Then Lefty reached a decision. "Ah, the hell with you, O'Neil." He clutched his mangled shoulder and grimaced in pain. Johnny stepped to the man and wrenched the gun from his hand.

At that moment, Luke Lawson stepped off the boardwalk, pulling the big-gutted Beason along behind him, Dr. John Grant, alerted by the firing, trailing behind. The sheriff, red-faced and panting, mopped his face with a dirty bandana, his eyes wild.

*Some historians say that Cole "Lefty" Tandy attempted a border shift, a play where a gunman shifts his gun to his uninjured hand. In Lefty's case it's possible, though he never completed the move.

"Wha . . . what the devil happened here?" the sheriff wheezed.

"You can see it, Beason," Sean said.

"I see a man lying in the street and another shot through and through," Beason said. "O'Neil, was this your work?"

"You could say that. I shot Lefty."

"How did it start?" the lawman said, struggling to level out his voice.

Sean told him what happened without elaboration, and Luke Lawson, who knew and liked the young rancher, was happy to confirm that Frenchy Laurent had walked into the street first, and that Lefty had been the first to go for a gun.

The sheriff slowly shook his head. "I don't know what's happening to this town anymore. It's going all to hell." He placed a hand on Lawson's shoulder and motioned to the two injured men. "Luke, help Doc Grant take these men to his surgery. They need attention bad."

Grant, an earnest young man wearing horn-rimmed spectacles, said, "One shot and one run over by a freight train. You're right, Sheriff, they both need doctoring."

"That's sawbones humor, huh?" Beason said, scowling.

"Do you see me smiling?" Grant said. Then, "Help me, Mr. Lawson."

Lawson nodded. He and two other bystanders lifted Frenchy Laurent by his shoulders and feet and one of the helpers said, "Heavy son of a bitch, ain't he?"

Beason scowled again and then turned to the O'Neils. "You two better come down to my office. You've got some explaining to do."

"We were planning to do just that, Sheriff," Sean said. "And we have some questions to ask."

Johnny put on his coat and hat, wincing as his hand flared in pain. "Maybe we should get that seen to by Doc Grant first," Sean said.

But the big man shook his head. "It can wait. There's nothing broken, and I've had worse hurts before. But my ribs took a beating." Then, his expression conscience-stricken, "Sean, I lost my temper, and when I do that, bad things happen."

"It wasn't on you, Johnny. Frenchy couldn't wait to open the ball."

"Something came over me, and I wanted to pound him to a bloody pulp."

"And that's what you did, Mr. O'Neil," Bob Beason said. "You sure as hell did."

Chapter 12

Another shooting! Corinda Mason stood at her window and smiled. There was no hope of doing business in this hick town, the population was too busy gunning each other.

Earlier that morning, Corinda had gotten a mix of good and bad news from the desk clerk.

The good was that tomorrow the Patterson stage would leave for San Antonio at seven in the a.m. and the driver, a man named Rowdy Roberts, was a stickler for punctuality.

The bad news was that the Apaches were still out, and two days before had killed and scalped a peddler less than two miles east of town.

"Maybe you should wait a few days, ma'am," the clerk said. "The savages will move on or get rounded up by the army."

"I don't want to spend another day in this town if I don't have to," Corinda said. "Besides, I have pressing business in Philadelphia."

"It could be a dangerous journey, ma'am. The Apaches

are running buddies with the Comanche and a sight meaner."

"This stage driver . . ."

"Rowdy Roberts."

"Is he willing to make the trip?"

"Yes, he will. Fear doesn't enter into ol' Rowdy's thinking and his shotgun messenger is Dan Keys. When he worked as a lawman in the Indian Territory, Keys killed every member of the Plunkett gang on the same day. Those were the brothers Ace and Bart Plunkett, the brothers Elias and Ethan Beckman and Jed Traynor, a mad dog who'd killed more than his share."

Bored out of her mind by Mustang Flat, Corinda was willing to listen to anybody. "Oh my," she said. "Mr. Keys must be quite a man."

"He was and still is. Nice enough feller, but mean as a caged cougar."

"How did he kill five men, outlaws I guess, on the same day?"

"Officially the Plunkett gang was in the bank robbing profession, but they'd turn their hand to anything crooked and Traynor was their fast gunman. Then they stopped at a burg called Last Hope up there on the Canadian and pretty much tried to take over the town. Then they say Traynor killed a man in a saloon and cut the whore who was with him, and that's when Keys cracked down."

Her professional interest roused, Corinda said, "Five men . . ."

"All of them hard cases."

"Five hard cases. How did Keys do it? Or don't you know?"

"I know. I heard it from Rowdy Roberts who heard it from Keys his ownself."

The clerk poured a glass of water from the jug on the desktop, drank to wet his pipe, and said, "How it come up, after the shooting, Ace Plunkett and the others were hanging out in front of the barbershop when who came down the boardwalk but Dan Keys. Keys told Traynor to raise his hands because he was taking him to jail on a charge of murder and whore cutting. Well, Traynor said. "'I will not and be damned to ye fer a lowdown hick star strutter.'"

"You do the accent very well," Corinda said.

"I'm saying it as Rowdy said it to me."

"Then go on. What happened next?"

"It seems that Keys was not in the mood for a cuss fight, so he hauled iron and shot Traynor right between the eyes. Traynor's body hadn't hit the ground before the sheriff, that's what he was, triggered Bart Plunkett and dropped him like a sack of . . . a sack of . . ."

"Dirt?"

"Yeah, that's it."

"And then?"

"Well, Keys ran into the barbershop, and Ace Plunkett went after him. Keys got out the back door into the alley and crouched down behind a pile of empty packing cases belonging to the general store next door. Then Ace Plunkett came out and stepped into the alley, turned to his left, and Keys let him have a bullet in the back. Killed him stone dead."

"He shot him in the back?"

"Yes, ma'am. See, that was the only part of Ace that faced him."

"That makes sense," Corinda said. "Two down, three to go."

"Then it gets strange. Elias and Ethan Beckman didn't like what was happening and made a dash for the livery where they'd left their horses. But don't you know it, the livery man's dog took a set against Ethan and grabbed him by the top of his boot. The livery feller came out and said, 'What are you doing to my dog?' Ethan said, 'Git it off me,' and Elias said, 'I'll shoot that damned dog' and the livery man says, 'And I'll shoot you.' Well, Keys came on the scene while the three men yelled at each other and the dog worried Ethan's leg. He took advantage of the situation and shot both brothers, Bang! Bang! and then he shot the dog."

"Why did he shoot the dog?" Corinda said.

"Nobody knows. Maybe he figured it was dangerous."

"And what happened to the fifth man?"

"That was Bart Plunkett. Oh, he raised his hands and tried to surrender, but Keys shot him anyway. The folks in Last Hope said it served him right."

"Then it seems I'll be in good hands on my trip to San Antone," Corinda said.

"And Rowdy Roberts can't be stampeded either. I recollect the time . . ."

"One story was enough for today. Maybe Mr. Roberts will tell me some more on the journey to San Antone."

"Be assured he will, ma'am, but I still urge you to stay here at the Red Dust Inn until there's no longer an Indian threat."

"Time and tide wait for no man, or in my case woman,"

Corinda said. "I must get to San Antonio." Corinda smiled, and because the clerk had amused her, she leaned over the desk, giving him an up-close view of her corseted breasts and kissed his forehead. "You're very kind."

The clerk nodded, but it took a while before he found his voice again.

Chapter 13

The O'Neil brothers walked in silence with Beason to his office, passing Clem Milk's funeral parlor where a black hearse, two black-draped grays in the shafts, stood ready to accept a casket. A small rat terrier stood at a distance and barked incessantly at the raised catafalque behind the side window, as though impatient to see the corpse hurried to its final destination.

In the daylight Bob Beason's office looked worse than it had the night before.

Papers and empty bottles littered the floor, and the walls, chairs, and desk were an inch deep in dust. The place smelled of piss, puke, man-sweat, and boiled cabbage.

Both brothers refused coffee. Beason poured himself a cup and sat behind his desk. "Now," he said, "will you kindly tell me what the hell's going on around here, and this on the day when Billy Kincaid is being put to rest."

"Billy will be buried in the Mustang Flat graveyard?" Sean said.

"Didn't you see Clem Milk's hearse ready to go once Colonel Kincaid arrives? And why not? We have a well-tended little cemetery. Got a former mayor and a couple of war veterans buried there and poor Aggie Murphy who was killed by bronco Kiowas that time."

"I reckoned the colonel would lay his son to rest on his own range," Sean said.

"There's no accounting for folks, is there?"

"Seems like."

"Billy will be a credit to the Mustang Flat cemetery."

"Is that what you think, Beason?"

"Not just me, there's a few others think along those lines. Luke Lawson over to the mercantile for one."

"Lawson didn't know Billy."

"Sure, he did, well enough to recall him as a high-rolling customer, and Clem Milk cottoned to him."

"The undertaker's friend, huh?" Johnny said.

Beason smiled. "Funny you should say that. Up Fort Worth way they call Luke Short the undertaker's friend because he shoots 'em where it doesn't show."

"Never heard of the man," Johnny said.

"I only met Luke once, that was in Fort Smith a few years before he married pretty young Mattie Buck. At the time I was thinking of taking up the bank-robbing profession, but he talked me out of it. He was just a little feller, was Luke, but good with a gun and nice enough if he liked you and he cottoned to most folks."

"We're not here to talk about Luke Short," Sean said.

"No, we're not. What were we talking about?"

"About Billy Kincaid being such a credit to the Mustang Flat boneyard."

"I'm sure the colonel will erect a fine monument, one of them marble ones with the crying angels and Billy's name picked out in gold. Folks will come from miles around to see a thing like that. Good for the town, I reckon."

Beason glanced at the clock on the wall. "It's already noon and I expect Colonel Kincaid is already on his way since the burial is at two. I guess them boys you had a set-to with were early mourners."

"Frenchy Laurent and Lefty Tandy weren't mourners. They were a couple of lowlifes looking for trouble."

Beason stared hard at Sean for long moments, and then said, "All right, then what happened. Speak to me. Say your piece, O'Neil. Air your mind."

"Frenchy picked a fight with my brother, and the two had at it out in the street."

"I saw what was left of Frenchy," Beason said.

"He had it coming," Johnny said.

"I wish I'd been there, Mr. O'Neil. I'd like to have seen that fight." The sheriff eyed Sean and said, "Now let me guess . . . Lefty saw what you'd done to his compadre, and he drew down on you."

"Yes. And Sean shot him."

"Self-defense, I'd say," Beason said. "In a manner of speaking."

"Lefty would've killed Johnny," Sean said. "I had to stop him."

"Brotherly love," the sheriff said. "That would have a jury in tears. Hell, it almost brings me to tears."

"You're a sensitive man, Beason."

"I know it. Too softhearted for my own good. My

sainted mother, God bless her, used to tell me that. 'Bob,' she'd say, 'you're too kindly for your own good.'"

"Now I need to tell you about last night, Sheriff," Sean said.

"Oh, dear Lord, you're not giving me another burden to bear."

Johnny said, "It's Sean and me who bore the burden. We're lucky to be alive."

"Then lay it on me. It's also my lot to be burdened, Mr. O'Neil."

"Sean will tell you how it was," Johnny said. "He's better at that kind of thing than me."

Sean said, "Then I'll begin at the beginning. Last night an old man stopped Johnny and me on our way into the livery stable. Now, what I'm about to tell you might be the truth, but it could be the ravings of a crazy old-timer."

"What was the old-timer's name?" Beason said.

"Sam Stolly. I think that was his last name. It was hard to make out since he'd been drinking."

"It is Sam Stolly, and he's as crazy as a bed bug. But I'm listening."

"Stolly said he saw the Crystal Palace bartender . . ."

"Tom Johnson."

"Yeah, that him. Stolly said Johnson stepped out the back door of the saloon just a minute or two before Billy Kincaid was shot and then stepped back in again. The old man reckoned the bartender had arranged to meet Billy in the alley and then drilled him."

"Arranged to meet Billy in the alley? What would a heller like Billy Kincaid and a lunger like Tom Johnson have to talk about?" Beason said. "They weren't exactly two peas in the same pod. Old man Stolly filled your head with nonsense, O'Neil."

"It's not so strange," Johnny said. "Johnson knew there was bad blood between Billy and Sean, and he may have told Billy he'd information about my brother and Nora Ann."

"What kind of information?"

"Information bad enough to justify a killing."

Beason shook his head. "It's as thin as hen skin and I don't believe a word of it. O'Neil, Sam Stolly told you a big windy and you fell for it. Somebody murdered Billy Kincaid all right, but it wasn't Tom Johnson. Hell, I have two better suspects sitting right here in front of me."

"Then we'd better take the bull by the horns and have a talk with Johnson," Sean said. "Beason, someone is staging events to control us, and we can't let that happen. How do you explain what happened last night?"

"What part of last night would that be?"

"The part where Johnny and I were bushwhacked on our way back to the ranch."

"Nobody told me about this," Beason said, frowning.

"Well now I'm telling you," Sean said.

"Who bushwhacked you?"

"Beason, sometimes I think you're half as smart as a wooden Indian. How the hell should I know who bushwhacked us? He didn't want to be seen, that's what made him a bushwhacker."

"You two are sitting right here, so he missed."

"He shot our horses out from under us, so he didn't do so bad."

"And now you suspect who?" Beason smiled. "It wasn't Tom Johnson."

"I suspected Lance Kincaid, but he and his hired guns paid me a visit this morning and denied any knowledge of it."

"Not Kincaid's style. He'll hang a man or shoot him, but he ain't into drygulching."

"He wants the man who murdered Billy."

"Don't we all."

"And he's given me two days to find him. This is the first day."

"And if you don't?"

"Then he's planning to start the biggest range war Texas has ever seen."

Sean was perversely pleased to see the sheriff blanch.

And Beason was shaken to the core.

A range war was the last thing he wanted to find himself in the middle of. Lawmen had a nasty habit of getting killed in range wars, and Beason wanted fervently to go on living.

Suddenly he was all business. "Now let me get this straight, this bartender, Tommy what-the-hell's his-name? You're saying he was the one punched Billy Kincaid's ticket?"

Sean smiled. "Let's put it this way. We got the word of one old drunk that Johnson left the bar moments before Billy was murdered. We know he didn't show up for work today, so we're putting two and two together and coming up with six."

Beason slurped noisily on his coffee. He winced, pulled his Colt from under his hip. "Goddam cannon, gets on my nerves." He shook his head slowly. "Why would What's-his-name?"

"Tom Johnson."

". . . want to murder Billy, for heaven sakes. He had no reason to kill him."

"Reason enough," Johnny stepped in, "if someone paid him."

"Aw, come on, why him? There's plenty of bums in this territory will do your killing for you, do it for the price of a whore and a bottle. No one knows that better than me. I've hanged enough of them."

"Listen, Sheriff, Billy was always in town late, either at the saloon or visiting his sweetheart," Sean said. "Maybe whoever hired Johnson figured a man who works nights had a better chance than most to lay for the kid. Besides, a hired gun in town attracts attention, and Johnson isn't a man you'd notice. Who would suspect a consumptive, skinny little bartender of being a hired assassin?"

Beason sighed and rose heavily. "I ain't buying this, O'Neil. I think you're mixed up in this whole mess to the hilt, and that includes Billy Kincaid's murder. But after I see Billy buried, we'll go talk to Johnson."

"And I can't make up my mind about you, Beason. I don't know if you're stupid or just plain pig-headed."

The sheriff grinned. "That makes two of us."

Chapter 14

The funeral of Billy Kincaid was so strange, so bizarre, so unreal that chroniclers chose to ignore it, or, as Bat Masterson once remarked, "Those newspaper boys swept it under the rug with a mighty big broom."

Sean and Johnny O'Neil stood outside Clem Milk's establishment with Sheriff Bob Beason and a dozen townspeople when Colonel Lance Kincaid rode into town with Nora Ann and a dozen punchers. As always, he was flanked by Zack Elliot and John D. Lowery. Over his dark broadcloth frock coat, the colonel wore a voluminous black mourning garment, then popular in Victorian England but seldom seen in the United States and never in West Texas.

By two o'clock the bright promise of the afternoon gave way to gray clouds that didn't threaten the overdue monsoon rains but dulled the day and cast a melancholy gloom over Mustang Flat. A south wind arrived with the overcast and made the male mourners around the hearse hold onto their hats while it slyly slapped at the skirts of the women. Billy's Mexican sweetheart, her unbound hair streaming in the breeze, stood a distance apart, ignored and unwelcome.

Colonel Kincaid, ashen-faced, dark shadows under his spiking blue eyes, came down on Sean O'Neil like the wrath of God. He drew rein, pointed a trembling finger and said, "You! You're not attending my son's funeral."

"That was not my intention," Sean said. His anger flared but he kept his voice even.

"You want me to move him on, Colonel?" Lowery said.

Johnny stepped in front of his brother, his face flushed with rage. "Better bring an army, big mouth. You'll need it."

Lowery smiled. "O'Neil, I can drop you right where you stand."

"There's two of us, Lowery," Sean said. "Want to try your luck?"

"Enough!" Lance Kincaid said. "I've had my say, now let it go. This is a sad day, a day for burying, not brawling."

"Some other time, O'Neil," Lowery said.

Sean ignored the man and exchanged a glance with Nora Ann, who managed a smile.

Clem Milk, looking solemn, stepped to the colonel's mount, and said, "Shall we bring out the dear departed now?"

"Yes, now," the colonel said. "We'll leave our horses here and walk behind my son to the cemetery." The little undertaker bowed and turned away, but Kincaid's voice stopped him. "And Milk, have your men bring a chair and your camera."

"My camera?"

"Yes, as I told you, bring your camera."

"And what kind of chair?"

"Damn you, Milk, the kind you sit in. Now do as you're told."

The undertaker wrung his hands and bowed again. "Anything you say, Colonel Kincaid, anything you say."

Nora Ann, riding sidesaddle, then popular, if not mandatory, in the East but seldom used on the frontier, urged her horse forward to the O'Neils and said, "I'm so sorry, Sean. Father isn't himself today."

"It's a sad day for the colonel and I can't blame him," Sean said. "But I didn't plan to attend Billy's funeral. I'd feel like a hypocrite, pretending to mourn a man I never did like."

Nora Ann nodded and smiled. "I understand. Billy could be difficult at times."

Dressed all in black, her face covered in a veil that fell from the brim of her top hat, Sean thought her devastatingly beautiful, a woman any red-blooded man on earth would desire to wed and bed. Then suddenly Nora Ann seemed distant, distracted, her attention elsewhere. Her lovely eyes stared beyond the hearse and the growing crowd, fixed on something behind Sean. Johnny noticed the same thing and, intrigued and less discreet than his brother, turned his head and saw what Nora Ann saw . . . a woman standing at the window of the hotel. She wore a pale blue dress, the color muted behind the dusty panes of the window, as she seemed to stare directly at Nora Ann and not the activity below. Finally, Nora Ann touched the brim of her hat with the handle of her riding crop, broke the eye contact, and then without another word to Sean swung her horse away and rejoined her father.

Sean gave Johnny a what-was-all-that-about look, and his brother said, "I don't know, she looked at a woman standing in a window of the Red Dust Inn."

"What kind of woman?"

"The usual female kind."

"I mean, was she young, old, or in-between?"

"The window is dirty, so it was hard to tell, but I pegged her as young. She wore a blue dress. Old ladies of my acquaintance don't wear dresses that color."

"She was probably Corinda Mason, the singer. She's staying at the inn."

"Maybe she and Nora Ann met back east at some time."

"That would be my guess," Sean said. "Did Nora Ann looked surprised to see her?"

"I don't know. What did you think?"

"I don't know."

"Then we both don't know," Johnny said. "But pretty women look at other pretty women."

Sean smiled. "Maybe Nora Ann likes blue dresses."

"I think you got your saddle on the right hoss. Pretty women also look at what other pretty women are wearing. And what do you know, they're bringing out Billy."

Sean turned his attention to the street where Milk and an assistant clumsily loaded the burdensome black and silver coffin into the hearse and a third top-hatted man appeared carrying a straight-backed chair, his bearded face solemn, and then a fourth, less well-dressed, with a bellows camera and stand.

If Colonel Kincaid thought the thing ill-done, he didn't let it show. "Dismount," he said. "We'll walk behind the hearse to the cemetery." Then, as though triggered by the words hearse and cemetery, he glanced at the gray sky and said, "Dear God in heaven, this is a dreadful day."

"Father!" Nora Ann had dismounted and ran to the colonel, but he pushed her away and said, "Let me be."

The girl seemed hurt but stepped aside.

Sean and Johnny O'Neil watched as Sheriff Beason took up the rear of the procession, his waddling walk kicking up dust from his boots. Heat lightning flickered in the somber gray sky, and the wind ceased to whisper, the ensuing silence profound.

"Are we going to watch or not?" Johnny said. He seemed ill at ease.

"We'll see Billy laid to rest, I guess," Sean said. "We can't do anything else until Beason gets back."

"We could go get a drink."

"The saloon is closed."

"Out of respect?

"No, because the colonel wanted it that way. Look, there goes Lucas Battles hurrying to the graveside."

"Who's he?"

"The proprietor of the Silver Palace. He served in General Sherman's staff during the war. I've never liked him much."

Johnny smiled. "Sean, you don't like anybody who wore the blue."

"No, I just don't cotton to two of them, Lucas Battles and Tecumseh Sherman."

But Johnny was no longer listening, his gaze fixed on the people at the graveside. "What the hell . . ." he said.

Sean followed his brother's eyes and said, "What do you see?"

"Clem Milk is opening Billy's coffin."

"Now I see it, Beason's fat butt was in the way. Milk is unscrewing the lid."

"Why?" Johnny said.

"Maybe the colonel wants to make sure that Billy is really in there."

"I don't know," Sean said. "But I guess we'll soon find out."

He turned his head and saw what he'd half-expected. The woman in the blue dress stared out the window again.

"Now remove my son, Clem," Colonel Kincaid said.

The little undertaker was aghast. "But, Colonel, tell me why? I prepared Billy in a winding sheet, all proper and respectful."

"Damn your eyes, Clem, do as I say. Take my son out of there."

Dick Peterson, Kincaid's tall foreman, grabbed Milk by the arm and said, "Do as the boss tells you."

"No, wait," Nora Ann said, alarmed, "Father, why are you doing this?"

"A family portrait." Kincaid said. "A fine family portrait. We don't have one and now we will." Then, "Clem put the chair over there on that flat spot and get your camera ready."

Horrified, Milk said, "But Colonel . . ."

As though he hadn't heard, Kincaid said, "Then you and your men raise my son from the coffin and set him in the chair, make him sit up real nice."

The punchers, a superstitious bunch, looked at each other with uneasy eyes, and even Lowery and Elliot, the normally stoical gunmen, seemed stunned.

Milk's assistants stood around the coffin looking lost, until the undertaker said. "You heard the man, get him out of there."

"Into the chair?" one of the assistants said, a tall, skinny man with the long-suffering face of a martyred saint on a Renaissance church ceiling.

"Yes, in the chair," Milk said. Then, "Let's have a family portrait."

"Father, I don't want to do this," Nora Ann said. Her full lips were pale.

"But you will," Kincaid said, a small step away from anger. "It's for posterity."

"What posterity?" Nora Ann said.

"For my sons and grandsons."

"You don't have any sons or grandsons," Nora Ann said.

"But I will. I'll wed again. I still have the hammer and tongs to produce a male heir and you will give birth to the grandsons."

Her father, still a strong, virile man, was capable of siring children, but, as Nora Ann suspected since her return to Texas, he had begun to cut the wire separating sanity from madness. A family portrait with a dead man was a symptom of that burgeoning lunacy and for now at least, she would have to cooperate. She stepped around the yawning grave and stood beside the chair.

Kincaid followed her, took up a position on the other side and then said, "Bring him. Bring my son."

"Not yet, Colonel, the camera . . . I have to set up," Milk said. He looked distraught, a funeral director in more distress than he'd ever known before.

"Then set up, damn you, and be quick about it," Kincaid said. "We'll wait."

Milk opened the tripod and aligned the large bellows camera with the chair, and then ducked under its black shroud for a long minute while he checked the focus. When he reappeared, he said, "I'm ready, Colonel."

Silent lightning shimmered in the leaden sky behind Kincaid as he said, "Bring my son."

Milk, by nature a timid man, ventured to say, "Colonel, the back of his head . . . he was shot . . ."

"Make your picture from the front," Kincaid said. He ignored Nora Ann's sharp intake of breath and added, "Get it done." He beamed. "We'll have a fine family portrait to hang above the mantel at Oaktree."

Sheriff Bob Beason looked like a man who'd just seen a ghost . . . or worse.

"They hauled Billy Kincaid out of the coffin and propped him up in the chair," Beason said. "His brains . . . his brains were running out."

"I know, we saw it," Sean O'Neil said. "I don't believe it, but we saw it."

"The colonel wanted a family portrait, him, Billy and Miss Nora Ann." Beason was a haunted man, his normally ruddy face ashen. "His eyes were open, Billy's eyes, as though he watched everything that happened."

"Clem Milk made the picture?" Sean said.

"Yeah. And he told everybody to smile. What a damned idiot."

"Did they?"

"Nobody smiled. Nora Ann cried, I couldn't see for sure, but I'm sure she was shedding tears."

"After Milk made the picture, they put Billy back in the box and screwed him down," Beason said. "By nature, I'm an equable man, but then I got angry."

"How angry?"

"Angry enough that I told Milk I'd put a bullet in him if he tried to unbox Billy a second time."

"And then what happened?" Johnny O'Neil said, interested despite himself.

"I got chunked out of there. The colonel told me what happened to Billy was none of my business and to light a shuck."

"And so you did," Johnny said.

"Well, I'm here, ain't I? You should have seen the lightning glitter in Billy's eyes like he was still alive . . . I need a drink."

"Later, Sheriff," Sean said. "Right now, we've got some cussin' and discussin' to do with Tom Johnson about Billy Kincaid's murder."

"A drink first, jawing after," Beason said.

"A range war and people's lives are at stake here," Sean said. "We talk with Johnson and then you can drink all the whiskey you want."

"Hell, Sheriff, I'll even buy the first round," Johnny said. "That is if you come along with us and behave."

"O'Neils, you're hard men," Beason said. "Mighty uppity and hard."

"And hard times are coming down," Sean said. "I'd say men like us have a right to be uppity."

Chapter 15

It was Sheriff Bob Beason's business to know where people lived in town. Tom Johnson's shack was on the fringe of what the townspeople called Little Sonora, a sprawling ghetto of wood-frame and tarpaper shacks running from behind the saloon all the way west to the town limits. Unlike the town itself, the village was noisy, alive with the sound of men, women, children, and dogs. As always, the spicy aroma of cooking hung over the shacks, and Johnny O'Neil, his stomach growling, suddenly realized he was hungry.

"Is it always as noisy as this?" he asked Beason.

The lawman nodded. "Yeah, I'd say always. Friday night is worst of all. Usually there's a cutting on Friday, maybe a shooting or two, but mostly I leave 'em strictly alone. Like in the Dark Ages during a plague, I ride over Saturday mornings and holler, 'Bring out your dead!' The fat man laughed at his own joke and looked disappointed when Johnny didn't join him. "I read about the plague in a book, you understand. That's how come I know what happened in them days."

"People shouldn't have to live like that," Sean said.

Beason shrugged: "Ain't much can be done about it. It's always been this way, and it always will. That's the order of things."

"Decent work and better housing might make a difference."

"Maybe so, O'Neil, but this is cattle country, and at best the work for the Mexicans is seasonal. It's something that can't be helped."

Sean was about to say more, but the sheriff held up a pudgy paw. "Please. I ain't no bleeding heart, only the law here. Look—" he pointed to a shack a little better than the rest with clean lace curtains in the window— "that's where Billy's little sweetheart lives, her and her padre. Her name is Maria Perez . . . the old man named her for a saint, you know . . . and she's the prettiest little gal you'd ever want to see."

There was no sign of life from the house as they rode past though Sean thought he saw the curtain twitch. "That's Johnson's shack over there," Beason said. And the young rancher forgot about the girl and why she'd loved a wastrel like Billy Kincaid.

Johnson's shack was no better than the others. Its single window was covered inside with a piece of sacking, and the door was slightly ajar on its leather hinges.

"Why would Johnson choose to live here," Sean muttered aloud. "He must earn enough to get himself a room at the hotel."

"He's a strange one, all right," Beason said, as if that explained everything. Then as he swung off his horse, he added: "Maybe when a man is slowly dying from consumption, he wants to surround himself with life. Who knows?"

The O'Neils sat their horses as Beason walked to the door. "You there, Johnson?" he yelled. There was no answer, and he stuck his head inside, pulling it back in a hurry. "He ain't there. God, it stinks. He lives in a pigsty."

Sean, recalling the state of the sheriff's office, decided the place had to be bad to offend the nostrils of the lawman.

Beason turned to the brothers. "Well, he ain't here. Now what?"

"Maybe he's flown the coop," Johnny suggested.

"Could be," Beason agreed.

Sean looked around. There was an undersized boy of about ten intently watching them from under a shock of straight black hair. The young rancher smiled and called the child over. Shy as a fawn, the boy walked slowly toward him. "You know the man who lives here?"

The child nodded.

"Know where he is?"

Another nod.

Beason's voice took on its official tone. "Come now, boy, this is the law talking and a man as hates boys, nasty, vicious creatures that they are. Tell me where Johnson went. Tell me directly now or face the consequences."

The child did not reply. He shot a frightened glance at Sean and looked as though he was about to turn and run.

"Shut up, Beason," Sean said. Then he smiled at the boy. "Where is Mr. Johnson, son?"

"He left," the boy said, "on a gray horse."

"How long ago?"

The boy shrugged.

"Which way did he go?"

The child turned and pointed south, in the general direction of both Sean's ranch and the Kincaid spread.

"Was he carrying anything? A trunk, maybe, or a bag?"

The boy shook his head. "Nothing. He just rode the gray horse."

"Well, what do you think, O'Neil?" Beason climbed ponderously onto his mount. "Want to go look for him? As if it matters a damn."

"It matters and we'd better find him," Sean said. "He's got some questions to answer."

Johnny patted his stomach and nodded in the direction of the saloon. "Maybe we should get us a sandwich and a beer first. I'm about to starve to death, and all I can smell is food cooking."

"I second that," Beason said.

"Later." Sean swung his horse around in the direction Johnson had taken. "I reckon we'd better find the bartender before it's too late. I've got a hunch he was hired to kill Billy Kincaid, and now he's gone to collect his blood money. But unless I'm very much mistaken, it won't be in gold—it will be in lead."

"But there's miles of open country south of here," Beason whined. "We could ride all day and never find the little runt."

Sean smiled without warmth. "I know, Beason, but we'll keep riding due south and pray we find a man on a gray horse before whoever is behind all this finds him first."

"O'Neil, a hungry man is an angry man," the sheriff said. "You ever hear that?"

"Not until now, and I don't want to hear it again."

"I won't make it. Hunger and thirst, I'll fall off my horse and perish."

"Beason, you could live on nothing but water for a six-month. Now let's ride."

The boy was still watching the three men. Sean waved to him, then turned to Beason. "Pay him, Sheriff."

The fat man spluttered. "Why me?"

"You just got through saying you're the law around here, so pay him a reward for his information."

"What information? That Tom Johnson rode south on a gray horse? That ain't information."

"It's more than we had a couple of minutes ago."

Beason grumbled as he fished in his vest pocket. "I only got a dollar."

Sean nodded. "That'll do fine."

"A whole dollar?"

"Pay the kid, Beason."

The sheriff flipped the coin to the boy who caught it expertly. He bobbed his head. "Gracias, señor, gracias."

Disgruntled, the fat man growled, "Buy a bushel of green apples with it, kid. Give yourself a bellyache."

The child's mocking laughter followed the fat man as he spurred after the retreating O'Neils.

Noiseless lightning still flashed in the gray sky, and the featureless land rolled ahead of them, cattle country, vast, open, and shadowed with secrets.

The three men rode steadily south for more than two hours, skirting the boundary of Sean's ranch to the north. Johnny unused to riding, was galled by his saddle and muttered under his breath about horseflesh, hard leather, and all things western. Beason, who seldom if ever rode, was in equally bad shape. Both men grew tired and hungry, and it was Sean alone who seemed as though he could go on forever.

Finally, Beason reined in his horse. "That's it for me, O'Neil. I'm heading back. If'n we keep this up, we'll ride clear to the Rio Bravo." He took off his hat and wiped his face with a sleeve. "Besides, Johnson's probably back in town by now sitting in the bar drinking cold beer and smoking a stogie."

Sean studied Beason. The man was right. He was done in. Even Johnny looked gray, and Sean remembered that he'd been through a lot that morning. The fight with Frenchy Laurent had been no picnic, like tying a knot in a mountain lion's tail.

The young rancher removed his battered Stetson, stood in the stirrups, and used the hat to shade his eyes against the declining sun. There was nothing to be seen for miles but the immensity of the plains. Here and there the land was slashed by dry washes, and among stands of mesquite and wild oak there were a few Herefords grazing. In this part of the range, they would be Colonel Kincaid's beef.

Sean closed his eyes, a sudden longing in him to ride north, leave West Texas and its feuds behind and head into the mountains where the silver-trunked aspen grew, and a man could spread his blankets under a roof of lodgepole pine and stars . . .

"O'Neil! Hell, man, are you listening to me?"

Sean slowly became aware that Beason was talking to him.

The fat man sighed and repeated, "Are you calling it a day?"

Reluctantly the young rancher agreed to end the search.

"But I'll ride back to town with you," he said. "Maybe Johnson got back alive."

"What about your brother?"

"Johnny, you'd better head back to the ranch," Sean said. "I'll point the way."

"All in all, I've had a busy day." The relief on the big man's voice was obvious.

He stood in the stirrups, easing himself in the saddle and looked to the west, as though something had attracted his attention. But he then sat down again so abruptly the little mare showed her irritation by bucking wildly. Johnny grabbed the saddle horn with one hand, his hat with the other and held on desperately till the horse decided it had made its point and came to a standstill.

"You all right, big feller?" Beason grinned.

Johnny ignored him. "Sean, just before this gut-twister started pitching, I saw something," he said. "Look over there where those trees grow beside the wash."

Sean followed his brother's pointing finger to a stand of mesquite some hundred yards away. He looked hard at the trees for a few seconds. "I don't see anything."

The big man was agitated. "I saw something move in there, I tell you, something white."

"Jackrabbit," Beason said. "It's gotta be a jackrabbit."

"It wasn't a rabbit," Johnny said. "I know what a rabbit looks like."

"No point in standing here talking about it," Sean said. "We'll go take a look."

Beason hung back, his face concerned. "Wait, it could be a trap."

"What kind of trap, Beason, for God's sake?" Sean said. "If somebody wanted to kill us, they could have done it while we stood around here jawing. Let's go."

The young rancher spurred his horse and was first to reach the trees. Johnny was right, he did see something white . . . the wind teasing the flapping left sleeve of Tom Johnson's shirt. The sleeve was about the only white part left, because the entire front of the man's chest was stained bright red with blood.

Sean dismounted and kneeled by the skinny bartender.

Beason crowded up next to him. "Oh dear, oh dear, this is terrible," he said. "Is he dead?"

"He's close to it."

"Another one! Oh, for heaven's sake not another one."

"Hobble your lip, Beason," Sean said. He lifted the dying man's head. "I think he's trying to say something." His ear close to Johnson's mouth, he said, "Who shot you, Johnson? Who did this to you?"

The man tried to raise his head farther. His impossibly thin hand grabbed the young rancher's arm. He whispered haltingly between racking coughs that stained the front of his shirt with more blood. Finally, his throat rattled, and his head slumped back.

"He's gone," Sean said.

"He's dead?" Beason asked.

"As he's ever gonna be."

Johnny pulled off his derby and crossed himself. "May Jesus, Mary, and Joseph have mercy on his poor soul."

Beason asked, "What did he say, O'Neil? Did he tell you anything?"

Sean picked up a couple of cartridge cases and then shook his head. "He tried hard, but I couldn't understand him."

"Maybe he shot himself, couldn't live with the guilt of murdering young Billy Kincaid," Beason said.

"His gun is in the holster, and he was shot in the chest," Sean said. "It doesn't look like a suicide."

Sean stood and found Beason studying him closely, stroking his stubbled chin, looking wise. "Strange that we found him here, ain't it, O'Neil? I mean the kid said Johnson headed south, but after a mile or two he could have taken any direction. How were you so danged sure he'd keep on riding this way?"

"I wasn't. I had a hunch was all. Call it a sixth sense, I don't know, call it luck maybe."

"Luck of the Irish." Beason's voice was without humor.

"That's it, Beason, luck of the Irish," Sean said.

"I don't believe in luck. A man makes his own luck."

"Luck is another name for opportunity, and when it comes along a man's got to be prepared for it. I was prepared to find Tom Johnson, dead or alive."

"Maybe too prepared," Beason said. "Like you had it all planned out."

Sean said, "So, you reckon we shot Johnson, then dragged you out all this way so you could find his body? Sheriff, if that was the case, we'd have done it a sight closer to Mustang Flat."

"Damn right we would," Johnny said. "Ask my aching butt about that."

"You're a daisy, O'Neil, mighty slick with the words," Beason said.

"I wish I could say the same about you," Sean said.

"We'd better get the stiff back to town," Beason said. "I want you to remember one thing, O'Neil, I'm going to be watching you. I'm going to be watching you mighty close and I mean within hollerin' distance. You catch my drift?"

Sean smiled. "That's your job, Sheriff."

"As long as you know," Beason said. "Now help me get Johnson on the back of my horse."

Johnny took the dead man by the shoulders and Beason moved to grab his legs. But Sean stepped between them.

"Wait. There's something I want to see."

He kneeled and ripped open the front of Johnson's shirt, exposing the bloodied chest.

"For pity's sake, O'Neil!" Beason said. "Have you lost your mind?"

"The man's no longer got a need for a shirt," Sean said. He pointed to the dead bartender's thin, wasted upper body. "Look at that."

Beason looked. "I looked. Now what?"

"It looks like Johnson was shot twice just above the heart. The wounds are so close together I could cover them with a silver dollar."

"What are you driving at, O'Neil?"

Sean stood up. "Just this . . . I don't know of any rancher or farmer in the valley, myself included, who could place two shots that close with a rifle." The young rancher looked steadily into the sheriff's eyes. "I know of only two men in the area who might be able to shoot like that."

"You're talking about John Lowery and Zack Elliot," Beason said.

"Right, Colonel Kincaid's hired gunmen."

"You're barking up the wrong tree, O'Neil. Lowery and Elliot are draw fighters, like Wes Hardin and Clay Allison, and they like it belly to belly with revolvers. They're pistoleros, not riflemen."

"The killer was close enough. I'd say within six feet and decided to use his Winchester. Maybe it amused him. Whoever he was, Johnson trusted him and allowed him to get within spitting distance."

"How handy are you with a Winchester, O'Neil?"

"As good as the next feller," Sean said. "But I didn't murder Tom Johnson."

"All right, then the colonel caught up with Johnson, found him here and executed him. How does that set with you?"

"I don't think so. Kincaid had no way of knowing it was Johnson killed his boy. I didn't tell him, and sure as hell the old drunk from the saloon didn't ride out to Oaktree and tell him either."

The sheriff shook his head, once to the right once to the left. "O'Neil, I think you're whistling Dixie. Are you trying to tell me them draw fighters of the colonel's acted on someone else's orders to kill Johnson? That same third party of yours who's trying to start a range war?"

"You're saddling the right horse, Sheriff. It ain't certain, but it's possible someone paid for the services of one or both gunmen after they went to work for Colonel Kincaid. Sure, the mysterious outsider already had hard cases working for him, killing cattle, and burning barns, but the war wasn't starting fast enough for his liking."

"Whose liking?" Beason said. "Third party, outsider . . .

damn it, boy, you're trying to buffalo me, and I ain't easily buffaloed."

"I have no idea who he is, just an unknown man who so far is content to stand in the shadows. He got to Johnson and paid him to kill Billy. And then Lowery or Elliot, maybe both, were told to kill me and Johnny, and the blame could be laid at Colonel Kincaid's doorstep."

"And Johnson?"

"When Johnson, on his way to wherever, came here first to collect his blood money he was shot. Call it an insurance policy to make sure he kept his mouth shut. I believe he was killed by the same man who bushwhacked Johnny and me, the same man who hired Johnson to kill Billy Kincaid."

The lawman looked confused. He motioned toward the body. "How long you reckon he's been lying there?"

"Judging by how his wounds are bleeding, not long. I think we missed the killer by an hour or less."

Beason looked round nervously. "Here, do you figger he's gone?"

"He's gone, long gone on a fast horse."

Beason sighed. "O'Neil, don't tell me anymore about who maybe killed who. I'm too tuckered to think. Once I get fed and likkered up, I'll sit down and study on things."

"Do all your thinking, Sheriff," Sean said. "Just think straight and cut this one thought out of the herd . . . it's possible the mystery man lives in Mustang Flat, and you pass him by in the street every day."

Beason nodded. "I'll keep that in mind, not at the front of my mind, but somewhere."

"You still think Johnny and me are the killers, don't you?"

"As I already told you, I haven't got to studying on it yet, but I will."

"Then study on this. I reckon the man behind this has a razor-sharp brain and he's probably smarter than all three of us put together. He's got ice water in his veins, and he'll stop at nothing to get what he wants. Do you know anybody who might fit the bill?"

"Only you, O'Neil. You're as smart as a whip and you got ice water for blood," Beason said. "You proved that today."

"When I shot Lefty Tandy, I suppose."

"No. When you drug me and Mr. O'Neil out all this way without even a thimbleful of whiskey or a bait of grub. Now help me get this carcass on my horse."

The moon began its climb into the evening sky when the distant lights of Mustang Flat came into sight and the O'Neils bade farewell to Beason. Now that Johnson had been found, there was no need for Sean to go into town, but, despite his aching butt, Johnny had decided to stick with him.

"Too many dead men and too many suspects," he said. "I wouldn't set easy in my mind if I left you alone."

The sheriff waved, then drew rein and called after the brothers, "Now you boys keep in touch, you hear?"

The lawman heard Sean yell back, "Count on it, Sheriff!"

Beason shook his head and kicked his horse into a walk, muttering to himself as was his habit, "Wish I knew what's happening around here. Bad thing when a man doesn't know who he's supposed to hang." He grinned, turned in the saddle, and slapped the dead man on the butt. "Hold on, pardner, we'll be home soon."

Beason kneed his tired mount into a reluctant canter and twenty minutes later dumped his grim load at the undertaker's office and then headed for the Crystal Palace.

Chapter 16

Johnny O'Neil had been unusually quiet all day since his fistfight with Frenchy Laurent, and the long ride had done little to improve his mood. But when he saw the lights of Sean's cabin through the darkness he brightened visibly. His good humor was mostly restored when he walked through the cabin door and greeted Rusty Chang.

The little man studied Johnny with little enthusiasm and said, "Where's the boss?"

"In the barn unsaddling the horses." Johnny said.

"How come you ain't been kilt yet?"

Johnny grinned. "Earlier today a feller by the name of Frenchy Laurent tried his best to do that and believe me, he came mighty close."

Rusty said. "Wish I'd seen that." Then, "Did you see Billy Kincaid planted?"

"At a distance. Me and Sean weren't invited to the funeral."

"How come?"

"Colonel Kincaid still thinks we could've had a hand in Billy's death."

"And did you?"

"You know better than that."

"I guess I do."

"But you're suspicious. You Celestials are all the same."

Rusty nodded. "Ah, but do you know why all Chinese look the same?"

"No, tell me."

"God made every person different, but he got tired by the time he got to China."

Johnny grinned and shook his head. "Rusty, you're one strange Chinaman."

Sitting at last in a comfortable chair, the smell of cooking food in his nose, Johnny refused to be baited any further by the little Chinese. He pulled off his boots and sighed as pain almost instantly fled his feet. "Now, me lad, what's for dinner?"

"Still ain't got no horse. But maybe I can rustle you up a tasty mule for tomorrow. You like mule cooked blue?"

Johnny smiled and shook his head. "Ah Rusty, Fighting Johnny O'Neil, the Boston Battler, is a tired man this night so please don't chide him. He won a terrible scrap this morning and for the rest of the day rode all over God's creation on a saddle made of barbed wire." Johnny looked at the little man and winked. "So how about some sympathy for his poor, weary soul?"

Rusty softened a little. "I've got a beef stew, real tasty, buttermilk biscuits, and a gen-u-ine Texas cowboy cake that'll line your flue. Meantime coffee is on the bile, so help yourself."

"Rusty, you're as sweet as a grandmother's kiss, and you talk Texan well."

"When living in a foreign country, learn the language."

"And Texas is a foreign country?"

"So the Yankees say."

"And what do you say?"

"This may be a shade beyond your understanding, slugger, but Texas isn't a country it's a state . . . a state of mind. A man doesn't live in Texas, Texas lives in a man."

"I always pegged Celestials for philosophers," Johnny said.

"Good. Then maybe I can teach you something, but I doubt it."

Johnny poured coffee into his cup as Sean walked in. "Things quiet today, Rusty?" he said.

The old man nodded. "Dug out the saddles, then checked on the herd, and they seem *esta bien*, and our big Hereford bull is as sleek as a newly weaned calf." He busied himself with plates. "Rode as far as the colonel's ranch house and looked the place over. Nothing moving there. The shades were drawn in the house and the bunkhouse windows were covered in burlap."

"I guess everybody from Oaktree was in town for Billy's funeral," Sean said.

"Does Colonel Kincaid still reckon you pulled the trigger?"

"I don't think so. With a man like Kincaid, it's hard to tell what he's thinking, but yeah, I believe he's changed his mind about that."

"Confucius, the great Chinese philosopher, says only the wisest and stupidest of men never change their mind about anything."

"We did find the guilty party, or at least the man who pulled the trigger on Billy." Sean told about finding Johnson's body, and then said, "He'd been murdered to silence him, and I suspect it was one of Kincaid's gunmen who did the killing."

"I don't understand," Rusty said. "The colonel caught up with the man who murdered his son and killed him, so it's over."

"I said I believe one of Kincaid's gunmen killed Tom Johnson, but the man who ordered Billy's death is still a mystery."

"I guess you better go tell all that to the colonel," Rusty said.

"Aim to, but that can wait till tomorrow. Right now, I want to eat."

Johnny chewed on a mouthful of beef and waved his fork in his brother's direction. "You think that's right? I mean he buried his son today. Seems to me you'll be intruding on the poor man's grief."

"I agree, but I don't have the time for the social niceties, brother. I'm trying to prevent a range war here and the colonel didn't give me much time."

"You're right, I can see that. But I'll . . ."

"Fast rider coming." Rusty's head was cocked to the side, listening.

Sean rose to his feet like a cat and drew his Colt.

"Kill the light!" he said.

Johnny blew out the lamp, plunging the cabin into darkness.

Sean opened the door and stepped to his left into darkness.

Chang stood in the doorway, his scattergun up and ready.

The rider yanked his lathered horse to a violent stop in the yard and swung out of the saddle.

"Stop right there, mister, and keep your hands high and away from your sides."

The cold command froze the man in his tracks. "That you, Sean?" he said. The man craned his head trying to penetrate the darkness. When there was no answer, he said, urgently this time, "It's me, Steve Pierce."

Sean stepped down from the porch. He knew Steve Pierce, a small, timid man who worked for a feisty little Scottish rancher named Sandy McPhee. But he kept his gun leveled until he could clearly make out the man's white, frightened face.

Sean holstered his weapon. "What's the trouble, Steve?"

The little man gulped. "It's Mr. McPhee. He's . . . I think he's in bad trouble."

"You'd better come inside and tell me what's happened."

"No time for that. You'd better get into town fast."

Sean spoke over his shoulder to Chang. "Saddle me a horse and one for Johnny." As he turned again to Pierce, he heard his brother groan. "What kind of trouble has Sandy got himself into this time?"

In a high, agitated voice, the little man explained that

McPhee had lost several cattle the day before, all of them top breeding stock. Early this morning he had found them, or what was left of them after they'd been butchered. He blamed it on Colonel Kincaid and had called his neighboring ranchers to a war council.

"Including you, Sean. But when I came over to fetch you, you wasn't here."

"Go on."

"Well, Mr. McPhee and about a dozen others, Jamison, Durant, Putnam . . ."

"I know the men. Just tell me what happened."

"Well, they had a meeting that lasted most of the day. They was getting pretty likkered up and talking about what they was going to do to the colonel and his hired draw fighters. Then Mr. McPhee, he tells me to ride into town for more drinkin' whiskey. When I got back . . . oh God help me, I still don't know why I said it—"

"Said what, Steve?" Sean prompted.

"I said I'd seen that Texan, the one they call Lowery. He'd just rode in on a tired horse and was drinking at the Crystal Palace. I heard him say he planned to spend the night at the Red Dust Inn."

Sean turned to Johnny, "He made good time, if it was him killed Johnson."

The big man nodded his agreement.

Pierce was puzzled, looking to the brothers for an explanation.

"Forget it," Sean told him. "Now what about McPhee?"

The drover swallowed hard. "I rode here as fast as I could. When I left, Mr. McPhee was saddling a horse to ride into town. He said with his bare hands he'll beat the truth about his dead cattle out of Lowery. His wife was crying, begging him to stay home, but he rode away like the hounds of hell were after him. He's aiming to brace Lowery and nothing can stop him. What's going to happen I don't know. I mean, what do you think . . ."

But Sean O'Neil didn't answer, already running to his horse, his brother bounding close behind him.

Chapter 17

Johnny later recalled little about that reckless ride across a dark prairie lit only by the pallid glow of a bashful moon. Sean set a killing pace, and the big man could only hold on to the saddle horn and let his horse have its head. Nor did the pace slacken when they hit Main Street. Sean barreled up to the Crystal Palace and yanked his gray to a halt. The big animal skidded to its haunches, protesting the sudden violence of the bit. The young rancher jumped from the leather, looped the reins over the hitching post, and vaulted onto the boardwalk.

He burst through the saloon door and saw with relief that McPhee was still alive. The little Scot stood at the bar brooding over a bottle of whiskey and a filled shot glass. McPhee's usually ruddy face was even redder, both from the whiskey and the anger inside him.

Sean glanced around the place. Within its walls the atmosphere of danger was palpable, like the charged air before a monstrous thunderstorm. Lowery sat at one of the tables, a silver coffeepot and a blue-and-white china cup and saucer in front of him. The draw fighter was playing solitaire with a greasy deck of cards, but his eyes were watchful. His glance slid over the young rancher and rested briefly on the holstered Colt at his waist.

He smiled.

"Howdy, O'Neil. What are you doing out this side of your bedtime? Kind of late for a straight arrow like you, ain't it?"

Sean ignored the gunman.

He stood next to McPhee. "Don't you think it's time you were going home, Sandy?" he said.

McPhee shook his head stubbornly. "Got some unfinished business to attend to first." He turned and pointed a finger at Lowery. "With him, that lowdown son of a bitch."

The draw fighter shook his head and said nothing. Beyond him sat two men Sean had not seen before, by the look of them, drifters passing through town. The men stirred uncomfortably in their chairs, talking in low whispers as if afraid to draw attention to themselves. A couple of townsmen stood at the bar, and beyond them, studiously ignoring Sean, was Frenchy Laurent. His face looked like raw meat, but he seemed to have recovered some from the beating Johnny had given him that morning. There was no sign of Lefty Tandy.

Lowery pulled an expensive gold watch from his vest, glanced at it, and snapped it shut. The sound was very loud in the silence. "It's gone ten," he said. "Take him home to his bed, O'Neil."

"When he's good and ready," Sean said.

"I see you brought your brother along," Lowery said. "For protection, maybe?"

"The day I need protection from the likes of you, Lowery, is the day I hang up my gun forever."

"Tut-tut and tut, don't push me, O'Neil. I can shade you any hour of the day, any day of the week. A damned dollar-a-day waddie like you should watch what he says when he's around his betters."

"Then here's what I say, you bushwhacked Tom Johnson earlier today, Lowery, and I aim to see you hang for it," Sean said.

That last seemed to strike a nerve in Lowery, but the gunman smiled it off. "I bushwhacked nobody, and this is not a good time to be a smart alec, O'Neil. I may have to kill a man tonight, and I don't particularly mind adding another."

"And then I'll put your name on the list, Lowery," Johnny said, his massive fists clenched.

"I have no quarrel with you, pug," the gunman said. "So stay the hell out of it."

"Johnny, let him be." Sean said.

"Sound advice, O'Neil," Lowery said. He directed his attention to McPhee. "If you have business with me mister, you'd better get to it fast."

"Are you talking about me, gunslinger?" McPhee said.

"Why, of course I am. What do they call you, Limey?"

To call a Scotsman "Limey" was a deliberate insult and Lowery knew it.

"They call me Alexander McPhee, and I bear my father's name because I'm not a whoreson like you."

"Fighting words, Limey. Can you back them up with the gun you wear?"

McPhee flushed, his blue eyes shot red with rage. He

turned to the bar and downed a glass of bourbon, refilled, and drank again. Then he swung to face the drawfighter, his eyes wild and accusing. "I lost cattle today, Lowery, and I'm holding Kincaid responsible. You're one of his hired guns and I say it was you who stole and butchered, them."

Lowery was relaxed. He smiled slowly and shook his head. "You're crazy, little man."

McPhee drew himself up to his full height. He reminded Sean of a little red rooster ready to do battle with a hawk. "I say again, you stole my cattle and butchered them. They were some of my best breeding stock, Herefords, and I'll ask you kindly to fish in your pockets and pay for them."

A look of incredulous amazement spread over Lowery's face. The drawfighter stood up. He unbuttoned his coat pulling it away from the holstered guns under his armpits. "You're crazy," he said. "You're just plain crazy."

"You say you didn't take my cattle?" McPhee said, his throat tight.

Lowery sighed and shook his head, but he never took his eyes from the little Scotsman. Sean, watching, saw the gunman for what he was—a cold-blooded predator who had his victim trapped and very badly wanted to kill.

"I'll tell you one time and one time only," Lowery said, "I never took your cattle. The colonel called a truce, ask your friend O'Neil there." The gunman turned his head a fraction. "Tell him, O'Neil."

Sean laid a hand on McPhee's shoulder. "It pains me to say this, but I think he's telling the truth. There's Apache off the reservation. They're hungry and I guess they killed and butchered your cattle for meat. Lowery doesn't have a spot of blood on him." The young rancher turned to McPhee, looking straight into the man's eyes. "Leave it be, Sandy. Lowery has other questions to answer, questions a lot more serious."

"You accusing me of something, O'Neil?"

Sean smiled thinly. "Not yet, Lowery. But I think given time I'll find evidence enough to hang you."

The drawfighter laughed. "You're as crazy as the Limey."

Again, Sean ignored the man. He took McPhee by the arm. "Let's go home, Sandy."

The little rancher's shoulders slumped. He could not dismiss the logic of the Apache raiding party. He nodded dumbly and turned toward the door.

Lowery's voice, suddenly cold and harsh cut across the silence of the saloon, stopping the man in his tracks.

"Our business isn't over yet."

Sandy McPhee turned to face Lowery. "What do you want?"

Lowery looked like a rabid wolf. "An apology. I want to hear a humble apology for smearing my good name."

"You go to hell," McPhee said.

In the deathly silence that followed, the two drifters rose and walked to the bar away from any possible line of fire. One of the townsmen, a Dutch gunsmith named DeHooch, turned his pale frightened face to Sean. "This is no good. Me, I'll go for sheriff."

But before the man could move, Frenchy Laurent, who seemed to appear out of nowhere, placed a huge paw on his shoulder. He grinned, his broken face a grotesque mask, and shook DeHooch like a terrier with a rat. "Now, now, there ain't no need for that. All Mr. Lowery wants is a simple apology. Ain't that right, Mr. Lowery?"

The gunman nodded. "Quite right, Laurent, just an apology."

Sean leaned over and whispered urgently in McPhee's ear. "Apologize, Sandy. It doesn't mean a thing."

At first it looked like the little man would balk. But then he sighed deeply as if willing himself to relax and whispered, "Okay, I apologize."

"Didn't hear you." Lowery had his right hand cupped to his ear, his head cocked.

"He said he's sorry," Sean said, anger edging his voice.

"I was speaking to the Limey, not you." Lowery's chin jutted toward McPhee. "I said, I didn't hear you."

In the white heat of anger, McPhee could be dangerously, recklessly brave. But now the anger was gone, driven away by the possibility of an Apache raiding party. Besides, the little man was tired. He wanted badly to go home to his wife and children, and the beginnings of a massive hangover was driving knives into the back of his neck and head. The little man's chin dropped to his chest. Slowly and distinctly, he said, "I apologize for what I said and the accusation I made."

A sudden, churning sickness in his belly, Sean put his arm around the man's shoulder and said, "It's all over, Sandy. We're going home."

But Lowery would not let it lie.

"Hold it right there." The gunman's eyes were the color of ice, and he was no longer smiling. He stepped away from the table, about ten feet separating him from Sean and McPhee.

"You walked in here on your hind legs like a man. If you want to stay alive, you'll leave like the yellow worm you are . . . on your belly."

Stung by anger, Sean's hand dropped close to his Colt. "Damn you, Lowery, if you're spoiling for a gunfight, get your work in, and I'll give you all the gunfighting you want."

For the second time since entering the saloon, Johnny spoke. Like Sean, he was pale with anger. "You better be ready to accommodate both of us."

The drawfighter grinned. "If you boys are taking a hand in this game, I hope you're ready to pay the stakes."

"Are you going to talk all night, Lowery?" Sean said, ready for the draw and shoot. "You're heeled, so let's get to it."

"No!" McPhee stepped quickly between Sean and the gunman. He turned to the young rancher. "I will thank you, Mr. O'Neil, to let me fight my own battles." Then his voice softening, he whispered, "There will be no more killing on my account, there's been enough death already." He stared hard at Lowery. "I have given you my apology, and now I want to tell you something. I am almost forty-six years old, and I have an ailing wife and seven children, so . . ."

The little man did something totally unexpected, an action that men talked about for years, including famous Texas Ranger William "Bigfoot" Wallace who said, shortly before his death in 1899, "I wasn't there that night, but no matter, if I'd seen it, I wouldn't have believed it."

McPhee dropped to his knees and flattened himself on the floor. Tears streaming down his cheeks, he crawled on his belly toward the door.

For long seconds there was a stunned silence. Even Lowery looked amazed. Then Frenchy Laurent took off his hat, waved it over his head and hollered, "Yahoo! Look at the little worm go!"

Lowery slapped his thigh and roared with laughter, and Laurent joined him. No one else made a sound. The faces of the two drifters, the bartender, and the townsmen were frozen into sick, stunned masks.

"That's enough!" Johnny O'Neil said. "Lowery, you've had your fun." He stepped to the crawling man and took him by the shoulders. "Come on, Sandy," he said. "You're going home."

Sobbing, McPhee tried to push him away. "Let me be! Just let me be."

Sean turned on Lowery with the fury of a wounded cougar. "You're a pig, Lowery," he said between clenched teeth. "And I'm going to kill you like a pig! Haul the iron and get to your work."

The gunman, taken aback by the young rancher's red-hot anger, hesitated a split second before going for his gun and that moment's hesitation probably saved Sean's life because the saloon door slammed open and Sheriff Beason barged through, a scattergun in his hands. He took in the situation at a glance and yelled, "I'll kill the first man who moves!"

Instantly, Lowery's hands spread away from his guns. "I'm not looking for trouble, Sheriff. I fell in with bad company as you can see."

Sean, the killing rage still in him, kept his hand near his holstered Colt. He felt the cold muzzle of Beason's shotgun against his neck. "If'n I was you O'Neil, I wouldn't try that, I surely wouldn't." The young rancher still enraged saw the grinning Lowery through a black crowding fog. It was his brother's quiet voice that cut through his anger and dragged him back to sanity.

"He's not going for his gun, Sean," Johnny said. "Kill him now and it's murder, and he isn't worth hanging for."

Sean relaxed slowly. He straightened from his half crouch and turned white-lipped to Beason. "You ever stick a gun in my face again, Beason, I'll make you eat it."

The sheriff, reading the warning in Sean's eyes, decided to retreat into bluster. "I knew there would be trouble when I saw that big gray of your'n outside," he said. He decided he'd saved enough face and lowered his gun.

Beason turned to McPhee. The little man sat on the floor his face buried in his hands, and he sobbed quietly.

Displaying an unexpected gesture of compassion Beason took McPhee by the arms and raised him to his feet. "You've no call to be out this time of night, Sandy. Best you go home and sleep it off." Then, "Give my regards to the little lady."

The man did not protest. Without a backward glance, he staggered through the open door and into the night.

Beason waited till he heard McPhee's horse leave, then he turned to the grinning Lowery. "What the hell's going on here?"

"Nothing much until O'Neil barged in here. No one was aiming to harm the little man." The gunman sat at his table and poured himself a brandy. "We were only having a little fun. Why don't you tell the sheriff yourself, O'Neil?"

Beason dug deep inside himself, and to everyone's surprise found sand. "O'Neil doesn't need to tell me anything. I saw what happened. If that's your idea of fun, Lowery, you got a twisted sense of humor."

Lowery bowed his head and toasted the sheriff with his glass, a mocking smile on his lips. "Everyone needs a laugh now and then."

Bemused by his own courage, Beason motioned toward the bottle in front of Lowery with the 10-gauge. "That's it for the night, Lowery. The bar's closed."

Frenchy Laurent opened his mouth to protest, but Lowery waved him into silence. The gunman smiled, picked up his hat from the table and said, "Happy to oblige, Sheriff. We don't want any trouble with the law." He waved a hand toward Laurent and said to Johnny, "Frenchy was no oil painting to begin with, but you sure rearranged his features into uglier."

"He called the play," Johnny said.

Lowery's eyes sought Sean's, and he said, "Frenchy, it's a fatal mistake to brace a man who's a sight better at backing his play than you are. Someone who's faster with his hands, I mean. Let that be a lesson to you."

He beckoned to Laurent and together they stepped toward the door.

Sean's voice, brittle with suppressed anger stopped him. "Heard you came in on a tired horse tonight, Lowery. Been riding some?"

Lowery turned to face the young rancher. The gunman's

mouth was twisted in an insolent grin. "Sure, I rode today. I ride every day. It's good for a man."

"Were you riding south of here on Kincaid range, meeting somebody maybe?"

Lowery's grin slipped. "That's my business."

Sean's face was a stiff bloodless mask. "I'm giving you fair warning. I'm making it my business."

"Okay, boys, that's enough." Beason shoved his big belly between the two men. "We've had enough excitement for one day."

Lowery nodded. He walked to the door and let Frenchy Laurent through first. Then he turned to Sean. "We'll meet, O'Neil, depend on that. We'll meet real soon." The doors opened and closed, and the gunman was gone.

Beason whistled between his teeth. "O'Neil, you surely have a way of getting yourself into a peck of trouble."

Without looking at the sheriff, Sean answered, "Sure looks that way, doesn't it?"

Beason shook his head. "O'Neil, I done some studying on it, and I think you just got a bug up your butt about Lowery and Elliot." He saw the sudden coldness in Sean's eyes and shrank from it. "Now don't get me wrong, what you say might be true, I mean about someone else being behind what's happened an' all. But hell, you ain't got a scrap of evidence to prove it." The lawman sighed. "Give me something to work with, anything, and I'll make sure the law takes care of this whole sorry mess. But don't ask me to go chasing phantoms."

Sean felt tired. For the second time that day he longed

to get on his horse and ride for the mountains. Just go and leave all this feuding and death behind.

"Listen to me, Beason," he said finally, choosing his words with care. "I saw Lowery get set to try to kill a man in here tonight." There was murmured agreement from the men at the bar. "I believe he already killed today when he put two bullets into Tom Johnson to shut him up. Speak to Lowery, Sheriff. Pin him down and maybe you'll find the man behind what's happening on the range." Sean's shoulders slumped, and his weary gaze found Beason's bloodshot eyes. "Don't go asking me how I know these things . . . I just know."

"All right, bring me the proof, and I'll do the rest."

"Proof? I just told you I don't have any proof, at least nothing that would stand up in court. But I'll tell you something, Sheriff, one way or another I'm going to nail Lowery's hide to the wall and do the same to the man behind him."

"That's a job for the law, O'Neil." Beason turned dramatically to the men at the bar. "You heard me warn this man—the law will do the punishing if there's punishing to be done!"

Sean looked sadly at the lawman. "Know something, Beason, I almost discovered some respect for you tonight, but it was misplaced. You're still a jackass."

Beason, unpredictable as ever, found that last amusing, and he grinned. "Hell, O'Neil, I like you. One day, I'll probably hang you, but dang it all, I like you."

"And you're a sweetheart, Beason," Sean said.

The young rancher turned on his heel and left the saloon. He leaned against a post supporting the porch and slowly, with steady hands and great care built himself a smoke. As Johnny joined him, he thumbed a match into flame, fired the cigarette, and said, "All in all, quite a day."

Johnny nodded. "I'd say so. Can't remember having too many like it."

"Then let's go home," Sean said.

The two men untied their horses from the hitching rail and climbed into the saddle.

Beason came out of the saloon and stood wide-legged and big gutted on the porch. "One thing, O'Neil, afore you go. Lefty Tandy died early this evening in Doc Grant's surgery. I guess a shoulder wound like that was just too much for the little man."

"And now you plan to arrest me?" Sean said.

Beason shook his head. "Nope, it was a clear-cut case of self-defense. I can't arrest a man for that."

"I'm sorry it went down the way it did. Lefty gave me no choice."

"That's what I heard. Anyway, I don't much care. I never liked the man."

Sean touched his hat brim. "Thanks for telling me, Beason."

He was glad of the darkness. The sheriff couldn't see how the news troubled him. It was never an easy thing to kill a man.

"Just thought you'd want to know," Beason said. "I confiscated the eight dollars in his pocket, enough to bury him decent."

Sean nodded and swung his horse away from the hitching rail.

Beason watched the brothers ride off and then shivered as something rose dank and black to his nostrils, the stink of the grave. Suddenly he needed a drink. "Hey you, bartender," he yelled. "Don't close up just yet. You got a customer. "

Chapter 18

Sean O'Neil was content to keep his tired mount to a walk as he and Johnny rode down the dark main street of Mustang Flat under the waxing crescent moon.

His brother gave him a sidelong look and then said, "What do you plan to do?"

Sean flicked his cigarette butt away, watched it arc in the darkness, then hit the earth in a shower of sparks. "Tomorrow morning, I'm riding out to see Kincaid," he said. "I'll tell him what I suspect, ask for his help, and hope he sees reason."

"You reckon Kincaid'll be willing to help?"

"I sure hope so. The man is ruthless, and he's filled with rage and grief, but he's fair. At least he was up until recently, and maybe all that's changed. I hope he'll help me investigate Lowery even if it's just to prove his gunman's innocence." Sean's hand went to his shirt pocket and took out the makings.

"You smoke too much," Johnny said.

The younger man smiled. "I know it. But Dr. Grant says tobacco is good for the heart and lungs."

"I've been told that, but it cuts down on the wind,

you know." The big man saw Sean was unimpressed by the warning and added, "When Kincaid hears about a third party being involved, my guess is that he'll be glad to cooperate."

Sean nodded. "As of now, he's got a dozen drovers on his payroll. Chances are one of them knows something that will help us nail Lowery and whoever is paying him. Kincaid—"

"Swine!"

The rock sailed out of the night and thumped solidly into Johnny's derby. The hat sailed off the big man's head and dropped somewhere in the darkness.

"What the hell!" Johnny roared, grabbing for the saddle horn as his bay mare decided to act up again.

Sean's Colt was out leveled at the darkness between a false-fronted dress and hat shop on the edge of town and a tent that served as an office for a newly arrived attorney.

"You better come out with your hands in the air," Sean said. "Or you're coming out dead."

A figure emerged from the darkness, and to Sean's surprise the rock thrower was a girl. Right then she was more screaming wildcat, but there was no mistaking the silken sheen of her hair and the swell of her breasts under the simple gingham dress.

"Murderers," the girl yelled.

Johnny, seeing she had another rock in her hand, backed his horse away warily. "Now look here, young lady . . ." His voice choked off as he ducked the second rock.

Sean swung from his horse and ran to the screaming

girl. He grabbed her by the shoulders and shook her hard. "Listen to me. Just calm down and tell me what this is all about."

"You know what it's about, you, you . . . killer! If I had a gun, I would've shot you, both of you."

Johnny also dismounted. He picked up his hat and looked closely at the girl, his face puzzled. "Young lady, we don't know what you're talking about. Who are we supposed to have killed?"

"I think I know." Sean told him. He took his hands from the girl's shoulders and said, "You're Maria Perez, aren't you?"

The girl's eyes were hard, accusing. "Yes, Maria Perez, and the man you murdered was to have been my husband."

"Maria, we did not kill Billy Kincaid—"

The girl screamed something in Spanish, and her tiny fists beat on Sean's chest. "You lie! I know you're lying to me."

Sean took hold of her wrists and held them. "Listen, the man who shot Billy is dead, but the man who ordered his death is still alive. My brother and I are trying to find that man. You've got to believe us."

Maria's face was very pale, her eyes flat and hard as obsidian. "I do not believe you. Billy told me he was afraid. He said someone wanted him dead, and he feared that his sister was also in danger."

"Had he gotten threats?" Sean said.

"He said notes were left at Oaktree that told him he was a dead man."

"I guess they weren't signed."

"He showed me one and it was signed. It said, *The Avengers*."

"That was none of my doing," Sean said.

The girl tilted her chin defiantly. "You hope to benefit from Billy's death, you and the ranchers who hired you."

Johnny stared at the girl in wonder. She was small and she was young, but she had courage. He could not keep a note of admiration out of his voice. "Maria, I think when you hear the whole story, you'll realize we had nothing to do with Billy's death. Someone wanted him dead, that's true, but we believe it might be a man we don't even know or have even heard of. That man could be here in Mustang Flat, and he could be anybody, the saloon owner, the man who has the hardware store, or how many others?"

"My brother is right. There's probably forty grown men in this town, and the brain behind Billy's death could be any one of them," Sean said.

"And he might be a rancher or a farmer," Johnny said. "I know it's unlikely, but anything is possible."

The girl looked closely at Johnny. In the darkness she thought he looked enormous like a great bear. But even though his face was cruelly battered, his nose broken and set askew between high cheekbones, his eyes were kind, and his voice was gentle. A nagging doubt entered Maria's mind—could this big, simple man commit murder? Could his tall brother shoot a boy in the head and plan the execution of his victim's sister?

Maria shook her head, trying to compose her thoughts, and then said, "I think you're lying to me, trying to put the blame for Billy's murder on somebody else."

"Listen, we know who likely killed Billy Kincaid," Sean said.

"Tell me, I'll find him."

"He's dead."

"Dead? I don't understand."

"We believe that Tom Johnson, the Crystal Palace bartender, was paid to kill Billy. Now Johnson is dead, probably killed by the man who hired him. The man we're trying to find."

Maria wet her lips and blinked, absorbing what Sean had just said.

She said finally, "Then tell me the whole story, and let me decide."

Johnny turned to Sean and saw his brother nod in agreement.

"I will, but I don't think this is the time or place," Sean said. "Maria, why don't you go home and get a good night's sleep? Try to forget about Billy's death for a few hours, and we'll meet again tomorrow."

Maria's laugh was forced, bitter. "Sleep? Where will I sleep? I have no home." She saw the question in Sean's eyes and said, "My father threw me out of his house tonight. He called me a whore." She raised her head in a defiant gesture. "I carry Billy's child."

Sean let his surprise show. "I guess I didn't expect that."

"Why? Do you think unmarried women no longer have babies?"

"I mean . . . what I was trying to say . . ."

Johnny came to his brother's aid. "I guess there's always the hotel," he said.

Again, the girl's strained laugh. "The hotel? Who has money for hotels? And will the hotel rent a room to a penniless . . . a penniless greaser?"

The big man laid a huge hand on the girl's shoulder.

"Don't worry about a thing, little lady. I'll get you a room at the hotel. You can stay there until, well till you make up your mind about where you want to go from here."

The girl shook her head. "No, I will not stay at the hotel. I will not be welcome there."

Johnny sighed. "Then there is only one thing to do, if you feel you can trust us. You must come to my brother's ranch and stay there." The big man caught the startled look Sean threw him and shrugged. "There's nothing else to be done."

The hopelessness of Maria's situation got through to Sean, and he nodded. "As my brother said, if you feel you can trust us, then you are welcome to stay at my ranch."

Maria studied the two men's faces for a moment, then said, "I will be no trouble to you. If you have a barn, I will sleep there, and I will leave in the morning. As for trust, a woman trusts only when she fears harm. What can harm me now? What can harm me ever again?"

Johnny's sentimental soul was touched. "You poor girl, you must have loved Billy very much."

Maria surprised him again. "No, I did not love Billy Kincaid. He drank too much, and he could be cruel sometimes. But he was young, and he was rich, and he promised he would take me from . . . this." She waved a hand toward the shacks in the darkness behind her. "And for that I was willing to live with him and bear his child. I could never have loved Billy, but he was hope, hope when I needed hope and escape when I wanted so badly to escape."

The big man was stuck for words, but Sean filled in

the silence. "We'd better ride. It's getting late and there's much to do tomorrow."

Maria retreated into the darkness and reappeared with a battered suitcase that obviously held her entire possessions. Johnny swung into the saddle and extended his hand to the girl and pulled her up behind him.

Sean took the suitcase and nodded in the direction of his place. "Better get your little family home, brother," he said.

Johnny laughed, and even Maria Perez, unseen in the darkness, smiled.

Chapter 19

The hour was early, and the Patterson stage didn't showboat out of Mustang Flat, but rolled unseen and unheard through the gray, new-aborning day onto the prairie in the direction of the rising sun. The sky was streaked with ribbons of scarlet and jade above an endless sea of grass, and the air smelled fresh. The morning was coming in clean.

Corinda Mason was the only passenger, booked through to San Antonio.

She wore a simple traveling dress of brown cotton with white collar and cuffs, high-heeled boots, and a straw boater perched on top of her pinned-up hair.

That last morning of her life, Corinda looked beautiful enough to be a famous actress or courtesan, not the coldly efficient killer-for-hire she was. Ahead of her lay a long, arduous journey to Philadelphia, but it was worth every minute of her coming train travels. The most passionate, exciting lover she'd ever known planned to meet her in the city, and they'd never again be parted.

Lost in visions of her future, Corinda endured the hot, dusty, jolting misery of the stagecoach ride, and she dozed off and was asleep when they reached the first stage station, twenty miles east of Mustang Flat.

Rowdy Roberts, wearing a stained, ragged Confederate greatcoat over his buckskin shirt and woolen pants, climbed down from the box and opened the stage door.

"Baxter's Station, ma'am," he said. "Fifteen minutes for grub. Outhouse in the back." He touched his hat brim. "Beggin' your pardon, ma'am."

A tall, gangling youth with vacant blue eyes stepped out of the cabin to help Roberts change the team as Dan Keys, hard-faced and taciturn, assisted Corinda from the stage.

The small, low-roofed cabin had curtained-off living quarters and a table and benches to accommodate six skinny people. A blackened coffeepot smoked on a stove in one corner of the room and a serving dish of what Bill Baxter claimed was beef stew sat in the middle of the table, next to it a fork, spoon, and tin cup.

Baxter, a big-bellied man with a round face set in a perpetual smile that revealed a gleaming gold tooth, ushered Corinda Mason to a seat at the table and said, "I mind from the last time you were here, ma'am. You was headed for Mustang Flat. I recollect Buttons Muldoon and Red Ryan were on that run."

"Yes, and they were perfect gentlemen," Corinda said as she sat.

Baxter's smile gleamed. "Red is mighty popular with the ladies."

"I imagine so," Corinda said.

"Beef stew on the menu, ma'am."

"Just coffee, please."

"Comin' right, up." And to Keys, "Stew, Dan?"

"If it's like the last one of yours I ate, I'll give it a pass. I'll have coffee with the lady. That is if you have no objection, ma'am."

"None at all. Please join me," Corinda said.

Baxter poured coffee and looked long at Keys and, after some hesitation, said, "Dan, a drover stopped by for coffee earlier this morning and he brung some bad news you should hear."

"Then let's hear it."

"He says he saw Apaches camped a mile to the east of here. At least eight, maybe more."

"They may have moved on by now," Keys said, his eyes on the tobacco and papers in his fingers. He built the cigarette and said to Corinda, "May I beg your indulgence, ma'am?"

"Of course, please smoke if you wish."

Keys thumbed a match into flame, lit his smoke, and said to Baxter, "I'll tell Rowdy, see what he thinks."

Corinda laid her cup on the table and said, "Do I have a say in this?"

"As far as the Patterson stage company is concerned, no, you don't. But I'm the messenger and I'll listen."

"I want to leave Texas as soon as possible."

"I understand."

"I won't be delayed by savages."

"Apaches are a handful, ma'am. They learned a lot from the Comanche."

"No matter how learned they are, I must reach Philadelphia and I won't brook delay."

"I'm afraid that's up to Rowdy."

Baxter said, "Rowdy's fit Apaches afore and still got his scalp."

"Eight, maybe more, the puncher said?"

"Yup, that's his very own words."

"I don't like the odds."

"You know what I think?" Baxter said.

"No, but you'll tell me."

"The drover said there's cavalry on the way from Fort Concho."

"So, wring it out, Bill."

"All right, then I suggest you head back to Mustang Flat until the army gets here."

Keys shook his head. "I'll tell Rowdy, but I don't think he'll buy it. He's got a schedule to keep."

"And so have I," Corinda said. She said to Baxter, "Good coffee."

"A handful of Arbuckle in the pot and let 'er bile," the man said.

"What's your recipe for stew, Bill, or don't you have one?" Keys said.

"A handful of beef in the pot and let 'er bile."

"I kinda figured that."

Rowdy Roberts stepped into the cabin, poured himself coffee, and drank it down scalding hot. He wiped off his mustache with the back of his gloved hand and said, "Team's changed. Time to roll, Miss Mason."

"Baxter has something to tell you, Rowdy," Keys said.

"Say your mind, Bill, but make it fast. I have a schedule to keep."

"A passing drover said he spotted Apaches a mile to the east of the station," Baxter said.

"How many?"

"Eight. Maybe more."

Keys said, "The army is on the way, but Baxter thinks we should head back to Mustang Flat until the savages are rounded up."

Roberts frowned, his mind working. Then, "What do you think, Dan?"

"The passenger doesn't favor that idea."

"I'm asking you, Dan," Roberts said.

"If the Apaches are out looking for mischief, I reckon they'll have moved on by this time."

"That's my thinking. Young bucks don't stay long in one place."

"Are you willing to risk it, Miss Mason?" Keys said.

"I told you already, like Mr. Roberts, I have a schedule to keep."

"What if I told you I think you're making a big mistake?" Baxter said.

"And what if I told you to mind your own business, Bill?" Roberts said. "The safety of a Patterson stage passenger is my concern, not yours."

"Hell, man, ain't you scared?" Baxter said. "You don't mess with Apaches. Nobody messes with Apaches. They're kissin' cousins to the Comanche and a whole lot meaner."

"There's two things you can't do to an employee of the Abe Patterson and Son Stage and Express Company," Roberts said. "You can't bribe him, and you can't scare him."

"But I can warn him. I can tell him that if he meets them savages out on the long grass, he'll mighty soon run out of room on the dance floor. And I'll tell him there's nowhere to hide on the prairie."

Roberts smiled. "You're a joy to talk with, Bill."

"When all hell comes undone, don't say you weren't warned," Baxter said.

Chapter 20

Under a high, hot sun, trailing a gray dust cloud, the Patterson stage was three miles east of Baxter's Station when the Apache showed up, nine warriors split into two groups riding parallel to the coach.

When he first sighted the Indians, Rowdy Roberts slowed the six-horse team to a walk, conserving its strength for the running firefight he knew lay ahead. Dan Keys traded his scattergun for the Winchester, placed it across his knees and said, "Looks like trouble, Rowdy."

"Uh-huh," Roberts said. "Tell the passenger, if'n she ain't seen them already."

Keys leaned out of the box and yelled, "Indians, ma'am. We may be in for a fight."

Corinda Mason stuck her head out of the window and said, "I see them."

"Lay low, ma'am," Keys said. "We'll handle this."

The woman ducked back inside and removed the Bulldog revolver from her purse and readied herself. She wasn't afraid. That would come later.

From a distance, the Apaches looked like Comanche except for their headbands, and unbraided hair. Most carried rifles, but three of the younger men had bows, and all the warriors were painted for war.

"I think they mean business," Roberts said.

"Seems like," Keys said. "Six horses are a prize worth fighting for."

"Do you think they've seen the woman?"

"Damn right they have."

"If we can't outrun or outshoot them, you know what to do."

"I know, Rowdy. I won't let them take her alive."

"Then let's get the hell out of here."

Roberts manipulated the lines in his hands and sent the team into a gallop . . . and that was the moment the Indians attacked. The warriors were young, but all of them had raided deep into Mexico with their Comanche allies and killed hundreds. Old-time army scouts talked of the Sioux, the Cheyenne, and others, but always claimed that in a fight Apaches were the most warlike and dangerous of all the tribes. Now nine of those wildcats were out to prove them right.

Long-range rifle fire opened the ball and a few bullets thudded into the side of the stage. Up in the box Dan Keys shot steadily but scored no hits. Roberts kept the team at a run but knew his horses couldn't keep up the pace for long and would flag eventually. After the first few moments of the counter, the driver knew things were not going well. It was all too obvious that the Apaches couldn't be scared off and would press the attack.

Inside the coach, Corinda Mason understood the limitations of the British Bulldog revolver and held her fire. She was excited, almost exhilarated, a killer in her element, and felt no alarm.

The Apaches pressed closer, within bow range and an arrow thudded into the wooden armrest of Keys' seat, and the guard cursed as another flew inches over his head. The warriors were now so close the messenger could make out the heraldic totem animals painted on their buffalo-hide shields. Clouds of dust rose around the galloping Indians, and their war whoops rose above the rumble of the stage and the crash of rifles.

One warrior, younger and more reckless than the others, broke from the rest and rode directly at the coach. He came from behind, through the dust cloud, where Keys couldn't draw a bead on him and rode next to the door's open window. The young buck wore red lightning symbols on both cheeks, the color that among the Apache and Kiowa stood for violence, blood, and success in war. Making what Rowdy Roberts would later describe as a "dumb as a stump grandstand play" the Indian jumped onto the door, letting his paint pony run free, and, grinning at the woman, tried to climb through the window. At a range of about three feet, Corinda triggered the Bulldog and blew the man out of there. The .44 bullet crashed into the left side of the man's rib cage and exited under his armpit, spraying blood and bone. The warrior shrieked but still clung to the door. Corinda rose, shot him again and pushed him. The Indian fell away from the stage and disappeared into dust. Covered in gore, the woman's hands were stained red, and she wiped them off on the fabric of the seat opposite. It had not been a clinical hit-and-run kill at a distance, the kind she was used to, but up close and personal, and suddenly she felt sick to her stomach. The interior of the coach was splashed with the dead Apache's blood, as though it was lined with scarlet silk, and her hands were sticky. Now bullets slammed into the woodwork around her. Corinda had made herself a target, and the Apache had marked her, now aware that the woman inside the stage was a shooter.

Up on the box, Dan Keys took a hit. A bullet burned across the front of his right shoulder, taking a chunk of meat and with it his ability to handle a Winchester.

Rowdy Roberts yelled, "You bad hurt?"

"Bad enough." Keys reached for his scattergun. The fight would now be close.

A moment later Roberts took a hit to his right thigh, the bullet stopped by bone.

"Damn!" he yelled, his face shocked by pain. "We're being shot to pieces."

A warrior, his shield painted with the image of a black thunderbird, came close enough to use his bow, and Keys scored a kill. Firing from the waist, both barrels of his Greener blasted the warrior off his pony just as the man loosed an arrow that went nowhere.

Rowdy Roberts, his face ashen under his beard, yelled, "Two down."

"Only one," Keys said, feeding shells into the scatter-gun.

"The passenger shot one."

"The who?"

"The passenger. You're bleeding all over."

"So are you. They're drawing back."

"Two dead, and they're rethinking their strategy. That generally means shooting a leader and slowing us to a stop." Roberts slowed the team to a walk. "Let them rest a spell." He leaned over the side of the box. "Are you all right down there, ma'am?"

"Have they gone?" Corinda yelled back.

"For now. But they'll be back."

"When?"

"I don't know. Apaches are mighty notional."

Several minutes passed, and the Indians fell into single file out of rifle range.

Roberts used the break to tie his bandana around the leg wound, but he was losing blood and his movements were slow and clumsy.

"How are you holding up, old-timer?" Keys said.

"They won't take me alive, Dan. If they've a mind to it, Apaches can take three days to kill a man."

"We're hitched to the same plow on that score," Keys said. "When the time comes, I'll use my pistol."

"How about the passenger?"

"Should we tell her?"

"She won't want to be taken by Apaches. You ever seen a woman after Indians have finished with her?"

"Too many times I guess," Roberts said. Biting back pain, he leaned out of the box and yelled, "Ma'am!"

"Yes?"

"Ma'am, there's no easy way to put this . . ."

"I know what you're trying to say," Corinda called back. "I'll do whatever has to be done."

"Just so you know, ma'am," Roberts said. He sat upright in his seat. "Brave lady."

"Sure is, for someone so gently raised," Keys said.

"They're coming again!" Roberts stuck out his gloved hand. "Been good knowing you, Dan."

Keys took the proffered hand. "You, too, Rowdy. You, too."

Three events followed quickly.

The Apaches attacked, the offside leader went down, dragging the stage to a halt, and Dan Keys took a bullet under the front brim of his hat that spattered Rowdy Roberts with blood and brains.

As bullets and arrows thunked into the stage, Roberts drew his Colt and . . .

The attack faltered and then stopped.

Amazed, Roberts watched the Apaches stream at a gallop westward, yipping defiance as they fearfully glanced over their shoulders.

And then Rowdy saw the reason why.

Two army scouts, Navajo wearing yellow headbands, galloped toward the halted stage, a troop of Buffalo Soldiers from Fort Concho close behind them. As the cavalry chased after the fleeing Indians, a gray-haired, white soldier wearing captain's shoulder straps broke off and trotted toward the stage. He took in what had happened at a glance, dismounted and led his horse to where Roberts sat hunched over in the box and said, "I'm Captain John Young, Tenth Cavalry medical officer. Can I be of assistance?"

"My messenger is dead. See to the passenger, Captain," Roberts said. "She may be distressed."

The soldier saluted, stepped to the stage door, and glanced inside. He looked up at Roberts and said, "I'm afraid it's too late for her."

"I'm coming down," the driver said.

Rowdy Roberts then saw what Captain Young had seen.

Corinda Mason sat upright in her seat, her open eyes wide in horror. An arrow had struck her in the chest between her breasts, and its strap iron head was buried deep.

"The lady didn't know what hit her," the soldier said.

Firing sounded in the distance as Roberts said, "Look at her face. She knowed what hit her." He shook his head. "She knowed all right."

"Let me take a look at that leg wound of yours," Captain Young said.

Cavalry troopers took Corinda Mason's body and the stage to Baxter's Station, and an army rider dispatched to Mustang Flat informed the citizenry that the Indian menace had passed and that they could now dismantle their defenses, prompting Sheriff Beason to say, "I didn't know we'd mantled any in the first place."

A large sum of money and a fine revolver were found on Corinda's body, and Beason confiscated both and she was buried in the Mustang Flat cemetery at city expense. Because it was his duty to be there, the sheriff was the only mourner. Not to mention, no one else knew her.

Chapter 21

John D. Lowery was a patient man. That he had lived so long in a competitive and deadly business was a testimony to his composure. Since long before dawn, he had lain on the crest of a shallow, brush-covered rise overlooking Sean O'Neil's cabin, remaining still and quiet in the darkness like a hunting animal. Lowery watched the sun come up, saw it burn away the shadows from the crannies and corners of the cabin as it sketched in the shapes of the corral, barn, and outbuildings.

Now the gunman fixed his eyes on the cabin door where Sean must eventually appear. He casually fondled the worn stock of the .44-40 Winchester beside him, the oiled, pampered instrument of death that would shortly send O'Neil to a better world than this.

A better world than this.

The gunman smiled at his own thoughts. There wasn't much wrong with this world so long as a man had money. Once this job was done and his boss firmly in control of the vast Kincaid holdings, he would take his wages, gun wages, about ten times what a thirty-a-month drover broke his back for, and head east. He would go to

New York, perhaps Boston, and live like a king till the cash was gone and then head west again and earn more scalp money.

Lowery's eyes never left the cabin door. As yet, there was no sign of life. The place was asleep, like the castle in a storybook he had read as a child. The castle had slept for a hundred years 'til a handsome prince wakened the sleeping princess with a kiss and woke everybody up.

The gunman grinned. In another couple of weeks, once this range war business was all over, he would dress like a gentleman again, feel the touch of silk against his skin. The thought of silk brought a stirring of desire in him. Women, those fancy eastern women, were waiting. Yes, his first stop would be New York. He'd take a carriage to Madame Zelda Arquette's cathouse, enjoy her fine champagnes . . . then . . . ah yes, then . . . but not too old of course. Maybe some high-stepping little filly about nineteen or twenty. Lowery licked suddenly dry lips. He felt the thickening blood rush to his loins, and the feeling pleased him. Yes, about twenty, with smallish breasts but hips as round and white as a new moon. Madame Zelda would again complain, of course. She'd claim that her girls were badly used, torn, bitten, and bruised so they couldn't work for weeks. But he always paid the damages, and then Zelda would smile and stuff the bills between her breasts. Lowery's money was good, and it was plentiful, and Zelda knew it.

But first, there was O'Neil.

Lowery sighed and brought his mind back to the job at hand. O'Neil must die. Lowery's boss had ordered his execution and it must be today. The gunman admired his employer, who had sought him out in Boston when his bankroll was all but blown, grubstaked him, and given him this job.

Lowery smiled. This new boss of his was like himself, cool as ice, money hungry, and deadly.

First O'Neil.

Then there would be nothing to stop the range war his employer wanted. Colonel Kincaid would die in that war, he, Lowery, would make sure of that just as he had arranged the death of his drunken son. After that, who was left to oppose his boss's takeover? Just the small people, the weak, the ones who would die like cattle or move out.

Of course, Nora Ann Kincaid might . . .

The cabin door swung open.

Lowery was instantly alert. The gunman slowly eased his rifle up toward his right shoulder. The rise gave him a fair measure of cover and the grass was long, but he didn't want a sudden movement to give away his position to the men in the cabin. Lowery's lean jaw dropped a fraction when he saw the elder brother, the big dumb pug they called Johnny, run out of the cabin wearing nothing but long johns and a derby hat.

Fascinated, Lowery watched for ten minutes as the big man went through what was obviously a morning ritual. He ran in circles, grunting and puffing, did deep knee bends, then finished the strange performance by ducking under the spigot of the pump and splashing water over his head. He then yelled something toward the sky and ran back into the house.

Lowery slowly shook his head. He could have killed the big ox easily. But that was not in his orders, and John D. Lowery was a man who followed orders to the letter.

The gunman waited patiently.

The crickets were busy in the long grass sanding down their legs. He heard a bird off to his left somewhere, and the rising sun was warm on his back. Sweat beaded his forehead, but he ignored it. He was now the ultimate predator, tense, intent, ready to kill . . .

Fifteen minutes passed before the door opened again. Lowery had the rifle to his shoulder sighting along the barrel at the dark doorway. The big man was the first to appear followed by a girl. The gunman saw with some surprise it was Maria Perez, the little Mexican whore Billy Kincaid had been sparking. Then Sean O'Neil came out, settling his low-crowned hat on his head. Lowery felt his belly twist with excitement. He centered the rifle in the middle of the young rancher's chest where he knew the heavy .44 slug would tear out his heart. His finger slowly tightened on the trigger. He took a deep breath, held it for a second or two then slowly exhaled. He closed off his lungs, holding the sights rock steady. His finger began to squeeze the trigger . . .

Wait!

Where was the Chinaman with the scattergun that everybody talked about in town? He was said to be deadly with the Greener, and for years had been Sean O'Neil's shadow. Lowery swore silently and lowered the rifle. He didn't trust the Chinaman. He felt a prickling sensation in the back of his neck. Maybe the little yellow devil watched him right now, sighting on his unprotected back with a double load of buckshot. Lowery looked round slowly. There was nothing to be seen. His horse was tethered out of sight at the bottom of the rise grazing quietly on the buffalo grass. So where the hell was the Chinaman?

Lowery looked back to the cabin. Sean O'Neil stood on the porch talking with the girl and his brother.

The gunman cursed savagely. All right. He would take a chance on the little man with the shotgun. The plan . . . kill O'Neil and then run to his horse, a rangy thoroughbred and the fastest in the territory. He'd be in town or back at the Kincaid ranch long before any posse got started. But Lowery was not a man to take chances, and the thought of the stealthy Celestial bothered him. He'd been told by some puncher or other, no, it was Billy Kincaid, that the little man patrolled the O'Neil place, and moved around like a wraith. A gunshot might bring him running.

Lowery had one other choice open to him. He could wait till O'Neil left his ranch, then follow and kill him somewhere out on the open range. The thought did not please him particularly, mainly because after he'd bushwhacked the O'Neil brothers, he'd discovered how handy the young rancher was with a rifle. But the job had to be done today so he had a choice . . . the Chinaman or O'Neil's rifle.

Lowery sighed and laid his Winchester beside him. He saw Sean walk to the corral and saddle his big gray. The gunman watched the young rancher mount, saw him say something to his brother, then ride out. He was headed southeast.

The gunman smiled. O'Neil could be going to only one place, the Kincaid ranch. Lowery nodded to himself. His choice was made and now he had him. The colonel would soon show him the door, and he'd kill him on his return from Oaktree, on Kincaid range . . . and the blame would be laid at the colonel's doorstep.

It was perfect. O'Neil had begun to die the moment he rode out of his corral.

The gunman waited till Johnny and Maria went back into the cabin. He eased off the crest of the rise then rose and walked slowly to his horse. He was in no hurry, he had plenty of time. Lowery looked around warily before climbing into the saddle. The Chinaman still bothered him. Seeing nothing he kicked his mount into a walk and swung the thoroughbred's head in the direction of the Oaktree . . .

Chapter 22

Sean rode southeast for thirty minutes till he cut the wagon road to the Kincaid spread. He settled his gray into an easy canter following the road due south. He estimated the gray's ground-devouring stride would get him there in less than two hours. As he rode, the young rancher thought about last night and the new problem that had presented itself in the pretty shape of Maria Perez.

The girl had been silent during the ride from town. She had spoken only when they reached the Running-S, when she'd balked at Johnny's suggestion she sleep in the cabin.

Maria had insisted on bedding down in the barn, but Johnny had gently overruled that idea, and she had finally consented to enter the house.

Sean smiled, recalling how his brother had fussed around the girl like a mother hen, and how he'd fallen over himself to have Rusty whip her up something good to eat. The girl had been hungry, but she had also been tired, so when the little Chinese man left on his nocturnal prowling, he and Johnny curtained off part of the cabin with a blanket, letting her use the spare bunk.

The gray was getting lazy. Sean felt the horse's pace

slacken, and he kicked the big animal to wake him up. The gray laid his ears back briefly, then resumed his fast canter. His thoughts turned once again to Maria as he swung his eyes back to the road.

She had spoken only twice at breakfast. Once to ask Johnny about Billy Kincaid's death. The big man had promised to tell her everything after they had eaten. The second time was to Sean when she asked if he would lend her enough money to take a stage west to one of the mining towns, where she could get work as a laundress or cook. Johnny, although he obviously did not like the girl's plan, had jumped in and promised to stake her. The girl vowed to pay the money back as soon as possible. Then she had dropped her eyes to her plate and said no more.

Sean sighed. A mining camp was no place for a pregnant girl still in her teens. But for the tenth time since last night, he told himself it was no business of his. Still, he felt uneasy, as if letting Maria leave on a westbound stage was an act of betrayal.

The young rancher shook his head, clearing the girl from his mind. There were more urgent matters on hand, like sharing his suspicions with Colonel Kincaid that Lowery was being paid to destroy him.

Sean urged his horse to a gallop. Time was growing short.

The Kincaid mansion was a two-story, imposing wood-frame structure boasting some fifteen rooms. Like the southern plantation house Kincaid lived in as a boy, the front was dominated by four slender pillars fluted like the columns of a Greek temple. The house was a brilliant white in the late morning sun, and Sean remembered it well. He had visited there many times when the colonel's wife was alive, and the Kincaid place was welcoming and fun and Nora Ann always a sweet and lovely distraction. Back then, the colonel was good-natured and boisterous, and he laughed heartily and often, and no saddle tramp was ever turned away from his door without a good meal and a few dollars. He was on good terms with his fellow ranchers, and they visited his house often for hoedowns, Sheriff Beason, a surprisingly excellent fiddler, often providing the dance music.

But all that came to an end after Nina Kincaid died and the heartbroken and grieving Nora Ann had been hurriedly packed off to visit relatives in the east, in the hope that a change of surroundings and perhaps finishing school would help the girl heal.

But Lance Kincaid never healed.

With Nina's death, all the laughter and fun fled the Kincaid house, and the colonel became a lonely and embittered man who now saw his life only in shades of gray and black. And then came the rumblings of a range war driven by dark ambitions that had taken the place of love and light, and even Nora Ann's return failed to restore her father to what he'd once been. Billy Kincaid's murder tipped the colonel over the edge and, as one historian put it, threatened to make a second Antietam of the West Texas range.

That morning Sean O'Neil hoped to extinguish the coming inferno.

There were the usual buildings and corrals scattered around the main house and a huge, imported oak tree flourished in the front yard. A little buckskin mare, an ornate silver saddle on her back, was tethered to a ring in the tree, but Sean could see no other signs of life.

He rode to the front of the house, and as good manners dictated, sat his horse till someone should ask him to step down. Sean was about to forget manners and dismount when the front door opened, and he came face-to-face with Zack Elliot.

The gunman wore gray pants and a frilled white shirt open at the neck. He wore a holstered colt around his hips, the yellowed bone handle of the gun high and tilted forward.

Elliot nodded. "If you're looking to see the colonel, he ain't here, O'Neil."

"Where is he?" Sean asked.

"Left for town a while back."

Sean watched the man's eyes closely and decided he wasn't lying. "I guess you're telling the truth, Elliot. If I thought otherwise, I'd go through you to see him."

The gunfighter smiled. "I know you'd try."

"Who's out there, Elliot?" Nora Ann's voice came from the darkness beyond the open door. Before Elliot could reply, Sean called, "It's me, Nora Ann, Sean O'Neil."

Nora Ann Kincaid walked out beside Elliot, a look of disbelief on her face. "Sean, what are you doing here? I thought you and my father—"

"I've got urgent business with the colonel. I thought he might be here."

The girl smiled, but her voice was taut with anger. "He's in town. Where else would he be?"

Sean sighed. "Well, I guess I'd better head into town. I've need to see him today."

Nora Ann looked uncertain and shook her head. "No, not yet Sean. He'll be in Mustang Flat for hours. Wait till I change, there's . . . something I've got to say to you."

Sean was about to protest, but the girl had already run back into the house. He looked at Elliot, saw the gunman wink knowingly. Sean ignored the man, feeling in his shirt pocket for the makings. Nora Ann appeared ten minutes later. She wore a yellow shirt, boots, and brown riding skirt. Her breasts were unencumbered under the thin material of the shirt, and the girl read the expression on Sean's face and smiled. She walked to the little buckskin, climbed into the saddle, then swung the horse away from the house. "Come, ride with me, Sean," she said.

Once gone from sight of the ranch Nora Ann spurred her horse to a canter, and Sean kept his gray beside her. As they rode, he watched the girl closely, puzzled by the intent, bitter expression on her beautiful face. It was the same look he'd seen when she told him her father was in town, and Sean wondered at her anger. It was natural that the colonel should seek company after the funeral, understandable too that he would try to wash away his grief with bourbon. But this new, angry Nora Ann was totally strange to Sean, and that strangeness bothered him.

They had been riding for almost an hour when the young rancher saw a stand of bur oak and mesquite beside one of the dry creeks that crisscrossed the Kincaid range. Nestled within the trees was an ancient, abandoned cabin. The four log walls still stood, but the roof had collapsed long since. Sean broke the silence for the first time since they had left the ranch. "Is that where we're heading?"

Nora Ann nodded. "I used to come here when I was a

child." She smiled, remembering. "I called it my secret palace, and I used to imagine that a handsome knight on a tall white horse would come knocking at the door one day and take me away with him."

Sean said, "Away, Nora Ann? Away to where?"

The woman shook her head. "Oh, I don't know. Just away, far, far away."

"To his castle, I suppose."

"No, not a castle, a shining city on a hill."

Sean smiled. "Not many of those in Texas."

"No there's not, is there?"

There was a longing, a wistfulness in Nora Ann's voice, and Sean recalled the talk they'd had in town the day she'd arrived. She had talked about how wonderful the East was, and how dull the West by comparison. He was about to remind her that her roots were in Texas and that here, now her brother was dead, was where she was needed. But he decided against it. Nora Ann's life was her own. Only she could make the decision to leave or stay.

They rode to the front of the cabin and dismounted.

Looking over the decayed and mildewed logs, Sean guessed the colonel had built the cabin himself and had probably lived there for a time before he prospered and moved into the big house.

Nora Ann pushed the sagging door open. She saw Sean hesitate and said, "It's all right, there's no one here."

The young rancher followed her inside. The cabin was small. There was just one main room with what looked like a pantry or storeroom leading off from the back wall. A bunk stood to one side, covered by a tattered and dusty blanket. There was also a rickety table and a few stools. At some point the debris from the fallen roof had been thrown out, probably with an eye to renovating the cabin. If so, it never happened because the place was falling apart, and a huge packrat nest occupied the middle of the floor.

Sean opened his mouth to say something, but suddenly Nora Ann threw her arms around his neck and her lips hungrily searched for his. He kissed her, returning her passion, but then he pulled away. This felt wrong, all wrong.

Nora Ann would not let him go. Her breath was coming in short gasps, and her eyes were wild, unfocused. "I've dreamed about this day, Sean," she said. "I've lain awake at nights and dreamed of this day."

The flames of desire suddenly died in Sean O'Neil.

He had to talk with Colonel Kincaid. It was urgent. Men might die because he used this precious time to make love to a woman. He shook his head. "No, Nora Ann, not here, not like this. There can be another time, a better time. And a better place . . ."

The girl spat words at him. "You fool, Sean, the colonel won't see you today. He's in town in the arms of his whore." She saw the puzzled look in Sean's eyes and added viciously, "Yes, his whore. My mother and brother lie cold in their graves, and he takes a whore."

"Nora Ann, your mother has been dead for two years . . ."

The woman's harsh laugh was unpleasant. "You think he waited two years? Let me tell you something. He had the impertinence to write me about this . . . this whore . . . six months after he packed me off to Boston."

"The colonel grieved severely when your mother died. Perhaps he wanted companionship. It must have been lonely for him after she was gone."

"Companionship! All he wanted was a woman in his bed!" Nora Ann lifted her chin defiantly. "If the colonel can have what he wants, then so can I."

Sean sighed. "Who is the woman?"

Again, Nora Ann's scornful laugh. "Alice Wings. A whore who goes by the name Alice Wings."

Sean knew the woman, a tall, spare spinster who owned the dress and hat shop in town. She was such a model of propriety it was rumored that the legs of her piano were modestly covered by bloomers.

"I know Alice Wings," Sean began, "and she's not . . ."

"Don't tell me what she's not, I know what she is. God, I feel sick."

"Nora Ann, Alice Wings is a straitlaced lady, she's . . ."

"Don't say it! Don't mention that woman's name to me." Nora Ann covered her ears with her hands. "I don't want that whore's name mentioned ever again!"

Sean said, "I have to go, Nora Ann. I've got to speak with your father."

He turned to leave, but the girl caught his hand, pulling him back. "Don't go, Sean. Don't you see, it's way too late? My father wants the range, all of it. You're going to your death."

Patiently, as if talking to a child, Sean said, "I have to speak with him. It's my last chance to prevent a range war that could destroy all of us."

"You can't stop it! You can't stop the war because Father won't let you stop it. You don't know what he's like. He's twisted, immoral. Look what he's done to my mother's memory!" She grabbed him round the waist, looking wildly into his eyes. "Sean, it's not too late for us! Even now, even today, it's not too late. We can go away, go East, maybe even to Europe. The colonel might not survive much longer and one day all he owns will be mine. We could live, Sean! For the first time in our lives, we could really live like human beings instead of a bunch of provincial hayseeds."

Sean took the girl's hands from his waist. "I've got to leave now, Nora Ann. You don't know what you're saying because you're still not over the shock of your mother's death and Billy's murder. I . . ." He saw with numb fascination that the girl was slowly unbuttoning her shirt. She threw it off, baring her breasts.

"This is what you want," she said. She began to fumble with the buttons at the side of her skirt, but Sean yelled, "No!" and started toward the door.

"Don't leave now, Sean O'Neil. Don't turn your back on me," Nora Ann said.

"You're not thinking straight, Nora Ann," Sean said. "I won't take advantage of you."

"Watch your mouth, Sean. You can't take advantage of me. Cowboy, you have neither the guts nor the smarts."

Sean took a while before he spoke, then, "Nora Ann, I have a world of respect and affection for you. Don't make me throw it all away like dirty dishwater."

Behind him Nora Ann's ice-cold voice stopped him. "You had your chance, Sean. Now it's gone. When I came back to Texas, for a while I thought I might be able to love a man and I was sure that man was you. Well, it seems I was wrong on both counts."

"You weren't wrong, Nora Ann," Sean said. "We'll talk about this again."

"When peace comes to the range?"

"Yes. It will come because your father will see reason."

"And what a wedding we'll have, huh?"

"We'll have a fun wedding. You'll see."

"I already see it. We'll sit on haybales, drink moonshine from jugs, and dance quadrilles while Sheriff Beason plays on the fiddle. What a time we'll have, what laughs."

"You're teasing me, Nora Ann."

"You're a rube, Sean, easy to tease."

Then she laughed, a laugh full of malice that froze the blood in the young rancher's veins. "Sean O'Neil, you're already a dead man."

Sean stumbled through the door and into the sunlight. Fighting back a sudden rush of hot, stinging remorse, he climbed onto his horse and kicked the startled gray into a run.

Nora Ann's mocking laughter rang in his ears long after the cabin was lost from sight . . .

Chapter 23

"Damn it, what happened to Sean O'Neil?" John Lowery said.

"He was here," Zack Elliot said.

"I know he was here. Where did he go?"

"He and Nora Ann rode out of here and headed west." Elliot shrugged. "O'Neil wanted to talk with the colonel, so I guess they're headed for town."

Elliot and John Lowery stood in the Kincaid parlor, and Elliot drank coffee from a delicate china cup balanced on a saucer. Lowery, in a thoroughly bad mood, thought it made the man look effeminate . . . ladylike. He planned to kill Elliot one day and put a big-name shootist on his rep, maybe when all this range-war nonsense was over.

Lowery said, "I didn't anticipate this. I should've shot O'Neil at his place when I had the chance."

"Why didn't you?"

"I couldn't place the Chinaman."

Elliot smiled. "Everybody's scared of the Chinaman, even Billy was scared of him."

Stung, Lowery said, "I'm scared of nobody."

Elliot laid his cup and saucer on the table. "Put the crawl on you though, didn't he?"

"You trying to pick a fight with me, Zack?"

"No. I'm just telling you something as I see it."

"Yeah, well don't see anything else."

"Hell, man, lay for O'Neil on the wagon road out of town. He'll take that route before he cuts the trail to his ranch."

"How long will it take him to talk to the colonel?"

"Not long, the mood Kincaid is in. He wants a range war, not peace talk."

"Do you believe that?"

"It's obvious, isn't it. He hired us, didn't he?"

"The colonel doesn't want a war."

"Then who does?"

"I know, but I can't tell you."

"Could be I signed up with the wrong man. Maybe I should make a switch."

"There's a way. We'll talk about it after O'Neil is dead."

"Then go kill him."

"You're ice, Elliot."

"And so are you."

"Then we're two of a kind."

"Me, I'd rather be one of a kind."

"What does that mean?"

"It means anything you want to make of it."

"On your best day, you can't shade me, Elliot."

The gunman smiled. "One day, you may have to prove that. We're in a competitive business."

Lowery said, "Can I turn my back on you?"

"Well now, John, I might stab you in the back, but I won't shoot you."

"You're a dilly, Elliot."

"Ain't I, though? Now get out of here and do your job."

John Lowery lay behind the solid protection of the western rim of an ancient buffalo wallow about twelve feet in diameter. He'd chosen his ambush site well, concealing his horse a quarter mile away in a grove of mesquite. From where he lay, the wagon road from Mustang Flat was a double ribbon of white some hundred or so yards away. Lowery had an unrestricted view of about a mile of the trail so when Sean O'Neil came in sight, he would have plenty of time to ready his Winchester . . . all the time in the world.

Despite the pounding heat of the sun, made worse by the lack of a breeze in the wallow, Lowery was a contented man, and he hummed softly to himself as he waited for his victim to appear.

Time passed. The day faded to late afternoon, and the sun lowered in the candy-striped sky. Lowery was hungry, thirsty, and his searching eyes grew strained. He eased his outstretched legs, grunting as he ironed out a charley horse in his right calf muscle. Then, with a sudden indrawn hiss of breath he saw Sean O'Neil appear.

The young rancher was riding at a fast canter, and that pleased Lowery.

There was something poetic about a man rushing headlong toward his own death.

He jacked a shell into the chamber of the Winchester,

he sighted, whispered softly, "Come on, O'Neil, just a little closer, just a leetle bit closer . . ."

The rifle barked once. The well-remembered jar of the recoil thudded against the gunman's shoulder, and he smiled and lowered his weapon. It was a killing shot, dead center chest, and he felt no need to check on his handiwork and perhaps be seen.

No, the job was done, and there was an end to it.

As Sean O'Neil took the wagon road from Mustang Flat there was a cold, empty feeling inside him. Colonel Lance Kincaid had refused to talk with him, using Alice Wings, standing at the door of her large adobe house, to relay his words.

"Tell him my talking is done!" he yelled.

"You heard that," Alice said, a woman in her mid-thirties with severe features made attractive by beautiful brown eyes.

"I heard it," Sean said. Then, louder, "Colonel, we have to talk. I believe your life is in danger."

"Alice, tell O'Neil to go away," Kincaid yelled. "Lives are in danger, all right, but not mine."

"Colonel, you're wrong," Sean said.

"Alice, ask him if he found the man who murdered my son."

"Not yet," Sean said. "But I have a suspect."

"Alice, shut the door and lock it."

The door banged shut in Sean's face, and he heard a bolt slam home.

He stood for a while, looking down at the toes of his boots, his shoulders slumped in defeat. Colonel Kincaid was not in a mood to listen to reason. It seemed his mind was fixed on war and would not be moved. Then it was time to call a meeting of the local ranchers and the farmers, too, if they'd come and tell them it was time to buckle on their guns and prepare for the conflict that was now just over the horizon. The range would echo to the sound of gunfire and the wails of widows. There could be no winners or losers. If Kincaid planned to sow the whirlwind he'd reap a range ablaze, fertilized with the blood of dead men.

But Sean corrected himself. There would be winners, big winners, men like John D. Lowery and the mysterious man who hired him and made him turn traitor.

Sean O'Neil rode away from Alice Wings' house, and he felt his back crawl. He was sure the colonel watched him from a window, death and destruction in his heart, his once bright soul made dark by grief and madness.

Chapter 24

Sean O'Neil rode out of Mustang Flat, his heart heavy, his failure with Kincaid made worse by the thought that Nora Ann had snatched something away from him, something once warm and precious, and left nothing in return.

He kept his horse at a steady canter and tried to rationalize the girl's behavior. Losing the mother she adored, coupled with her father's affair with another woman may have unbalanced her. And the strain of the impending range war had done little to help. If he'd been able to talk with the colonel, he'd planned to tell the man that Nora Ann needed a long rest, a time away from Texas and the memories it still held for her. Perhaps she should return to Boston for a while, at least till she got things straight in her own mind. Nora Ann must face the fact that she had her own life to live, and her father had his . . .

A sledgehammer blow in the chest came first, followed a split second later by the roar of a gun. Sean felt himself reel under the impact of the heavy bullet and he clutched for the saddle horn to steady himself. But his hands were moving slowly, painfully slowly, as though he watched them in a dream. Then he was falling . . . falling backward off the horse . . . backward and downward . . . sinking to the earth, settling into a soft, warm bed of soft grass. There was a single yellow flower close to his face. He reached out and touched it, surprised when he saw it turn red.

"I shouldn't be here," he whispered. "Not on the ground like this. He felt no pain and he'd no feeling at all in his arms and legs. He thought about it, even though the effort made his head spin. Then he remembered. He was going on a far journey, all the way to the mountains.

Sean had thought the mountains were hundreds of miles away, yet he saw they were very close. He was about fifty or sixty yards from the timberline where the tall pines spread a cloak of darkness around their feet. He looked up toward a mountaintop. There was no snow, and the peak of the mountain was bathed in sunlight, splashing its slopes with molten gold. He jumped to his feet and started to run then, toward the trees, eager to reach the sunlight. He stopped. Wait, slack up on the reins, Johnny should be here. Johnny should be with him. Then he remembered. Johnny had something to do, something to finish. It was a task they'd begun together, but now Sean couldn't recall what it was. When he stopped and tried to remember his chest hurt and he knew the higher altitude was to blame.

Well, he'd call for Johnny to see if he had finished the job. "Johnny!" He called his brother's name. There was no answer. Sean shrugged. The big fellow would be along later. He'd arrive late, like he always did.

The mountaintop was very bright. Sean laughed as he started to run again, running toward the tall timber into the brightness of the sunlight . . . and then into darkness.

* * *

"What was that?" Johnny O'Neil tilted his head to one side as he looked at Maria Perez.

"I didn't hear anything," the girl said.

Johnny stepped to the door and walked outside. He looked around him and said, "I thought I heard Sean's voice. I thought I heard him call my name."

Behind him, Maria said, "I didn't hear a thing. It was probably the wind."

Johnny came back into the cabin and closed the door behind him. "Strangest thing." He shook his head and sighed. "I guess I'm hearing things. You're right, it was just the prairie wind."

Chapter 25

"Pa, there's a horse up ahead," young Ben Lieberman said.

"I see it, and its rider," Adam Lieberman said.

"He's lying on the ground."

"He sure is."

"Maybe his horse threw him."

"Maybe. We'll soon know."

Lieberman, one of the many Jewish peddlers who brought goods and services to every far-flung ranch and farm in the West, drew rein on the paint nag in the traces of his wagon and he and his ten-year-old son stepped down and walked to the body.

"I know this man," Lieberman said, taking a knee beside the still form. "That's Sean O'Neil, the rancher, and he's one of my regular customers, or his Chinese cook is."

"Is he dead, Pa?" Ben said, a kid with a shock of black hair and huge brown eyes.

"He's been shot. And yes, I think he's dead."

"I don't think he's dead, Pa."

"He's not breathing, son."

"Yes, he is, Pa. I saw his chest move. I know I did."

"Bring the canteen."

The boy returned with the canteen, and only then did Lieberman lean over and press his ear to Sean's chest. "He has a heartbeat," he said. "But it's very weak." He turned the unconscious man and looked at his back. "Bullet went right through him, Ben, front to back."

"Will he live, Pa?"

Adam Lieberman used canteen water to vigorously wash Sean's blood from the side of his face and hands and then said, "I don't think so."

"What do we do?"

"We'll take him into Mustang Flat where there's a doctor, but if he lives it will be a miracle." He smiled at his son. "Sometimes doctors perform miracles, but they must work very hard for them. Now let's clear a space for Mr. O'Neil in the wagon."

"Who shot him, Pa?"

"I don't know, son. It seems that everywhere we've gone on this trip there's been talk of a range war. Maybe this has something to do with it."

"Is a range war dangerous for us, Pa?"

"It could be. But if a war comes, we'll stay well clear of it."

"What happens in a range war, Pa?"

"You ask too many questions. Now help me get Mr. O'Neil in the wagon. We need to hurry."

"I hope he lives," Ben said. "He has a good face."

"So do I hope he lives," his father said. "On our way we'll say a prayer for him."

* * *

"All I can do is dress his wounds and make him as comfortable as I can, and then we wait and see," Dr. John Grant said.

He stood in his surgery near Sean O'Neil who lay on the operating table, his bandaged body covered by a sheet. Sean's face was ashen under his tanned skin, and he lay unmoving on his back,

"Will he live, Doctor?" Adam Lieberman said.

"He's young and he's strong and by all accounts a fighter," Dr. Grant said. "If he was otherwise, I'd put his chance of recovery at ten percent."

"It's not encouraging," Lieberman said.

"No, it's not. But I won't give you false hope. His wound is very serious. Are you and Sean friends?"

"No, he's a regular customer."

The doctor smiled. "The best kind. I don't have many of those, among the male population anyway."

"What's going on here?"

Sheriff Bob Beason barged into the surgery, an enormous presence in such a confined space.

"Luke Lawson told me he saw a body delivered here like a side of beef. Is that him on the table under the sheet?"

"That's him, Sheriff," Dr. Grant said.

"Who is it?"

"Sean O'Neil."

"Lawson said there was a gray horse tied to the back of a peddler wagon. I should've known it was O'Neil was brung in. That was you, Lieberman?"

"It was me. I found him lying on the wagon road leading into town. He'd been shot."

Beason looked at Sean's face and then lifted the sheet. "He don't look too good. How is he, Doc?"

"He's badly wounded, shot through and through. I'd say a rifle shot."

"Will he make it?"

"I give him a twenty percent chance. If the bullet was still in his chest, he'd have no chance at all."

"When will he be able to talk?" Beason said.

"I don't know. Maybe never."

"Doc, you're a cheerful feller."

"No matter how dreadful they are, some things need to be said."

"That's all right. I never took you for a blabbermouth anyhow," Beason said. He looked at Sean's gray face. "I guess someone should ride out to the Running-S and tell his brother what happened."

Dr. Grant smiled. "And I guess that should be you, Sheriff."

"County sheriff's job, if we had a county sheriff."

The doctor stared at Beason, his left eyebrow raised.

"Adam," the sheriff said, looking away from Grant, "you got a jug of that Tennessee moonshine?"

"I sure have, fresh in stock two weeks ago, and I'm selling it at cost to my regular customers," Lieberman said.

"Then fetch me a jug. I got some riding to do," Beason said.

Chapter 26

Johnny O'Neil sat with Maria Perez at the table in Sean's cabin, and the big man said, "I'm sorry the truth hurt so much. But you wanted to know."

Earlier he had told Maria the whole story of a mysterious, sinister, and faceless man behind the threatening range war and how Billy's murder had been a major part of his plan.

"And that's the fellow Sean and me are trying to find," he said.

At first, the girl had been reluctant to believe Johnny, but the more he talked, the more she couldn't bring herself to believe that the O'Neil brothers would be involved in the cold-blooded murder of a drunken boy to start a war that could destroy the range and the Running-S with it.

She said, "I want to believe you. I want to believe that whoever is trying to destroy the range had Billy killed. But now it matters so little. It is all over for me."

Johnny was concerned. "Don't even think that. For you and the baby, it's only the beginning. You have a long happy life ahead of you."

The girl's eyes were red, and Johnny, unused to the tears of women, especially pretty, pregnant women, felt big and awkward and useless.

"If you will allow me to stay one more night, I will catch the stage . . . anywhere . . . in the morning," Maria said.

"Now, you've no call to do that, young lady. Believe me, a mining camp is no place for a girl your age, especially one in your condition."

"There is work in a mining camp. And I must have work to support my child."

The big man placed his hand over Maria's. Her small hand was lost under his scarred, big-knuckled paw, but she didn't pull it away. "Look, let's talk about this when Sean gets home. We'll work out something, maybe even arrange for you to work here." Then hearing the eagerness in his voice, he added hastily, "Or . . . or in town. Don't worry, Sean's as smart as a whip. He'll figure something out."

The girl was unconvinced, but she returned Johnny's smile. "You love your brother, don't you?"

"Well, he's kinda skinny and a mite bossy at times . . . but you're right, I love him. He's all the brother I've got."

He turned as the door opened and saw with distaste it was Rusty Chang. The little man nodded briefly to Johnny, smiled hugely at Maria. He placed his Greener in the corner and threw his battered hat on the table. "The boss isn't home yet?"

"Not yet," Johnny said. "Maybe the colonel's taking a heap of convincing."

The little man sniffed. "The only way to convince him is hot lead. I told Sean that plain enough myself, but he never listens. He's not hard of hearing, but he tries mighty hard not to hear advice from this old Chinaman." He walked to the stove. "Anyway, he'll be home soon so I'd better get dinner cooking."

Maria rose from the table. "Please let me help with that. I feel I should do something for my keep."

Rusty closed his lips around an objection, and he grinned and willingly relinquished the cooking chore. Within an hour the girl weaved her own magic on the unpromising beef, beans, and peppers she had to work with. As they sat eating, Johnny nodded to the girl over his fork. "Maria, I've eaten in a lot of places, but even in Delmonico's I never tasted anything this good." He gave a sly sideways glance at Rusty. "When you can spare the time, a certain party needs some lessons on how to cook."

The little man rose to the bait. "When a certain party wants to eat a horse, there isn't much another certain party can do for him, no matter how good a cook he is."

Johnny smiled, and Maria joined him. It was the first time he'd seen the girl genuinely smile, and it pleased him. He put down his fork, rubbed his belly, and sighed. "Sean's going to love this grub, so keep it hot for him." He pulled out his watch and glanced at it. "Almost six-thirty. He's late."

The big man suddenly felt uneasy. Since he thought he had heard his brother's voice calling him he had been unable to shake the feeling that something was wrong. Now that feeling was suddenly growing stronger, a kind of insistent gnawing at the pit of his stomach that wouldn't let go.

Johnny rose, found his coat and hat and turned to the little Chinese. "Rusty, I'm heading out to the Kincaid place. I'd appreciate it if you'd saddle a horse."

The man looked up in surprise. "Sean can look after himself. He's been late before."

A trace of anger crept into Johnny's voice. "I guess I can saddle my own horse." Then realizing he was being testy and unfair, he added more civilly, "Rusty, don't ask me why, but I have a feeling something's wrong."

The little man jumped to his feet. "Then I'm coming with you." He grabbed his hat and shotgun and walked to the door. "I'll saddle the horses."

When Rusty left, Johnny turned to Maria. "You'll be all right here till we get back. Just keep the door bolted, and don't open it for anyone."

The girl nodded. "Being alone is something I'd better get used to."

The big man did something then that surprised himself. He took the girl by her slender shoulders and kissed her on the forehead. He stepped back, and to cover his confusion, said gruffly, "Just remember what I told you, about the door."

"I won't forget. I hope your brother is not in danger."

Johnny grinned. "He's probably sitting with the colonel right now, drinking brandy and smoking cigars. When a man gets to my age, he's apt to imagine all sorts of things. It's one of the penalties of growing old."

"You're not old. I don't think you'll ever grow old. To stay young, that's a gift from God."

Realizing he was blushing like a teenaged boy, Johnny was relieved when the door opened, and Rusty stepped inside. He wore a yellow slicker, and he carried a second over his arm that he handed to Johnny. "Looks like there's a big storm coming. The sky is as black as a cow's tongue." He stepped outside again.

Johnny took his leave of Maria and waited outside the door until he heard the bolt slide home. He nodded and then joined Rusty in the corral. The Chinese man tightened the cinch on the little buckskin and turned when he heard Johnny step toward him. "Do you really think Sean is in trouble, bad trouble?"

"I wish I knew for sure." Johnny shrugged into the slicker. "It's just a feeling I have, and I can't shake it." Then, almost as an afterthought, he added, "I thought I heard him call me."

Rusty had been ready with a taunt, but seeing the grimness in the big man's face, he felt a sudden spike of concern. "Let's ride," he said.

The two men followed the same trail Sean had taken earlier, riding in silence till they joined the wagon road to Oaktree. Johnny looked at the sky and spoke for the first time since leaving the corral. "Sky's full of stars. Thought you said there's a storm coming?"

Rusty nodded. "It's comin'." He jerked a thumb to the north. "It's comin' from far off that way, out of the New Mexico Territory badlands."

"You can see that far, huh?"

"Like yourself, I get feelings about things. It's the Chinese way."

The sky to the north looked clear, but Johnny shrugged and said, "I guess you know best."

"Yes, I do. And that's a natural fact," his eyes fixed on the vague gray ribbon of the wagon road.

"I bet Sean's decided to stay the night at Oaktree," Johnny said. "Nora Ann would insist on it, I reckon."

"Maybe so," Rusty said.

"She's a nice lady."

"Very pretty."

"And nice."

"She's Colonel Kincaid's daughter."

"What does that mean? Damn, this saddle is made of cast iron."

"It means she wants her own way. She was a strong-headed girl, and now she's a woman."

"And what does that mean?"

"It means she still wants her own way. Not very smart, are you?"

An indication of how worried Johnny felt was the fact that he let Rusty's insult pass. They rode for an hour, their eyes constantly probing the surrounding darkness.

"How far?" Johnny said.

"An hour if the storm doesn't hit. But it will."

"Chinaman, you're wishing thunder and lightning on us, but there will be no storm. You Celestials are too super-stitious, that's always been your problem."

"And the Paddies I worked with on the railroad were not?"

"They could tell when a storm wasn't coming and so can I, so take that to the bank."

Thirty minutes later the skies opened.

Thunder crashed and lightning scrawled across the sky like the signature of a demented god. Shifting glass rods of rain glittered, and the air smelled of ozone and wet grass.

"We're lightning targets, the highest points in the damn prairie," Johnny yelled, rain hammering around him. He was angry at being wrong and angry at the sudden danger.

"You're the highest point, not me," Rusty said.

Whatever Johnny said next, and it was not polite, was stomped into silence by a roll of thunder.

Then Rusty said, "Lights ahead."

"The Kincaid place?"

"It ain't El Paso."

"It ain't El Paso . . . I wish you'd learn to speak like a Chinaman."

Rusty yelled into the storm. "I gave that up. Nobody knew what the hell I was talking about."

"Most of the time I still don't know what you're talking about."

"I hope the colonel has hot coffee ready," Rusty said.

"Now that"—Johnny waited until after the thunder boomed—"I do understand."

Chapter 27

Johnny O'Neil and Rusty Chang dismounted at the Kincaid ranch house and knocked on the door, loud because of the storm. There was no answer, and Johnny tried again. He saw a curtain twitch in a window and stepped away from the door into view. After a few moments, the door opened and Nora Ann, standing in the lamplit interior, showed her surprise.

"Mr. O'Neil, what are you doing here?"

Lightning flashed followed by a crash of thunder before Johnny answered. "I'm looking for my brother," he said.

"Sean's not here," Nora Ann said. "Who is that with you?"

"Rusty Chang."

"Then come in, both of you out of the rain."

"Miss Nora Ann, I'll put the horses in the barn, if that's all right with you," Rusty said.

"Yes, please do. There's hay and oats. You needn't knock when you're finished with the horses, just come right in."

"I'm obliged to you, ma'am," Rusty said.

As the little man gathered up the reins and led the horses away, Johnny stepped into the foyer where there was a coatrack and a side table with an oil lamp.

"Just hang your slicker on the rack," Nora Ann said. "We can dry the floor later."

Johnny did as he was told and followed Nora Ann into the parlor. She seemed to be alone.

"Where is the colonel?" Johnny said. "Sean said he was coming here to talk with him."

"My father is in Mustang Flat," the woman said. Her nose wrinkled. "He's visiting a friend."

"Then Sean must be staying the night in town," Johnny said.

"If he spoke with my father that's likely," Nora Ann said. "The talks probably dragged on for a long time." She clapped her hands. "Polly!"

A plain-looking girl who looked to be all of sixteen appeared in the doorway. She wore a maid's uniform, black dress and shoes, and a white pinafore and hat.

"Coffee for our guests, Polly," Nora Ann said. "That's for two, the other will be here shortly."

The girl smiled at Johnny and said, "It's an awful night, sir."

"Yes it is, Polly," Nora Ann said. "Now do as I told you and bring a plate of those cookies that you baked earlier." When the girl left, the woman smiled at Johnny and said, "My father hired her, and God knows why. She's as thick as a plank." Then, "I wouldn't worry about Sean. I'm sure he and the colonel had a constructive conversation."

"Sean believes there's someone who wants to profit by your brother's death."

"Who, for heaven's sake?"

"A man hiding in the shadows while he bankrolls all the killings he wants done. Who that may be, we don't know. Sean thinks this man is trying to start a range war and plans to take over everything, including Oaktree, when the gunsmoke clears."

Nora Ann shook her head. "I think Sean is wrong. Study on it, Mr. O' Neil, there's no one in Mustang Flat with that kind of power and influence. I mean, we're talking about a bunch of hicks who have trouble making ends meet from one day to the next. Ah, here's Polly with the coffee. And do come in, Rusty. Don't stand in the doorway like a stranger."

"How are you, Miss Nora Ann?" Rusty said.

"Pinyin wo hen hao."

Rusty smiled, pleased. "You haven't forgotten your Chinese."

"I am fine, isn't a lot, I'm afraid. You must teach me more."

"It's been a while."

"Yes, it has."

"Remember, I tried to teach Sean?"

"He was a very poor student. I used to make him stand in the corner."

Nora Ann poured coffee, offered cookies, and then said, "The man in the shadow could be a rancher."

"From what Sean tells me, they're no richer than the people in Mustang Flat," Johnny said. "Tom Johnson, the Crystal Palace bartender, pulled the trigger on Billy, but we need to find the man who paid him."

Lightning flashed and for a moment flickered sizzling white in the parlor, striking close. Thunder banged, and then Nora Ann said, "I already miss Billy. He had his faults, but he was my brother and I loved him."

Johnny placed a hand on Nora Ann's shoulder and said, "I'm so sorry. His murder was a terrible thing."

"I hope Sean and my father put their heads together today and come up with a plan to find the man in the shadows soon."

"I'm sure they will. It's our only hope."

"Have another cookie," Nora Ann said.

"Thank you, dear lady, but Rusty and me must be on our way."

"You're more than welcome to stay the night."

"Thank you kindly, but we left Maria Perez at the ranch, and I'm concerned for her safety."

Nora Ann was surprised. "Billy's lady friend?"

"Yes. And she's carrying his child."

The woman's shock grew. "She's pregnant?"

"Indeed, she is. I'm trying to convince her to live with Sean and me until she can find something better. She's worried about raising the baby without a husband."

"My father wants a grandchild, especially a boy."

Johnny smiled. "Then he may want to bring Maria here to Oaktree, at least until the child is born."

"Yes, I'll suggest that to him. Listen, the storm is passing."

Still growling, the thunder grew more distant, and the lightning flashes were less dazzling, but the darkness was still intense.

"And that's our cue to leave, Miss Kincaid," Johnny said, rising to his feet. "You've been a very gracious host."

"Are you sure I can't tempt you and Rusty to stay?"

"Alas, no. Perhaps some other time."

"You'll always be welcome at Oaktree," Nora Ann said. "And so will Sean."

Rusty brought the horses and Johnny climbed into the saddle. "Nice lady," he said.

Chapter 28

A meaty fist pounded on the door and Maria Perez said, "Who is it?"

"Me, Sheriff Beason."

"What do you want?"

"For a start, I want to come in out of this rain. I'm soaked here."

"Hold on a minute."

"Make it a quick minute."

Maria took a shotgun from the gun rack to check the loads. There were none. The Greener was empty. She tried one of the drawers, found a box of revolver cartridges, tried another, and discovered what she looked for, a scattering of shotgun shells. The girl loaded the shotgun and stepped to the door, just as thunder crashed followed by the lesser thunder of Beason pounding.

"I'm dying out here!" he yelled.

Maria slid the bolt and stepped back just as Beason, wearing a gleaming yellow slicker, barged inside.

"I'm not coming with you!" she yelled, above the

relentless racket of the rain. She motioned with the scattergun. "I know how to use this."

Bob Beason stopped in his tracks, runnels of water running off the slicker and splashing around his boots. "What are you talking about, girl? I'm not here for you. I'm here to see Johnny O'Neil."

"He's not to home," Maria said.

"I can see that. Where is he?"

"Sean didn't come home today and by now Johnny and Rusty Chang are at the Kincaid place to see if he's there."

"Sean O'Neil's not coming home. Maybe he's never coming home. He's been shot."

Shock chalked the girl's face. "Is he badly hurt?"

"Wounded enough that Doc Grant gives him a twenty percent chance of making it."

"Making it?"

"Surviving. Go on living. Remaining alive. Now put the scattergun down and let me get out of this damned coat."

Maria laid the Greener on the table and said, "Hang it on the hook on the back of the door. You're dripping water everywhere."

"I can't control the weather, lady," Beason said.

Thunder roared as though applauding that last remark.

The sheriff hung his hat over the slicker and sat at the table and said, "Any whiskey? I'm chilled to the bone."

"I think there's a bottle in the cupboard. I'll get it."

Maria laid a bottle of Old Crow and a shot glass on the table. Beason downed a shot, poured another, and then said, "Why did you think I was here to take you back to

Mustang Flat?" He made a face. "As if I'd ride all the way out here to do that."

"My father threw me out of his house."

"Why?"

"I'm pregnant."

"Who's the father."

"Billy Kincaid."

Beason leaned forward in his chair. "Did he rape you?"

"No, we were lovers."

The sheriff sat back. "Seems like you make poor choices in men, young lady. Why are you here?"

"I had nowhere to go, and Johnny O'Neil brought me here. I hope to find a job so I can support my child."

"Mr. O'Neil is a gentleman. I wish I could say the same thing about his brother." Beason shook his head. "No, I mustn't speak ill of the dead."

"Sean isn't dead yet," Maria said.

"The doctor said he has a twenty percent chance. That's mighty close to no chance at all."

"You can be told that you have a ninety percent chance, or fifty or just one, but if you believe and fight, you can overcome any odds," Maria said. "I think Sean O'Neil is a fighter."

The sheriff nodded. "You're right, young lady, I guess he is, but right now it's all in the hands of God."

Two hours later, when the level of the Old Crow bottle was much lower, Johnny O'Neil walked in the cabin door and Sheriff Bob Beason's words hit him like punches to the gut.

* * *

"Rusty, saddle me a horse," Johnny O'Neil said. "I'll go to my brother and stand at his bedside and will him to live."

"Johnny, sleep for a few hours first," Maria said. "You're exhausted."

"The young lady's right," Sheriff Beason said. "You look tuckered."

"I don't need sleep," Johnny said. "I won't sleep until I know Sean will recover and then I'll find the man who shot him."

"Don't take the law into your own hands, Mr. O'Neil," Beason said. "I'll handle it."

Johnny ignored that and said, "Rusty, get me a horse."

"I'm coming with you," the little Chinese said.

"No, stay here with Maria."

"Sean is my boss, and as the Texans say, I ride for the brand," Rusty said.

"For once, do as you're told," Johnny said, frowning.

"And for once, you listen, big man. I want to bring Sean home where I can help him. If they aren't Chinese, I don't trust them. I can heal Sean's wounds and save his life. Dr. Grant wants to wait and see. Well, I won't wait and see."

"Where are your medicines?" Johnny said.

Rusty waved a hand. "Out there on the range are all the medicines I need."

"Damn it, Rusty, you're not a doctor," Beason said. "Grass ain't gonna heal a man whose been shot through and through."

"No, I'm not a doctor, but my father was. In the Forbidden City, he was number one court physician to his Imperial Majesty the Emperor Tongzhi, and he taught me the ways of Chinese medicine. Although I am not worthy, I can use that knowledge to save my boss."

"Saddle me a horse," Johnny said again, exasperation writ plain on his face.

"Ah, then you have a decision to make, big man," Rusty said. "You can come with me on the buckboard, or you can ride the only fresh horse we have available. He's a mustang Sean named Rat's Ass because he hates everybody and he'll kick, bite, and try to murder you every way he can."

"Damn Celestials, you're full of deceit and treachery," Johnny said.

"We learned that from white men."

"Or it's the other way around."

"Have you made a choice? Rat's Ass, eight hundred pounds of pure horsy evil, or the buckboard?"

"You know I'm not a good rider."

"Yes, I know, and Rat's Ass will love you for it."

"All right, we take the buckboard. But I'll make the decision about whether my brother remains in town or comes here." Then, "What about you, Sheriff?"

"I'll ride back with you."

"Maria, I'm sorry to leave you by yourself again," Johnny said.

"I'll be fine. I'll say a novena for Sean while you're gone."

"And say one for me, little lady," Beason said. "I got a feeling that pretty soon I'm gonna need all the help I can get."

Johnny O'Neil climbed into the seat of the buckboard, dwarfing Rusty Chang, who sat with the reins in his hands. The vaulted sky had partially cleared, and some stars showed. The rain had washed down the dust and the night air smelled fresh and washed clean, but the night was oppressive and bore down on Johnny from all sides like a sodden cloak.

Rusty slapped the horse in the shafts with the reins and the animal immediately took offense and kicked wildly at the buckboard with its hind hooves.

"What the hell's wrong with that horse?" Johnny said.

"Nothing."

"Then talk to him. What's his name?" Johnny said.

"Rat's Ass," Rusty said.

Chapter 29

The buckboard was an hour from Mustang Flat when Sheriff Bob Beason brought his horse alongside Johnny O'Neil and said, "How are you holding up? Say, Mr. O'Neil, do you mind if I call you Champ?"

"The answer to your first question is that I'm barely holding up, and to the second, I never was a champ."

"How come?"

"There was always somebody in the way."

"What kind of somebody?"

"Somebody better than me."

"You mean bigger and stronger?"

"I mean better with his fists."

"I'd still like to call you Champ. You came close."

"Call me what you want."

"Tell me about you and your brother, Champ."

"What do you want to know?"

"Everything. Call it professional curiosity. I'm an inquisitive man."

"There isn't a whole lot to tell."

"Sky's clearing up. Tell it anyway."

"It's ashamed of its earlier display of bad temper," Johnny said.

"Now that's funny, Champ. I think it's a knee slapper."

"It isn't."

"Start with your parents, Champ. Enlighten me."

"Are you talking to me as a lawman or just a man?" Johnny said.

"A little of both."

"Since I've nothing better to do than stare at a horse's butt, and the Chinaman isn't much on conversation, I'll tell you the story of the fighting O'Neils. My pa, the first Sean O'Neil, died trying to make himself a success. As I remember him, he was a handsome, strapping man who left his native Tyrone to bring his wife and ten-year-old son, that was me, to a land where he was told men picked up gold from the streets. Well, there was no gold, only dust and heat and thin soil that stubbornly resisted the plow. Then one day something broke in my father's heart and they buried him on his own land. Kathleen, my mother, followed six months later of nothing more serious than a summer cold. She was laid beside her husband in alien ground, far from the green hills of Ireland."

"And you and your brother were orphans," Beason said.

Johnny nodded, remembering. "I was almost thirteen the year my parents died, almost man grown and strong as an ox. Sean was just a little tyke, barely able to walk, but even then, he was a quiet youngster not given to needless tears or tantrums. There were no lack of families in the area willing to give the O'Neil boys a home because boys grow into men and men are always welcome on the farms."

"Sodbusting is a healthy life for a boy," Beason said. "Although I never cared for it myself. Work behind a plow all you see is a mule's ass, work from the back of a horse you can see across country as far as your eye is good. And that's a natural fact."

"Well, we ended up with a Swedish couple who already had their own brood of youngsters. But I couldn't abide farm life. I stuck it out for six months before I left. I was heartbroken at leaving my brother, but I was determined to make my fortune in the East, a fortune I planned to share with Sean when the time came." Heat lightning shimmered in the sky before he said, "Sean had the hardest part. It was my ownself who took the easy road."

"Prizefighting isn't easy, Champ," Beason said. "You got scars on your face that weren't put there by a mother's kiss."

"No, I guess not, but I was never what you'd call a bleeder, but the more I fought, the more my old scars opened up. I owe my boxing career to the sporting bloods in Boston who saw potential in a big, rawboned farm boy, and I learned quickly. By the time the War Between the States began I was reckoned to be one of the top bareknuckle prizefighters in the nation."

"And with the gloves, Champ," Beason said. "You were wearing gloves when you beat Tom King, the Fighting Sailor, in eighteen and sixty-three, London Prize Ring Rules, twenty-five rounds. I know that because I read about the fight in the *Sporting Gazette*."

Johnny managed a smile. "Tom always had a tot of gin before a bout. I don't know if it helped him or not."

"It didn't when he fought you. His seconds threw in the sponge when he couldn't come out for the twenty-sixth."

"Tom planned to retire. His heart wasn't into that fight."

"Champ, tell me more about you and Sean," Beason said.

"Why are you so interested, Sheriff?"

"Sometimes it is good to talk about a man whose life is in danger, remember him as he was and full of vim and vigor."

Rusty Chang said, "And he will be full of vim and vigor again."

"John Grant is a good doctor. He's treated a lot of people," Beason said.

"No, he is not," Rusty said. "The good doctor prevents sickness. The middling doctor attends to people who are about to be sick. Only the inferior doctor treats those who are actually sick."

"And what kind of doctor are you?" Beason said.

"For Sean, I must try to be all three."

The sheriff thought about that for a moment, then said, "Only a Chinaman would say something like that."

"You don't understand?"

"No, I don't understand, and neither would anyone else. Champ, finish the story about you and your brother."

"Over the years, Sean and me wrote occasional letters, and I offered him a home in Boston and a job as my fight manager, but he always refused. Sean was fifteen when he left the Olsen farm to fight for the Confederacy and he was not yet eighteen when he joined his first cattle drive, pushing a herd from the Texas Blacklands to Kansas. Unlike most cowpunchers, he saved his money, banked every hard-earned dollar until he had enough to start his own spread. Sean chased his dream and found it. And now . . ."

"He'll go on living that dream," Rusty said.

"We'll make him live," Johnny said. "I won't let him die on me."

It was almost dawn. Blue fingers of light reached across the sky from the east and washed out the stars. The earth smelled good, fresh, renewed by the rain, and Mustang Flat had just shaken itself awake and lighted the lamps.

Chapter 30

"Oh, my God," Johnny O'Neil said.

Three words that expressed his fear, distress, and growing anger.

"Sean, stay with us," he said. "Don't you dare leave us."

"He can't hear you," Dr. John Grant said. The young man looked exhausted. "He hasn't moved or made a sound since he was brought in." The doctor saw the question on Johnny's face and said, "A peddler and his son found him lying on the wagon road to town. He'd been shot through and through by a rifle bullet that entered his chest and exited his back."

"What do you think, Doctor? Will he live?"

"Since you're his brother, my most hopeful diagnosis is that he has one chance in twenty of pulling through."

"And your least hopeful?"

"He'll be dead in a few days, maybe sooner."

"How soon?"

"By nightfall."

"What can you do for him?"

"Nothing I haven't done already. I've cleaned and

bandaged his wound and I'll give him morphine later if he needs it."

"There's nothing else?"

"He needs a miracle, Mr. O'Neil, and I don't have any on hand. Can I say it plainer than that?"

"No, I guess you can't."

Rusty Chang said, "We're taking him home."

"As good a place as any and better than here," Grant said.

"I won't let him die," Rusty said.

"Are you a doctor?"

"No, he's a cook," Johnny said.

"My father was a physician to the imperial Chinese court," Rusty said. "Sean is my boss and my friend. I will save him."

"The ride in a buckboard could kill him," Grant said. Stating fact. He wasn't seeking an argument.

"And not riding in the buckboard could kill him," Rusty said.

Grant said, "Mr. O'Neil, you're the next of kin. It's your decision to make."

Before he could answer that question, Sheriff Bob Beason stepped into the surgery. "How is he?" he said.

"Still the same," Grant said.

"Sheriff, have you any idea who could've done this?" Johnny said. "I want a name."

"A name? I don't have a name. It could've been a rancher or farmer trying to start the war. It could be Colonel Kincaid or one of his gunmen, or it could be the mystery man that your brother talked about. In all, I have a hundred suspects, but no name."

"Find him, Beason," Johnny said. "Find him, tell me who he is, and I'll take it from there."

"You'll do no such thing, Champ," Beason said. "You'll leave it to the law."

"Who are Kincaid's hired gunmen? Who are crowing on top of the dung heap?"

"I think you already met them. The two of note are Zack Elliot and John Lowery. Champ, leave them boys alone, they're fingers looking for triggers. Men like them never put off until tomorrow a man they can kill today, and they're poison, fast and deadly as rattlesnakes with the Colt's gun."

"And how are they with rifles?"

"I don't know. Elliot and Lowery are drawfighters. They like it up close and personal, and they'll give it to you in the guts."

"Sheriff, find out where they were when Sean was shot yesterday."

"I'll do what I can."

"Do better than you can. Surprise yourself."

"We go now. No more talk," Rusty said.

"Doctor?" Johnny said.

"I can't do much else for your brother. I wish it was otherwise, but on the frontier a bullet wound is a death sentence."

"Will Rusty's medicines help?"

"I don't know. The Chinese have practiced herbal medicine for centuries, so who knows? In medical school I was told their medical practices date to the Shang Dynasty, three-thousand years ago. If Rusty Chang gives your brother an extra chance, then let's give him a try."

Rusty said, "Kind words, Doctor, but you have items I don't have, gauze, bandages . . ."

"Morphine?"

The little man gave that some thought and said, "Can you provide it?"

"Yes," Dr. Grant said. "And syringes. I'll give you what I think you'll need."

"Sheriff, help me load Sean into the buckboard," Johnny said.

A big man and strong, Johnny picked up Sean from the surgical table and carried him outside with no more effort than a mother holding a baby in her arms.

Beason helped settle Sean in the bed of the wagon and then Johnny said, "I'm going back inside for a minute."

"I'll stay out here and keep an eye on him."

Johnny passed Rusty Chang on his way out, carrying a bundle of bandages and a box with a syringe and small bottles containing a tincture of morphine and opium, a powerful painkiller.

"How much do I owe you, Doc?" Johnny said.

"You owe me nothing, Mr. O'Neil. I didn't do much."

"For the morphine then?"

Grant managed a tired smile. "It's on the house."

Johnny nodded and produced his wallet. He dropped a twenty on the bed.

"It's very kind of you," he said. "But the O'Neils pay their way."

"Then good luck," Dr. Grant said. "I hope we get a miracle."

"Do medical men say prayers?"

"All the time."

"Then say a few for Sean," Johnny said.

Chapter 31

It was almost dawn, and the shadow of the buckboard lengthened as Johnny O'Neil and Rusty Chang stopped at the ranch house. Maria Perez came out immediately.

"How is he?" she said.

Over by the horse corral a couple of Herefords had wandered in from the range. Both sleek and fat, they watched Maria with intense bovine curiosity as she stepped to the back of the wagon.

"No change in him," Johnny said. "He seems to be no better and no worse."

"Bring him inside and we'll get him to bed," Maria said.

"Sean's gun, boots and hat are in the wagon," Johnny said.

"Yes, well, I don't think he'll need those anytime soon. Now, into bed with him."

Johnny carried his brother into the cabin and laid him out in the bed. "He's covered by nothing but the sheet, Maria," he said. "I think you should leave while I get him ready. It wouldn't be decent for you to stay."

"And I haven't seen a naked man before? You go get yourself a cup of coffee and tell Rusty to come here."

Johnny opened his mouth to object, but Maria had already pulled the sheet away and was examining the blood-stained bandages on Sean's chest and back. She glared at the big man. "Are you still here? Get Rusty like I told you."

"And who made you the boss?" Johnny said, frowning.

"I did."

"Did somebody say my name?"

The little Chinese stood in the doorway.

"Rusty, Sean's breathing is very shallow, and I can barely find a pulse," Maria said.

"Let's get the bandages off," Rusty said. "I want to look at those wounds." He turned to Johnny and said, "You're taking up three-quarters of the space in this room and using up all the air. We'll tell you when you can come back."

"He's my brother, Chinaman," Johnny said, irritated.

"And he's my patient," Rusty said. "Now go."

Johnny scowled. "Hey, get that damned barn cat off the bed."

A huge marmalade tabby settled himself beside Sean, pressing close, purring.

"No!" Rusty said. "The love of a cat is a precious thing and is not to be thrown away. His purr has great healing power, and he will share his strength of will with Sean."

"He's beautiful," Maria said, managing a rare smile. "What's his name?"

"Sean calls him Jeb Stuart, after the Reb cavalry commander, but most times he just calls him Jeb."

"I never saw that cat before," Johnny said.

"Jeb wasn't needed before," Rusty said.

"Look!"

Maria pointed at Sean's right hand. It was almost imperceptible, but his fingers moved slightly in Jeb's fur, and the cat's purr grew louder.

Rusty nodded. "*Zhu fu ni,* Jeb Stuart," he said. "I wish happiness and good fortune on you."

Johnny sighed. "Tell me when to come back." He shook his head. "Cats . . . Chinamen . . . bossy females . . . I hope you know what you're doing."

"We will heal him," Rusty said.

Maria Perez stared at Sean, her hands clenched, her mouth a straight, determined line, the skin of her face tight to the bone.

"Yes, we will," she said.

Johnny O'Neil splashed coffee into a cup and turned as Maria Perez stepped out of Sean's bedroom.

The girl said, "We must get a priest."

"A priest? For the Last Rites?"

"No, to pray over Sean. There is a Mexican priest in town, Father Diego Ortiz. He is a good man."

Johnny laid his cup on the table. "If you think it will help, I'll bring him here."

"It will help. Prayer has the power to heal."

"It can't hurt."

Maria looked hard at Johnny and then her gaze broke. "What will you do now?" she said. She seemed half afraid of the answer.

The big man's eyes were clear, and calm. "You know what I'll do."

"Johnny"—Maria pronounced it, Johnee, the first time she'd used his given name—"you must survive. For Sean's sake you must live."

A smile, then, "I don't intend to do otherwise."

"Colonel Kincaid has *pistoleros,* dangerous men. Paid killers. Billy stood in awe of them."

"You mean Zack Elliot and John Lowery?"

"Yes, those two. There are others, I think, but Elliot and Lowery are the deadliest. When my father saw them for the first time, he said the fires of hell burned inside them and had turned their souls to charcoal."

"One of them shot my brother. As your people say, he didn't face him *de hombre a hombre,* but ambushed him on the trail. That's about as low as man can sink."

"It might've been someone else. What is it Sean called him, the mystery man?"

"Whoever he is, and if he even exists, he wouldn't step out of the shadows to bushwhack Sean. He'd pay someone else to do his dirty work."

"But you still think it was Colonel Kincaid."

"Somebody paid. Maybe it was Kincaid, maybe another man, but the killer who stuck out his hand and took the money was either Lowery or Elliot, the only two hired assassins in this part of Texas."

"Maria! Come in here," Rusty Chang called from the bedroom. "I need you."

"Coming," Maria said. She gave Johnny a lingering last look and hurried to assist Rusty.

Outside in the darkness, a barn owl questioned the

night and an equally curious wind rustled around the cabin and tugged at the door, demanding entry. Inside, the oil lamps guttered in response and ghosted black smoke.

Maria returned after a few minutes, followed by Rusty who rooted around near the stove and came up with a small wicker basket.

"How is he?" Johnny said.

"No better, but no worse," Rusty said. He showed the basket. "I'm going outside to find things I need."

Johnny was instantly suspicious. "What kind of things?"

"Plants, night blooming wildflowers, herbs, and grasses."

"It's black as pitch out there."

"So?"

"You won't be able to see."

"I'll get a lantern from the barn, and I'll know what I want when I see it."

"I'm sure all that herbal stuff is bunkum," Johnny said, scowling. "It ain't going to work for Sean."

"Oh, but it will, Mr. O'Neil. And if you please, don't get mad at a man who knows more than you do. It isn't his fault."

"Be careful out there," Maria said. "The night is full of danger."

"From Colonel Kincaid's gunmen, you mean," Johnny said.

"If such men are out there, they won't see me, but I'll see them," Rusty said. "When white people look at Chinese folk, we're suddenly invisible."

"Don't count on it, little man," Johnny said. "They'll notice you well enough to lay rifle sights on you."

"Oh, please, take your shotgun, Rusty," Maria said, alarmed.

The Chinese man patted the rubber handle of the Colt stuck into his waistband. "I'll be all right, Mexican gal. I've got Mr. Sean's second-best *pistola*. It shoots straighter than his best one, or so he told me."

"It's not the gun that shoots straight, it's the man," Johnny said, determined to be testy. "Sean knows that, so he was joshing you."

"When it comes to revolvers, Sean never . . . what's that word? Joshes. Now, if you will kindly step away from the door and give me the road."

"Take care, Rusty," Maria said.

Johnny nodded, and then grudgingly, "Yes, take care. If I hear gunshots, I'll come running."

"No, Mr. O'Neil, if there are gunshots, I'll come running," Rusty said.

Chapter 32

That evening, as Rusty Chang stepped out of the O'Neil cabin, in Mustang Flat John D. Lowery killed another man.

A fastidious gunman who refused to spend time in a dung-smelling ranch house, Lowery held court in the Crystal Palace, sitting at a lace-edged, cloth-covered table with his customary Hennessy brandy and coffee. Historians agree with Western enthusiast Theodore Roosevelt that after the smoke cleared, Lowery became the frontier's premiere shootist. As the nation's twenty-sixth president said, "It was a title that bode ill for West Texas and the O'Neil brothers."

The man who died that night was the direct opposite of the meticulous Lowery, a massive, long-bearded, beetle-browed brute named Jordan Garrett, a bounty hunter by trade and inclination. Garrett stood seven inches over six feet, huge in the chest and shoulders, a mountain man who'd gunned twenty-seven victims. That he'd raped and murdered several women lies outside the scope of this narrative.

Garrett wore a black derby hat, overcoat and pants of

the same color, a brocade vest over a collarless shirt, and mule-eared boots. Not for him spurs on his heels that would announce his coming and going. He carried two .44 Smith & Wesson revolvers, one in each pocket of his coat, with which he was fast, accurate, and deadly. Hidden, was a sharpened steel machete that hung in a sheath from his waist.

Though he never sought a reputation as a shootist, no man had ever outdrawn Jordan Garrett or even come close, and that included Charlie Mourning, the El Paso gunman who was reckoned to be the fastest around.

Garrett stepped to the bar, pushed aside a couple of drifting punchers who took one look at him and gave him all the room he needed, and in a voice that sounded like a death knell, demanded whiskey, the best in the house. Lucas Battles, the owner, was bartender that night and he poured the stranger a shot.

Garrett downed the whiskey, rang a silver dollar on the bar and said, "That's the best you got?"

"Top shelf," Battles said.

The bounty hunter slowly turned his head and nodded in the direction of Lowery. "What's he drinking?"

"Hennessy brandy."

"Give me a shot."

"Sorry," Battles said. "The gentleman bought my last bottle. I've got good gin. I can mix you a nice gin punch."

Garrett ignored that, carried his glass to Lowery's table, poured himself a shot from the brandy bottle and swigged it down. He wiped his mouth with the back of his hand and said, "You weren't hard to find, Lowery."

The drawfighter raised his cold eyes to Garrett's face. "Is that a fact?"

"Fact. I followed the body trail."

"In my line of business, men get shot."

"Mine, too."

"You're a peach. What's your name?"

"Jordan Garrett."

"I've heard of you. Up El Paso way, you gunned Charlie Mourning that time."

"I would've let him go, but he gave me sass and back talk."

"Charlie was past his best."

"Hell, we're all past our best."

"Why are you here?"

"You know why I'm here."

"Who's paying you?"

"Gambling gent by the name of Hooper Rusk."

"Fort Smith?"

"The same."

"He's a sorry piece of trash."

"You must've thought that way about his son, seeing as how you drilled him. Didn't like his playing, huh?"

"Banjo Bob Rusk," Lowery said. "It was his card playing I objected to. He dealt from the bottom of the deck, and he was notified. But that didn't stop him."

"Your bullet stopped him permanent like. Now his daddy wants revenge."

"How much am I worth, Garrett?"

"Five hundred, a thousand if I bring Hoop your gun hand." Slowly, like molasses in January, Garrett opened his coat, drew the machete from its sheath and clanged the blade onto the table. "Naturally, I want the extry five hundred."

"I shoot with both hands."

"One will do. I'll take your left with the gambler's ring on the little finger. Hoop will enjoy that, a piquant touch."

"You're a lowlife, Garrett."

"Maybe so, but I have an idea."

"Spill it."

"Give me a thousand and I'll only take the hand."

"And leave the rest of me alive. Is that it?"

"You're smart, Lowery. You catch on quick."

"No deal."

"Well, it's my best offer. Now to business."

Garrett's hands slid into his coat pockets . . .

And John Lowery fired and fired again.

There were three eyewitnesses to what happened that night, two of them punchers riding the grub line who gave a garbled account. But most experts agree that Lucas Battles' version of what became known as the Crystal Palace Showdown is the most accurate. In a statement to Sheriff Bob Beason, later published by the *West Texas Telegraph,* Battles said . . .

> When the man named Jordan Garrett put his hands in the pockets of his coat, John Lowery fired a pistol from under the table where he sat. Lowery later told me he'd concealed the weapon there as soon as Garrett walked into the saloon, guessing, rightly, that the man was up to no good. Mr. Lowery's unerring bullet struck Garrett in the groin, to the right of his private parts. Garrett let out a terrible scream and then produced two murderous revolvers.

When asked by Sheriff Beason if Garrett, a notorious gunman, drew the revolvers from his pockets, Battles said . . .

> Yes, he did and at that juncture Mr. Lowery tipped over the table, startling Garrett, smashing a bottle of good brandy and a china coffeepot I may add, and fired at the gunman from behind the flimsy barricade of the tabletop. Once more Mr. Lowery's bullet met its mark and Garrett fell to his knees, groaning, a bullet in his chest. He then rallied for a moment and discharged both his pistols at Mr. Lowery but did no execution. He then fell forward on his face, let out a terrible moaning cry and expired.

At this point in the narrative, the editor of the *Telegraph* warned readers that ladies of delicate breeding and gentlemen of a nervous disposition should read no further.

Battles said:

> Upon examining the body, Mr. Lowery ascertained that all life was departed. He then retrieved the machete from the floor, chopped off Garrett's hands and threw them down beside the corpse. "Damn you, you scurvy son of a bitch, you won't dog my footsteps with that blade again," or words to that effect. Sheriff Beason said Mr. Lowery clearly

killed Garrett in self-defense, and no further inquiry was needed, and I agree with him. It is believed, the news carried far and wide by the Patterson stage, that Mr. Lowery's fame as a pistol fighter grew. It is a pity he did not live long enough to boast of it.

This account was written by my own hand, witnessed by David Quinn, drover, and Sid Bell, wrangler.

Lucas Battles, Esq.

Chapter 33

Rusty Chang returned to the O'Neil cabin, the wicker basket full of grass, plants, and herbs.

"What's in your poke?" Johnny said. "Weeds?"

"Stuff I need," Rusty said.

"What are you aiming to do with it?"

"First thing is to make poultices for Sean's wounds, front and back. Do you know what a poultice is?"

"Yes, I know what a poultice is, but I've never seen one made out of grass."

"Then you'll see one soon. Now step aside. I've got work to do."

Maria Perez walked out of the bedroom and said, "Sean stroked the cat again. I'm sure he did."

Rusty hurried to Sean's bedside and laid a hand on the wounded man's chest. "Boss," he said. "Boss, can you hear me?"

Sean lay silent and still.

Rusty was aware that Johnny stepped beside him.

"Boss, come back to us," he said. "It's Rusty."

Silence. Stillness. And from Johnny, despair.

"Chinaman, he can't hear you," he said.

"You speak to him," Rusty said.

"He won't be able to hear me either."

"How the hell do you know? Talk to him."

"Sean, it's Johnny. Can you hear me?"

Long seconds dragged past. Out in the night the barn owl repeated its question, and the wind whispered an answer. Maria stood at the foot of the bed, her breathing a slight, swift sound in the silence, and the marmalade cat slowly turned its head and stared at her with eyes the color of topaz stones.

"Sean, do you hear me?" Johnny said again.

And again, there was no answer. But then . . . Sean's lips moved under his mustache.

"He's trying to talk to us," Johnny said.

"No," Maria said. "He smiled. It was a *poco* smile to be sure, but a smile nonetheless."

"She means little smile," Rusty said.

"I know what she meant," Johnny said. "And if my brother smiled, he heard me."

"Boss, do you hear us?" Rusty said.

There was no reaction from Sean.

"Sean, stay with us," Johnny said. "Listen, brother, I'm going to get the man who did this to you and the lowlife scum who paid him. I'll tear them apart with my own hands and . . ."

"Enough!" Rusty said. "You'll make the boss sicker with that kind of talk. Now go away while me and Maria get to work and try to save him."

"Not try, Chinaman. Do it."

"Then leave me to my work. Maria, we need hot water in a bowl for poultices, and then we must change the bandages again." He stared at the woman. "Infection is our bitterest enemy, and we must defeat it."

Maria nodded and left to find a bowl and a pot to heat water.

"There is nothing you can do here, Mr. O'Neil," Rusty said. "Please leave."

"I can pray, I guess."

"Yes, pray that Sean recovers, but don't pray for revenge or God will turn a deaf ear."

"I won't ask God to exact revenge. I'll take care of that myself."

"Lowery or Elliot?" Rusty said. "Which one will kill you?"

"I don't know. I reckon it will take both."

"Only one is guilty, the one who pulled the trigger. How will you know which one?"

"If I must, I'll kill them both. That way the guilty one will be punished."

Maria turned from the stove and her voice rose in alarm. "But . . . but that's murder. You'll punish an innocent man!"

"They're hired guns, and neither of them is innocent. Nor is their boss."

"What about the mystery man?"

"You mean the man who stands in the shadows, the puppet master? He doesn't exist."

"Sean believed in him," Maria said. "He said so himself."

"My brother made up the mysterious man in his own mind because he couldn't believe any of the people he knew could be so evil. Well, he was wrong about that.

There is evil, great evil, and it resides at Oaktree with Colonel Kincaid and his killers."

Maria rose and grabbed Johnny's hand. Her eyes frantically searched his face trying to fathom his emotions, scrambling to find words to reach him. "Please don't do this," she said, surprised at the weakness in her voice. "You'll do the very thing Sean tried to avoid. You'll start the range war!"

The big man gently disengaged himself from the girl's strong fingers. "Lady, I must do what has to be done, so let the chips fall where they may." His jaw flexing, he added, "The range war has already started."

Chapter 34

No one slept that night as Sean O'Neil remained in a coma. But according to Rusty Chang his pulse was stronger, he was breathing easier, and his wounds showed no signs of infection, the specter of gangrene an ever-present boogeyman.

Across the dark, moon-dappled rangeland, another man lay sleepless.

John Lowery lay on his back and stared at the board ceiling of the room Lucas Battles kept for overnight guests, at least those with two dollars. The gunman was pleased with the kill he'd made earlier. Jordan Garrett was a name ofttimes heard when Western men sat around general store stoves and talked of outlaws, lawmen, bounty hunters, and the bold new breed of Texas draw-fighters. He knew his reputation would be enhanced by the shooting, exaggerated enough to make him the top fast gun on the frontier, the man who put Wes Hardin and Wild Bill Longley in the shade.

But his triumph had been spoiled by news from the fat idiot Bob Beason.

His stare crawling over Lowery's face like a nest of spiders, he said, "Did you hear about Sean O'Neil?"

"No, I didn't," Lowery said.

The sheriff watched Clem Milk and his assistant carry Garrett's body, the man's amputated hands laid on top of his belly, out of the saloon and said, "O'Neil was shot today."

"What's that to me?" Lowery said.

"Nothing, I guess. But anyway, he's at death's door."

"He's not dead?" Lowery knew his shock showed.

"Not yet. His brother took him back to the ranch where there's a Chinee to look after him with herbs and stuff."

"I wish him well," Lowery said.

And tomorrow I'll finish the job.

"It's a pity. O'Neil was a nice enough feller."

"Who shot him?"

"I don't know."

"It was a robbery, I guess. Some drifter or a Mex looking for a few bucks."

"No, it wasn't robbery. Nothing was taken."

"All right, then he was shot by one of his own kind, a two-by-twice rancher anxious to start a range war."

"I don't think so. I agree with you that somebody shot O'Neil to get the war started, but I don't think it was one of the small ranchers."

Lowery's eyes hardened. "Then you figure it was a big rancher . . . and the only one around these parts is Colonel Lance Kincaid."

"I have my suspicions, but for now I'll keep them to myself."

"Keep them to yourself, Beason. That's a good idea. You'll live longer that way."

Beason smiled. "In the past, a sight of hard cases tried to kill me. But I'm still here."

Lowery didn't want to antagonize the man, plenty of time to gun him later if needed. "Can I buy you a drink, Sheriff?" he said.

"Sure. It's a hobby of mine," Beason said.

Lowery closed his eyes, deep in contemplation. He'd complete the O'Neil contract tomorrow. Wait. What time was it? He took his watch from the bedside table, held it close to his eyes and squinted. Just after midnight. Then it was today. He'd finish the job today. Then an amusing thought . . . if Sean O'Neil wasn't already a dead man, he soon would be.

Comforted by that notion, Lowery closed his eyes and soon slept.

The long night dragged by with sullen slowness, the passage of time marked by the *tick-tick* of the carriage clock on the ranch house mantel.

Johnny O'Neil dozed off and on, wakened every now and again by Maria or Rusty bustling in and out of Sean's bedroom. Then, at around four in the morning, the marmalade cat walked out of the bedroom, stretched, yawned, and spread out at his feet.

"Jeb, are you deserting my brother?" Johnny said. "Shame on you, cat."

"He's telling you something," Rusty Chang said. "Jeb says Sean doesn't need his strength any longer."

Johnny jumped to his feet. "He's not . . ."

"Sean is much better. There's no fever, and he seems to be regaining consciousness. Slowly for sure, a bit at a time, but his eyes are open."

Johnny dashed past Rusty into the bedroom. Propped up on pillows, Sean watched his brother come to his bedside.

"How are you doing, old-timer?" Johnny said.

"I'm . . . I'm . . . still alive."

Sean's voice was a wafer-thin whisper, his words as flimsy as a torn lace curtain, and his drawn face was gray under his tan. He looked like he'd aged a score of years in the past twenty-four hours.

"You ain't going to die," Johnny said. "Rusty Chang says you're on the mend."

"Glad to hear it," Sean said.

"Are you in pain?"

"Some."

"Doc Grant gave Rusty morphine."

"I'll grit my teeth. I don't want to get to liking that stuff too much."

"It will ease the pain, Sean."

"Life is pain. When I feel it, I know I'm still alive."

Johnny hesitated, then said, "Sean, did you see the man who shot you?"

"No."

"I think it was one of Kincaid's hired guns."

"Johnny, stay away from Kincaid. When I'm on my feet again . . ."

"You'll be in bed for a while."

"Leave Kincaid to me."

"No, I plan to talk with him later this morning."

"Help me get up."

"You're doing fine right there."

Sean lay back on the pillow. "Damn, I'm as weak as a kittlin'."

"And you will be for a while, boss, maybe weeks." Rusty Chang stepped from the doorway into the room. He nodded at Johnny. "The great O'Neil here says he plans to have it out with John Lowery. And Zack Elliot. No matter that just one of those boys is more than a handful."

"Stay away from gunmen, Johnny," Sean said, his wan face signaling his alarm. He closed his eyes. "I feel so tired . . . Johnny . . . stay . . . away . . ."

"Let the boss sleep now," Rusty said. "We've tired him out with all this jawing." Then, "Maria. I need you. We'll look at the wounds again and make fresh poultices. How are my herbs?"

"You have enough," Maria said. She looked tired.

Johnny thought as much. "Girl, you need some rest."

"And she'll get rest," Rusty said. "Just as soon as I know the boss is out of the woods."

"Out of the woods . . . hell, I never met a Chinaman who spoke better American than me," Johnny said.

"How many Chinamen have you met?"

"Not many."

"Then that explains it."

It explained nothing, but Johnny didn't press the matter.

He stepped outside and closed the door quietly behind him. Inside, Rusty said something that made Maria laugh, and it was good to hear.

The night was still dark, the sky ablaze with stars, and Johnny wondered if the dawn would ever come, possibly the last one he'd ever see. His anticipated death under the gun of a lowlife whoreson like John Lowery troubled him, but only in so far as he might fail to ensure that the man was dying when he pulled the trigger.

Sean would live, he was now sure of that, and Johnny's sacrifice would guarantee a better life for his brother and convince arrogant bullies like Colonel Kincaid that there were men like the O'Neils who would read to them from the book and fight them tooth and nail and never bend the knee to tyrants.

As a prizefighter, Johnny O'Neil had led an honorable life. Now he was determined to die an honorable death.

He looked at the sky, his battered features silvered by starlight.

How long would the night hold back the dawn?

Chapter 35

First light arrived onstage hesitantly, like the second act of a bad play.

And for Johnny O'Neil the killing time had come.

He shaved and dressed meticulously. If he was to meet his Maker this day, he planned to be a credit to the fighting O'Neils, a true descendant of the High Kings of Ireland.

"You're leaving now?"

Rusty Chang stood in the bedroom doorway, his face set and unsmiling.

Johnny nodded. "Yes, it's time."

"Zisha," Rusty said.

"What did you say?"

"It's a Chinese word and it means suicide. That's what you're about to do, O'Neil. Commit zisha."

"No, I'm about to fight."

He took the whiskey bottle from the table, held it up to the light, and said, "Good, there's a swig left. Well, here's to the health of my enemies' enemies." He drank and said, "I needed that."

"I'll saddle a horse for you," Rusty said.

"Thank you. As Chinamen go, you're the pick of the litter."

Rusty seemed baffled by that last, but he ignored it as Maria stepped out of the bedroom. "How is the boss?" he said.

"Sleeping," Maria said. "He seems stronger."

"That's what he needs, sleep," Rusty said. "And when he wakes, we must get some food into him. Later I'll make a beef broth." The little man shrugged. "Sean never ate anyway, a bite here and there. Although he was always right partial to bear sign."

"Rusty, I have to go," Johnny said.

"I'll get your horse."

"Wait." He produced his wallet from an inside pocket of his coat and gave Rusty a wad of bills. "If I don't come back, make sure Maria gets on a stage out of here. There will be enough money left over to keep you going for a while."

There was a sudden gasp from the girl. "But . . . but . . . I thought I'd stay here . . ."

"It will be no longer safe for you here if I'm dead and Sean is still bedridden. Colonel Kincaid is mad with grief, and he'll blame you for the death of his son. You've got a child to think about. You can't endanger the baby's life as well as your own."

"I don't want to think of you dead, Johnny," Maria said. "You'll come back to us. I know you will."

Johnny smiled. "Say a novena for me."

"Since you're set on going after them draw fighters by yourself, you'd better take this." The Chinaman spoke.

He pulled a Colt from his waistband. "It's Sean's gun. Put it in your pocket."

"And what would I do with a pistol? Throw it?"

"Then take my scattergun."

Johnny shook his head. He held up his huge, knuckle-scarred fists. "The good Lord gave me these, and these are the weapons I'll use."

Rusty Chang shoved the Colt back in his pants. There would soon be another grave in the Mustang Flat cemetery, an O'Neil in the cold ground.

"It's time to go," Johnny said finally. He turned to Maria offering his hand. She did not reach out to grasp it. "Take care of yourself," he said, dropping the hand to his side. "If you ever need anything . . ."

The girl nodded. "I'll know where to find you."

The irony in the girl's voice was not lost on Johnny. He turned away from her into the brightening morning.

Rusty held the reins of the saddled buckskin, then looked away from Johnny and peered into the distance, "Rider coming in."

Johnny knew better than doubt the little man's vision, and he waited tensely till the horseman came in sight. He saw with a shock of recognition that it was Sandy McPhee, the redheaded man who'd crawled out of the bar after his showdown with Lowery and Frenchy Laurent.

In fact, the memory of that humiliation had eaten at McPhee like a cancer. It had made him doubt his own courage, and worse, it had undermined his manhood. There was only one way the memory of that disgrace could be washed away and that was with blood—the blood of the men who had humbled him.

The Scotsman nodded briefly at Johnny and said, "We heard about Sean. Is he . . . ?"

"My brother is in bad shape, but we think he'll live."

"Bushwhacked."

"That would seem to be the right of the thing."

"It must've been one of Kincaid's hired gunmen."

"That's my suspicion."

McPhee said, "Lowery or Elliot, or both. Those two and the colonel. That's where the blame lies. The very ground Oaktree stands on is cursed and all who dwell there, seed, breed, and generation."

"I don't believe that Nora Ann wants any part of it," Johnny said.

"No, I don't think she does either, but she's a prisoner at Oaktree, the bars on her door and windows forged from her father's iron ambition to be the biggest rancher in the state. Mark my words, he'll kill anybody who stands in his way, and that's why Sean was shot. If Kincaid's plan succeeds, we'll all be dead, and he'll be master of the biggest ranch in Texas."

"I won't let that happen," Johnny said.

"Nor me, not in a thousand years. I'll have riders sent out and I can guarantee a score of well-armed men, both ranchers and farmers, will meet here on the Running-S before sundown."

"Then hit Oaktree in the dark?" Johnny said.

"Yes, with guns and fire. We'll burn that nest of vipers to the ground."

"What about Kincaid?"

"He'll die with the rest. Tomorrow the air will be cleaner, and his vile shadow will no longer stain the ground with its darkness." Johnny nodded and McPhee took that as his cue to speak again. "Then it's decided. We ride against the Oaktree and destroy that pit of evil once and for all." He looked speculatively at Johnny. "Sean would have led us. Will you take his place?"

"I'm a poor substitute for my brother."

"We need a leader, one man to encourage the others and make sure our attack carries the day. You were a famous prizefighter. They'll look up to you."

"You can do it, McPhee. And we both know you have something to prove. Now is your chance to show you're a man with sand."

"After what happened at the Crystal Palace, will they trust me?"

"I trust you. Get your fiery cross started and bring as many men as you can before sundown. One way or the other, the issue will be decided this day."

"If we'd done this months ago when the burning and killing began, your brother would not now be fighting for his life."

"Maybe so," Johnny said. To end the discussion, he swung his horse around, calling over his shoulder, "Be here at sundown."

"Depend on it," McPhee replied, "We'll be here."

Chapter 36

As Johnny O'Neil rode south, he had no definite plan of action in mind. He wanted Lowery dead, that much was certain, but he had to get to the man before the other ranchers moved in force against Oaktree. It would be just him and Lowery. No one else.

He would beat a confession out of the drawfighter with his bare hands, and the colonel would be a witness. Then, to settle the score, he'd kill him, and Elliot, too, if necessary. Just how he would achieve this with the Oaktree punchers around, he did not know. But it was a reckoning, and it had to be done.

Johnny had just cut the main wagon road to Oaktree, riding through gently rolling country partially covered in mesquite and post oak, a fine, morning mist in the hollows, when he saw a buckboard and a couple of outriders approach from the direction of the Kincaid ranch house. When the wagon was about a hundred yards away, the lead rider threw up a hand and the driver slowed the team to a halt. The rider spurred to Johnny and nodded. "Howdy."

Johnny returned the nod. "Howdy."

The man gestured with his chin toward the trail. "Seen any dead drunk or hungover drovers on your travels?"

"Nope, nary a one."

The man shrugged. "Name's Dick Peterson, I'm the Oaktree ramrod." He looked at Johnny quizzically. "Can't say as I've seen you around these parts afore. You just passing through?"

Johnny felt a pinprick of anger at the man's probing. But he knew he could blow his chance of getting at Lowery by picking a fight with Peterson. He also realized he was on Kincaid range, so the man's question was valid enough.

"Name's Johnny O'Neil, and I've got business with the colonel."

Peterson nodded. "You're Sean's brother."

"The same."

"Never see Sean much no more. Hear tell he's gonna sort out the goddam mess the range is in." Peterson waved toward the wagon. "All this war talk has scared away half my hands. There's more in town, been drinking steadily since Billy's funeral. The colonel sent me to bring them in. The ones as can't ride, I'm to bring back in the wagon. I sure hope Sean can solve this thing. Since someone killed his Hereford bull, the colonel's loaded for bear. He blames the other ranchers, says they're trying to force him off the range." Peterson grinned. "That'll be the day."

Johnny felt a surge of relief. This suited him perfectly. With the hands out of the way, he would have a clear field to deal with Lowery and Elliot. As casually as he could, he asked, "Those Texas drawfighters still with the colonel?"

"Hell yes. Them boys ain't no dollar-a-day drovers to go getting drunk in town. They clink glasses in the big house with the colonel himself, though Lowery stops by the Crystal Palace at times, probably to buy a woman. Hey, did you hear?"

"Hear what?"

"He killed a man last night."

"No, I didn't hear about that."

"Lowery rode in as we were leaving, and we talked some. It seems the man he shot was none other than Jordan Garrett."

"I don't know the name."

"A big-time bounty hunter. He was the man that killed the three Riddell brothers and their old man up in the Sabine River country that time. As I recollect, there was Donny, the youngest, then Amos and Grady." Seeing no recognition in Johnny's face, Peterson said, "I can't remember what their pa was called, Reuben, I think, but anyhow, it was right after they robbed a Wells Fargo stage and Garrett caught them camped out among some red oaks." The big foreman took the makings from the shirt pocket and began to build a cigarette. He looked up from tobacco and paper and said, "Garrett drew from the pockets of a greatcoat he wore and killed all four of them." He made a gun of his thumb and forefinger. "Bang! Bang! Bang! Bang! Just like that." Peterson lit the quirly and said, "Them boys had a jackrabbit on a stick and coffee on the bile. Ol' Jordy ate and drank, and then lay down and slept among dead men."

"Hard case," Johnny said.

"Damn right, and by all accounts a demon with a gun. No wonder John Lowery considers himself the cock o' the walk. But I guess he's earned the bragging rights."

"How did he kill Garrett?" Johnny said. The information could be useful.

"From what Lowery told me, Garrett drew down on him, but John was faster."

"Why was a bounty hunter after him?"

"Who knows? When you kill a man, you always stand a good chance of making enemies of his kinfolk."

"Or even when you try to kill a man," Johnny said.

Peterson hesitated and then said, "Yeah, I reckon that's so." He eyed Johnny steadily. "What kind of business have you got with the colonel, Mr. O'Neil?"

The buckboard and the other puncher had drawn closer, and both men were suddenly alert, as though a lot was riding on Johnny's answer.

"I've got a message to give him from Sean. He couldn't come himself."

Peterson was silent for a moment, but the answer seemed to satisfy him. "Maybe a bad time for that. The colonel isn't himself since Billy died and neither is Nora Ann."

"Is he ailing?" Johnny said.

"Let me just say he's not thinking straight. Remember the family portrait at Billy's grave? He's not been the same man since then, like he changed horses in the middle of a stream. Nora Ann is at her wits' end. I don't think she knows what to do with the colonel. He's talking about marrying Alice Wings, and it seems she's promised she'll bear him a boy child. Me, I reckon the lady is a little . . . ah . . . over the hill for that."

"He wants a son?" Johnny said.

"Yes, to take over Oaktree when the colonel's too old to fork a bronc."

"Nora Ann could do that, inherit the ranch and run it."

"No, that doesn't even enter into the colonel's thinking.

He says running a ranch is a task for a man. Hell, maybe it is. I don't know. I don't think it's ever been tried before."

"Maybe Colonel Kincaid will see things different after I talk with him," Johnny said.

"Don't count on it. He's not much in the listening mood." Peterson swung his horse away. "Well, good luck Mr. O'Neil. Give my regards to Sean when you see him."

Johnny watched the man leave, then kneed his mount into motion. The sun climbed the eastern sky, the mist thinned in the hollows, and the endless vista of green grassland and grazing cattle soothed his troubled soul.

His talk with Peterson had convinced him of one thing . . . if Lowery indeed took the wages of a third party, then he was working alone. The ordinary cattlemen like Peterson obviously wanted no part of a destructive range war, and the news of Sean being shot obviously hadn't yet reached Oaktree.

Who was he, this third man? He gave up trying to answer the question. Sean didn't know and his brother was smart, so what chance did a stranger to these parts? Then it dawned on him . . . Lowery was the obvious answer. The gunman had it all figured. Let Kincaid and the other ranchers fight it out and then he'd move in with his fast gun and pick up the pieces, a fortune in grazing land and cattle. Johnny chided himself. Of course, it was Lowery. The man was as crooked as a barrel of snakes, and he and Sean should've guessed that days ago and gotten rid of him. Well, it was too late now, but Johnny told himself he'd very soon put the matter to rights.

Johnny O'Neil rode with little grace, like a sack of grain, a tall, heavily muscled man riding a horse too small for him. His high-buttoned suit was mud spattered, and the pearl gray derby discolored to a dull ash by sun and rain. He badly needed a shave, and his battered face was drawn and tired. The buckskin settled into a comfortable rhythm, and Johnny willed himself to relax, refusing to dwell on the coming showdown with Lowery till he reached Oaktree. But as he rode, he kept seeing Maria's tearful face, and the girl's words to him burned into his brain like fire.

He shook his head trying to dislodge what she said, but it stayed in his mind, loud and insistent like a hammer on an anvil . . .

You're doing the very thing Sean wanted to avoid . . . you're starting the range war . . . starting the range war . . .

"No!" Johnny cried aloud.

Startled, the buckskin mare acted up again and Johnny reined her in. He wiped sweat from a suddenly flushed face and whispered, "It's not true . . . I want only revenge for Sean . . . for the peace of his mind and mine."

Johnny rubbed his temples trying to think, trying to figure it out like Sean would have done. He was going to beat a confession out of Lowery and then destroy him with his fists. That much was certain. Equally certain was the fact that the ranchers would ride against Oaktree in a few hours, and the only event that would prevent Kincaid clashing with them head-on would be the gunman's confession.

But suppose Lowery wouldn't talk before he died? Or suppose he didn't die?

The thought hit Johnny like a brick. There was a good

chance he could fall under the drawfighter's flashing guns. If either happened, a showdown between the ranchers and Oaktree was inevitable, and there would be no victor, only losers, dead men, and their widows and children. But Lowery, skilled as he was, could survive such an encounter. The mystery man who was trying to destroy the valley might well triumph in the end. With stark reality, Johnny knew that Lowery would not let Sean live. His brother would be shot in his bed.

Johnny groaned, took off his hat and ran his fingers through his hair, his mind working.

Ah, Sean, if only you were here to show me the way. All this thinking is making my poor head hurt.

Johnny turned his face to the brightening sky and whispered aloud, "Lord, this is himself. I would count it a great favor if You could spare the time to help me end this terrible business to the satisfaction of all concerned."

He closed his eyes and waited.

The range was silent save for a warm breeze that tugged at the buffalo grass and the rustle of the buckskin's tail as it turned cartwheels against marauding flies. Unnoticed on the timeless plains several slow minutes ticked past . . .

It came to Johnny O'Neil then.

Sean did not want revenge.

He wanted what he'd tried for all along, justice. The young rancher had been shot because someone was afraid he'd talk to the colonel and expose Lowery's scheme. It was the first time the mystery man had shown concern, a real fear his plan might fail. Now there was only one thing Johnny could do—forget killing Lowery for the moment and finish what Sean had started. He must get the colonel to listen to him, and he'd have to do it fast before the other ranchers rode against Oaktree. Together they could punish Lowery's treachery and vile ambition.

The big man smiled at the sky. "Himself thanks You kindly, Lord." Then remembering Lowery's reputation as a gunman he added, "And I think I'll still need Your help."

Only the buckskin whickered in reply.

Chapter 37

To Johnny O'Neil's surprise, Oaktree was silent and deserted, the windows of the big house staring into the glowing morning like blank, sightless eyes. The barn, bunkhouse, and other outbuildings stood lifeless and silent, and there was no breeze, only dead air that smelled of nothing.

Johnny dismounted and stepped to the door. He took a deep breath and rapped three times, hearing the hollow echoes of his knocks resonate in the quiet of the house. There was no answer, and he tried again but no one came to the door. He grabbed the handle and turned and pushed, and the door swung open. He stepped inside. A huge grandfather clock ticked loudly in the hallway, its brass pendulum making its steady way back and forth, and from somewhere in the house there was a funereal *thump-thump-thump* as though someone slowly beat on a muffled bass drum.

"Anyone to home?" The eerie echo of his voice mocked him, and the drum stopped for a few seconds, then resumed its monotonous beat, an insistent booming.

"Colonel Kincaid, are you there? It's Johnny O'Neil. We need to talk."

Only the drum, if that's what it was, answered.

Was some ranny, maybe Lowery himself, playing a game with him?

Judging by the sound, the drummer was holed up in one of the rooms upstairs. Johnny stepped to the bottom of the staircase, looked up at the landing and called out, "Who's up there? This is Johnny O'Neil, and I'm not a man to be trifled with."

Again, the persistent drumbeat, solemn, as though taking up the rear of a war hero's funeral procession.

Johnny swallowed hard. Rusty Chang's scattergun would've come in handy about now. Help quiet a man's fears. He started to climb the stairs, each one creaking a death knell, and with every step he took the drumming grew louder.

The landing was in the middle of a corridor with three closed doors on each side, leading, presumably to bedrooms. The rhythmic thumping was coming from Johnny's left and he stood for a moment on the landing and tried to place the sound's origin.

Then he noticed that the door nearest him was slightly ajar. He walked toward it slowly, stealthy as a cat burglar, but uncomfortably aware that every board in this house creaked under the strain of his two-hundred-and-twenty-pound frame.

Johnny stood outside the doorway, listening. The beat of the bass drum came from inside. It was a mystery that he was now about to solve. He threw the door wide and barged inside . . . and the muzzle of the .45 aimed right at his gut stopped him in his tracks. And he couldn't believe what he saw.

Zack Elliot was slumped in a corner of the room to the left of the door. Above his head, lace curtains framed an open window and billowed slightly in a rising breeze. The front of the gunman's once immaculate white shirt glistened red, and his face was gray as wood ash, the grinning lips dry and colorless. But the Colt in Elliot's hand, hammer back, did not waver an inch from Johnny's belly.

Johnny stood frozen in the doorway. He knew it was too late for peace talk. He'd charge the gunman and take his chances on surviving the hits. He tensed, ready to spring. The four clicks of Elliot's gun as he slowly eased down the hammer were loud in the quiet, the gunman, his eyes glazed, still grinning.

"Johnny O'Neil . . . what the hell are you doing here?"

"I'm here to speak with Colonel Kincaid."

Elliot shook his head and slowly beat the toe of his boot against the expensive wood paneling of the wall, a sound like a muffled drum.

"Where is the colonel?" Elliot said. "Well, he's here and he ain't here."

"I don't catch your drift."

"Colonel Kincaid is dead. Dead as a six-ace poker hand, dead as a rotten stump . . . dead as a doornail . . . can you think of anymore dead as's?"

Johnny crossed the floor and kneeled beside the gunman. Eliot's face had taken on a waxy pallor, and death already smeared black shadows in the hollows of his face.

"What happened to you?" Johnny asked.

"I got shot."

"Where is the colonel?"

"He got shot. And a young maid we called Polly got shot downstairs."

"Where is Nora Ann?"

"I don't know."

"Is she in the house?"

"No. I reckon she left sometime after the shooting began."

"Who did this to you?"

"Listen up, O'Neil, he's good, maybe the best there is."

"Who? Was it Lowery?"

"You ever hear of Clay Allison?"

"No, I can't say as I have. Was it Lowery who shot you?"

"Clay was a hell of a shootist. Came a time when I saw him beat a man on the draw and shoot. He was fast, but he didn't come close to the speed of John Lowery."

"Lowery shot you and Colonel Kincaid?"

"He surely did, killed us both and then he killed the maid." Elliot coughed and a runlet of blood stained his chin. "I've never seen anything like it in my life."

"Why, Eliot? Why did he shoot you?"

"Because I drew down on him, trying to protect the colonel."

"Why did he kill Kincaid?"

"Someone paid him, I guess."

"I think Lowery wants Oaktree."

Eliot managed a slight smile. "Lowery, a rancher? Not a chance."

"He could sell the land and cattle."

"Yeah, he could. Maybe that was his thinking. I don't

know." Eliot's voice dropped to a husky whisper. "Listen, O'Neil, I could've killed you when you walked through that door, but I didn't because I want you to spread the word. Tell them Zack Eliot was outdrawn by the best there is or will ever be, and his name is John D. Lowery. Beats me how he does it with his guns up under his arms like that, but he's lightning fast, hell on wheels with the six-gun. Damnedest thing I ever saw. Tell them, O'Neil, tell them, and for God's sake let them know I died game."

"Elliot, who shot my brother?" Johnny said, a sudden hardness in him.

"I don't know. I didn't even know he'd been shot. Is he dead?"

"No. He'll live."

"Glad to hear it. Now go away and let me die in peace. I already played dead for Lowery, now I'm about to do it for real."

"Where's the colonel?" Johnny said.

Elliot nodded toward the far end of the room. "This was his office. He fell over there between his desk and the wall." The gunman closed his eyes. "Hell, dying is easier than I thought," he said.

Johnny rose to his feet and walked to Kincaid's desk. The colonel was there all right, sprawled facedown on the floor between the bottom of the desk and the wall. He turned the man over. Whatever Lance Kincaid's ambitions and dreams might have been, they were now gone for all time. A bullet had been placed neatly between his eyes, and like a grotesque mask, the rancher's face was frozen into a look of shock and horror.

Johnny shook his head, crossed himself again and stepped back to Elliot.

The gunman was clinging to life, but the candle of Elliot's existence guttered, and its last, faint glow was about to light his way into eternity.

"Elliot, hold on, we need to talk," Johnny said.

"You need to talk with a dead man?"

"Yes, you're soon to meet your Maker. It's time to speak the truth."

"You know, O'Neil, he took us both. We didn't even have time to clear leather before he was shooting." The gunman smiled, a ghastly grimace that twisted his face. "Never seen a man so fast . . . so . . . gifted."

Eliot's time was running out, and there was urgency now in Johnny's voice. "Who hired Lowery to kill you and Kincaid?" he said. "Who's behind all this? Is it Lowery himself? Is he the man in the shadows?"

The gunman was far gone. A weak hand grabbed the lapels of Johnny's coat and he struggled to speak. "Listen, Lowery and Frenchy Laurent . . . you're next for the bullet, O'Neil. Then one by one the ranchers . . . all of them."

Johnny leaned closer to the man's ear. "Where is Nora Ann? Does Lowery have her?"

"Such a beauty, Nora Ann."

"Yes, I know. Did Lowery and Laurent take her with them?"

Then Elliot revealed a surprising knowledge of the language of the San Francisco waterfront and its hell ships. "You mean, did they shanghai her?" he said.

"Yes. Did they do that? Did they shanghai her?"

"I don't know."

"Did you hear her say anything? Did she scream?"

The gunman tried. He tried very hard. "I don't know where Nora Ann is. Get after her, O'Neil. Hunt down Lowery and Frenchy Laurent . . ."

"Will they head for the Running-S? Will they take Nora Ann there?"

"Hunt them down . . ."

The voice died, Elliot's hand dropped, and his candle burned out.

Johnny crossed himself and muttered a brief prayer for the souls of Zack Elliot and Lance Kincaid before he walked from the room and made his way downstairs and did the same for Polly who was sprawled on the kitchen floor, blood pooling from under her. The dead are silent and still, and the house was hushed, so quiet he could hear his own breathing. But not peaceful. It was as though the house was haunted by the restless, clamorous spirits of dead men.

The parlor door stood open, and Johnny O'Neil stepped inside. Decanters of bourbon and glasses stood on a side table, and he poured himself a drink and sat on one of the overstuffed chairs flanking the fireplace. He drank, laid his glass aside, and buried his face in his hands. For the second time that morning he wished to hell he'd been born with less brawn and more brains. No matter, he must try to figure this out, determine his next move.

Johnny had no idea why Lowery should take Nora Ann with him instead of killing her when he'd gunned down her father. Did he desire the woman? That was a possibility? No, if Lowery was to take over Oaktree and the rest of the range Nora Ann had to die. Elliot had said that he, Johnny, was also marked for death. And that figured because he knew everything that Sean knew, and his brother was shot because of that knowledge.

Johnny stood heavy on his feet, a dull ache in the back of his head. It looked like the third party, and that was Lowery, had won. Johnny realized that if he and Nora Ann, died the law, knowing nothing about the gunman's plans, would pin Lance Kincaid's murder on the small ranchers. Even Sean's shooting could be laid at their doorstep. Wasn't his brother striving for peace when all the ranchers so obviously wanted war?

Even now, Johnny could hear Bob Beason. "Colonel Kincaid was murdered by rival ranchers. After they paid to have his son Billy killed, they saw their diabolical plot through to the end. And that's a natural fact, plain as the nose on your face."

Bolstered by a second bourbon, Johnny finally figured that he had two options, both thin, but options, nonetheless. If he could rescue Nora Ann from her captors, they could go to the law, and the girl could tell Beason about the murder of her father. That, or he could ride to town now, tell Beason what he knew, and get the sheriff to round up a posse and start a search. Nora Ann's evidence could put Lowery's head in a noose.

Thinking it over, Johnny knew that going directly to Beason with what he knew was his only hope. Alone, he could never find Nora Ann Kincaid in this vastness. It had to be the sheriff . . . if he didn't run into Lowery and Laurent and could make it to town alive.

Johnny left the house and stepped to his horse when he suddenly stopped in midstride. Maria Perez was still at the Running-S. If Lowery and Laurent came looking for him there, she was a dead woman, and Rusty Chang along with her.

Johnny climbed into the saddle and kicked his horse into a gallop.

He had the terrible feeling he might already be too late.

Sheriff Bob Beason knew his limitations as a lawman, and they were many. But what saved him from total mediocrity were his instincts, as finely tuned as those of a lobo wolf. And as he looked, coffee in hand, out the window of his office into the street, his intuition, call it sixth sense, clamored at him. Something was amiss, as obvious to him as a day when the sun didn't rise.

He shook his head.

What the hell is gnawing at me?

Outside, everything seemed as usual, people on the street, a few tradesmen, pregnant Mrs. Alice Logan with a shopping basket on her arm, a towheaded kid leading a three-legged raccoon by a string tied round its neck, something not usual, but hardly enough to explain the clamor in his head.

Finally, he had to face the truth.

The range war had started or was about to start or someone was dead, and the likeliest candidate was Sean O'Neil. The repercussions would be enormous, a battle he needed to head off at the pass or nip in the bud or whatever the sayings were, before the range become a bloodbath and Mustang Flat with it.

Beason sighed. His instincts had never failed him before. He buckled on his gun belt and holster. He'd head out to the Running-S since it was closer and find out what was happening. He anticipated bad news.

Truly, there was no rest for the weary.

Chapter 38

As Johnny neared the Running-S, he saw to his relief that Sean's gray and Rusty Chang's horse were still in the corral. He drew rein on the buckskin and stepped out of the saddle as Rusty appeared at the cabin door, the Greener in his hands.

"Oh, it's you," Rusty said, lowering the scattergun. "I took you for one of them circuit preachers or something."

Johnny stepped closer to the little Chinese. "Do I look like a preacher to you?"

"Maybe, if you cleaned yourself up."

"Has anything happened while I was gone?"

"Yeah, the boss woke up and talked."

"What did he say?"

"He said, 'What am I doing here?'"

"He didn't recognize his own room? His own bed?"

"No. I guess he figured he'd wake up outside the pearly gates."

"Did you tell him he's still in Texas?"

"No. I didn't want him to think he'd woke up in hell."

"Colonel Kincaid is dead," Johnny said.

The resulting shock showed on Rusty's face. "Say it again."

"Kincaid is dead, murdered, him and Zack Elliot. And I suspect Nora Ann's been took."

"If that doesn't beat all," Rusty said. "Who done it?"

"John Lowery, him and Frenchy Laurent."

"You know that third man Sean talked about, the man in the shadows?"

"The boss spoke about him."

"That man is Lowery. He planned it all along. Get the colonel and the ranchers at each other's throats and then when the gunsmoke clears take over the whole range."

"Where does that leave us?" Rusty said.

"It leaves us dead, if Lowery has his way."

Rusty looked around him, at the dust still settling on Johnny's back trail, and then said, "We'd better go inside."

"Yeah, we'd better. We're targets out here."

As Johnny walked into the cabin, he felt a little pang of surprise that the thought of harm coming to Maria Perez had troubled him so much. He'd given Rusty money to get her on a stage out of here, but now it dawned on him that he didn't want the girl to leave . . . not now, not ever.

Did he love her?

Nah, that was impossible. He felt protective. That was it. He'd make sure that no harm would ever come to her . . . and her baby.

Despite her long vigil at Sean's bedside, Maria looked remarkably fresh and pretty that morning. She'd changed into a stone-gray dress that set off the color of her hair, and eyes and her high cheekbones were flushed a pale rose. Despite his tiredness Johnny smiled at her, a smile she did not return. Maria brought him a cup of coffee and both she and Rusty listened as he told them what had passed at the Kincaid ranch.

When Johnny finished talking Maria's eyes were concerned.

"What will you do now, Johnny?"

"I'll ride into town to see Sheriff Beason," the big man answered. "And you're going with me, Maria. You'll be much safer in town."

"What about McPhee and the ranchers?" Rusty said.

"I want you to head for the McPhee ranch and try to head them off, Rusty," Johnny said. "For God's sake keep them away from Oaktree till I get Beason out there. I don't want them to get blamed for the colonel's murder and allow Lowery to make war."

"Nora Ann is her father's heir and only she can declare war on the smaller ranchers," Maria said. "Lowery is a hired gunman and has no stake in this."

"Yes, he has, and now I know that's why he took Nora Ann. He can hold a gun to her head and use her as an unwilling puppet while he pulls the strings. When the range war is won, and the other ranchers dead or scattered, Lowery can forge her will, leaving Oaktree and the other spreads with their lands and cattle to him, and then quietly get rid of her."

"What kind of mind would come up with a scheme like that?" Maria said.

"An extremely clever and evil one," Rusty said.

"I can dance to that tune," Johnny said. "And the war could be a short one after Lowery hires a score of hired guns. Plenty of those kicking their heels around West Texas, I guess."

Rusty nodded. "We breed 'em like jackrabbits."

Johnny drained his cup and then said, "Maria, we need to be going. Rusty, I'm leaving you with my brother. I'm taking a big chance with both your lives."

"I'll stay with the boss," Rusty said. "Do you think I might leave him?"

"No, I don't think that. You're a good man, Rusty. Your heathen doctoring saved Sean's life and I'm right proud to have known you."

"Spoken like a white man," Rusty said, smiling.

"And I meant every word of it."

A note of caution crept into Johnny's voice. "Listen, if something happens to me and I don't make it, you and Maria will be the only people who can tell the law what really happened here. Whatever you do, Rusty, save yourself and Sean. Don't have it out with Lowery."

"I've got a sick man here, and I ain't going anyplace, so get the sheriff here fast. As for telling Beason what really happened, he ain't gonna listen to a crazy old Chinaman and a greaser gal. You know that."

"Johnny, I'm staying here with Sean and Rusty," Maria said. "Go get the sheriff. We'll be here when you get back."

Johnny was silent for long moments then said, "I want you where I know you'll be safe."

"I'll be safe right here," the girl told him. "Rusty called it. We're not leaving Sean. When he's well again, then I'll pack my bag and go."

Johnny looked up sharply. He started to speak, stopped, then tried again. "Maria, I don't want you to go. Why don't you stay here at the Running-S. After this is over, we can work something out."

The girl shook her head. "Is there anything left to work out, Johnny? It was all said last night and this morning."

"Listen, Maria, that . . . that wasn't me. I wasn't thinking straight and that was someone else, a stranger."

The girl dropped her eyes. "Then I'll stay for a while and afterward perhaps we can talk."

Johnny said nothing. Just as Maria did, he knew there was no sense in building houses on a bridge they'd still to cross.

Rusty said, "Johnny, seems to me you'd better get moving."

"Take care of yourself," Maria said.

The big man nodded, opened the door, and Maria followed him outside. Suddenly the girl gasped and her whole body stiffened in alarm.

Chapter 39

In the yard, sitting their horses, were John Lowery and Frenchy Laurent and between them Nora Ann Kincaid. Even tied up, the woman looked beautiful that morning, even if her expression was one of anger.

Johnny O'Neil stepped to the side, and placed his body in front of Maria. He saw Lowery glance at the girl and then dismiss her, as though she was beneath his notice.

Frenchy thought otherwise. His massive, hunched shoulders and terrible scar across his empty left eye socket made him look barely human. "If what I hear is true, she don't show much," he said. "Bet she's still a lot of fun, O'Neil, eh? What's it like to ride a pregnant Mex mare?"

Johnny knew he had to remain cool, thinking. He ignored Laurent's jibe and said, "What do you want, Lowery?"

The gunman smiled. "'What do I want? Why, you of course, Mr. O'Neil. I'm here to send you and your brother to a better place. Downright civil of me, huh?"

Lowery was tense, ready to draw. Johnny desperately

wanted the man to relax, to blur the sharp edge of his speed.

He heard himself say, his voice unraveling, "I warn you, Lowery, Sheriff Beason is due here any time. Give me Nora Ann and you can ride on out of here."

"Come on, O'Neil, you can do better than that. We know the man I put the crawl on . . . what's his name? Yeah, McPhee . . . is trying to round up a posse of ranchers, but he won't be here for a while yet." Lowery's smile slipped. "And by that time, you and your brother will be dead."

"You won't be able to pin Colonel Kincaid's murder on the ranchers," Johnny said.

Lowery smiled again, "Yes, I can. They killed the colonel and declared war on Oaktree and within a few days we'll have enough guns here to fight it to the finish. If the idiot Beason gets in the way, he'll regret it."

Johnny saw that Lowery was ready. He again tried to buy a little time. "Are you all right, Miss Nora?"

The woman didn't answer. And it was then that Frenchy Laurent opened the ball. The one-eyed man cursed and yelled, "Enough of the damned yakking! Let's get this thing started!"

Frenchy pulled a gun from his waistband and aimed at Johnny. Chang, who had been staring with basilisk eyes at Laurent from the cabin door jerked up his Greener and fired. The heavy load of buckshot caught Frenchy full in the chest and blasted him backward off his horse, a fountain of sudden blood fanning over his head.

Lowery had briefly turned in Frenchy's direction when the man yelled. It had taken only a split second, but it was all the time Johnny O'Neil was going to get. Twenty feet separated him from Lowery, and it took him just under two seconds to reach the gunman. But in that short time Lowery lived up to his reputation as a premier shootist.

As Johnny charged, Lowery's hands went to the holsters under his armpits. It was a cross draw and technically awkward, but the man was smooth, slick, and blindingly fast. In those two seconds the gunman snapped off six shots and only two events saved Johnny from instant death.

The first was that Lowery feared the Chinaman with the scattergun, and two bullets cut down the little man before Rusty had a chance to bring the second barrel of the Greener to bear.

The second was that the breeze had dropped and Lowery was forced to sight on Johnny through a haze of powder smoke. Some historians say the thin smoke screen had no bearing on John Lowery's shooting, but rather his face had been splattered by Frenchy's cascading blood and bone and it had unnerved him. Whatever the reason, Lowery's third shot kicked up a startled V of dirt between Johnny's pounding feet, and a fourth tore its way into the top of Johnny's right shoulder. The fifth burned across his back and the sixth took him just above the waistband, smashing into the top of his upper thigh bone.

Johnny O'Neil experienced those two seconds in slow sequence as though in a terrifying nightmare. He felt the heavy bullets hit as he ran, jarring him from head to toe like roundhouse punches.

Finally, he saw terror in the gunman's face as Lowery realized he was not shooting at an ordinary man but at an enormous fighting animal . . . a predator who'd learned his ferocious skills in the boxing ring and was in a rage to kill. Then Johnny's hands grabbed the man's coat, and he pulled him bodily from the saddle.

Johnny roared his anger as he threw Lowery over his head. The gunman landed heavily and the bone in his left arm broke with a sickening snap. Lowery tried to bring a Colt to bear but Johnny kicked the weapon out of his hand.

Now, to the horror of some archivists who later read this account, the killing time began.

Johnny O'Neil hauled Lowery to his feet, then drove several massive straight rights into the gunman's face. Lowery who had never been in a fistfight in his life tried feebly to ward off the blows. But it was useless. Johnny's rage was a white-hot thing, and he was murderous.

"This is for Sean," he said, breathing hard, punching. "This is for my brother."

"No!" Maria Perez yelled. "Johnny, stop it."

But Johnny O'Neil was beyond hearing, surrounded by a scarlet-streaked mist as black as night.

Lowery's face caved into a bloody pulp under the big man's punches. And the sledgehammer blows were breaking other bones, bones in the skull, in the neck, in the chest . . .

It was over in seconds.

Loss of blood from his wounds weakening him, Johnny trembled as he stared down at Lowery and then at the grazed knuckles of his fists . . . fists that had just killed a man. The gunman's face was unrecognizable, and his mouth opened around a soundless scream.

Weak from loss of blood and sickened by the damage he'd wrought, Johnny was unable to stand. He fell to his knees and looked up at Nora Ann—straight into the muzzle of a Colt pointed at his head.

"Nora Ann . . ." Johnny said, stunned, scrambling for words

"You big dumb ox," the woman said, "as though killing Lowery will make any difference. You're going to die anyway, you and that little greaser whore of yours."

Johnny looked to the porch where Maria kneeled beside the wounded Chang. The girl gazed at Nora Ann Kincaid in numb horror.

"But why? I don't understand," Johnny stumbled, shaking his head.

The muzzle of the .45 was steady. "Of course, you don't understand, you punch-drunk pug. But really, it's all so simple. You see when my mother died, I saw my father replace her with a whore, and to make it easy for himself he sent me east." Bitterness tinged Nora Ann's laugh. "Oh sure, he said it was because I was grieving some and should have a change of scenery. But I knew the real reason—he wanted more time with his kept woman."

"But that's not so," Johnny began. "Your father was concerned . . ."

"Shut up! I don't want to hear that. Your brother said the same thing, and that's when I knew he would have to die." Nora Ann sighed. "Now listen quietly because I want to send you to hell happy. That's where you'll go, you know. Like all men, you'll go to hell and burn and rot forever."

Johnny thought then that the woman was not right in the head. He also knew with awful certainty that he was too weak to grab for her. What Lowery had failed to do this slip of a girl would accomplish—and worse, Sean and Maria would die with him.

Nora Ann talked again. "When I got to Boston, I realized that was the kind of life I wanted. New York, Paris, Rome, the wonderful places, the gay places full of life that I had always dreamed about. There was only one problem."

"Visiting those big cities took money," Johnny said, "Money you didn't have."

"Correct. You're not quite as dumb as I thought you were."

"And there was only one way to get that money— inherit Oaktree."

"Right again. What a clever boy. But there were two people in my way. Brother Billy, that drunken child, and Father of course, the man who told me I'd never inherit the ranch, that it would go to Alice Wings' son, when she gave him one. I thought about all that for a long time then hit on the solution. Start a nice little range war and in the course of it make sure Billy and Father did not survive."

Johnny's face was puzzled. "But how . . . how did you get it started, the cattle killing, the night riders, the murder of the rancher?"

Nora Ann laughed. "That was the easiest part. The bartender, Johnson, badly needed money to move to Arizona for his lungs' sake. Frenchy Laurent and his sidekick wanted the price of a drink and a woman. Once I'd recruited them, the rest was easy. They began the whole thing, and it was Frenchy who finally talked Father into hiring some top gunmen like John Lowery and Zack Elliot."

"You mean you wrote those men from Boston? That

was a risk, wasn't it? They could have blown the whistle on you."

"A risk, yes, but a small one. I was sure of those men. They were all money hungry. Besides, I only wrote to Frenchy Laurent. He recruited Johnson to kill Billy. But I already had an assassin in mind. Her name was Corinda Mason."

"The singer who was killed on the Patterson stage by Indians. I don't understand."

"You don't need to understand. What would you know about a woman's love for another woman? We met at a party in Philadelphia, Corinda and I, and she later told me what she did for a living, and it wasn't singing, although she had the voice of an angel. Corinda was a paid assassin, among the best of her kind, and one night we talked and planned on my inheriting Oaktree. After I sold the ranch, we'd meet again in Philadelphia, and we would have, had she not fallen prey to the savages."

Johnny was growing weaker. His head felt light as if it was floating away from his shoulders. He could feel blood seeping down his back, and the wound in his hip burned like fire. But he had to keep this insane woman talking, in the slim hope that McPhee and the other ranchers would get there in time.

"And Lowery crawled out from under his rock and Frenchy hired him?" he said.

"No, I hired Lowery after I stopped off in Fort Worth on my way back to Texas. Corinda recommended him since they'd both worked an assassination in New Orleans." Nora Ann motioned toward the dead man with her gun. "He was a high-stakes gambler and was well-known in the city's brothels and saloons. Once I learned what his price was"—the girl grimaced, a look that momentarily destroyed the beauty of her face—"it wasn't too hard to send him to Father as a gun for hire. A fat bonus when the job was done, and he'd have gone back to Fort Worth quite happily. Too bad he didn't live to collect it, huh?"

"Lowery did the rest of your killing?"

Nora Ann sighed. She was getting bored and more dangerous. "Yes, he did the killing, the rancher, Johnson, your brother, that fool Elliot, and my father. Apart from messing up with Sean, which I'll finish for him, he did his job very well." The girl's eyes hardened. "Now there's only you, O'Neil. I gave your brother his chance to share at least a part of my life, but he refused. I'm afraid I can't extend the same courtesy to you."

Johnny tensed. He was not going to allow himself to be shot down like a dog. But as he measured the distance between himself and the woman, he knew he'd never make it. He tried again to play for time. "You'll never make this work. There's too many dead men, too much to explain."

She could not resist the last word. Nora Ann smiled pityingly at the big man and spoke to him as if he was a child. "You are a fool, O'Neil. You see, the whole thing was started by you and Sean. You wanted Oaktree and tried to arrange the range war. You hired Lowery, Elliot, and Laurent to help and then there was a quarrel over the spoils and Lowery shot Sean. After you murdered my father and Elliot, you kidnapped me and brought me here. There was another quarrel, and this time you and the little Chinaman killed Lowery and Frenchy Laurent. The Chinaman and your whore died in the fight, and I was forced to kill you in self-defense." Nora Ann smiled coyly. "I'm sure when I speak to the law, they'll believe li'l ol' me! Wouldn't you?" Her voice, hardened. "Now, O'Neil, it's time to go. Your brother will join you shortly!"

Johnny charged but stumbled facedown after a few steps.

He lifted his head weakly, saw the smiling woman's finger whiten on the trigger of the Colt.

A shotgun roared.

Nora Ann Kincaid was blasted out of the saddle, landed on her back, and screamed, a primitive shriek of anger and fear. Her back arched and she raised both hands as though attempting to clutch at the sky, then she whispered, "Corinda," and died.

Johnny turned and saw Maria, standing pale and trembling, Rusty Chang's smoking Greener in her hands. The big man rose painfully and staggered to where Nora Ann lay. The hailstorm of buckshot from the scattergun had practically cut her slender body in half.

Maria stepped toward the body, but Johnny held her back. "There's nothing there you need to see. She's dead."

The girl nodded dumbly and helped Johnny stumble to the porch. He sat on the stoop, the fierce pain in his shoulder and hip making him weak and nauseous.

"I guess Billy can rest easy now," he said.

"I didn't do it for Billy."

"How is Rusty?"

"Rusty is dead."

The girl's strong fingers ripped away his shirt, uncovering his wounds. "You need a doctor. There's a bullet in your shoulder, and the wound at your side is bad."

"I'll live. I think maybe I've found something to live for."

Maria touched his lips. "Don't talk now. You must save your strength till help comes."

* * *

Alexander McPhee and fifteen riders showed up an hour later. To Johnny's surprise Bob Beason rode with them, and he had Doctor Grant in tow. Although he was barely holding on to consciousness, Johnny grinned, "Could have done with you an hour ago, Beason."

The sheriff nodded. "Didn't take me long to figure out what the hell the ranchers was gathering for. I ain't much of a man of action, but I got spies everywhere." Beason looked at the dead men and at Nora Ann Kincaid's bloody and broken body. "I think you got some explaining to do, O'Neil. Better take it slow and don't miss a thing."

Despite Maria's protests that he was too weak to talk, with many stops and starts, Johnny told the lawman and the attentive ranchers the whole story. When he finished, Beason said, "I'll organize a full investigation and get this thing officially settled." He looked hard-eyed at Johnny. "If you had told me all this earlier, all this might never have happened."

"I didn't know this earlier," Johnny said.

"Damn it, O'Neil, you and your brother went the wrong way in this thing. You kept too many secrets."

"Only my brother's shooting made it the wrong way."

The sheriff coughed. "I'm sorry about Sean. But you should've told me everything."

Johnny looked at the man for long moments, then sighed heavily. "Like you said, Beason, you ain't much of a man of action. I had to do it my own way."

The sheriff looked as if he was about to say more, then he decided against it. He turned to the men around him and yelled, "Let's get these bodies into town. And you,

McPhee, ride on to Oaktree now and bring the dead men to Mustang Flat."

A couple of ranchers helped Johnny to his bunk where Maria undressed him and washed his wounds. He was then examined by Dr. Grant.

"How are the others?" Johnny said.

"They're all dead. John Lowery was unrecognizable."

"He was the one who shot me."

"He wounded you in two places and you still managed to kill him?"

"I was angry because he shot and nearly killed Sean."

"Don't ever hold a grudge at me," Grant said. "I wouldn't want to be your enemy."

"Was I wrong?"

"It's not for me to say. This is the frontier, Mr. O'Neil. Western men make up their own minds about what's right and what's wrong."

"John Lowery was a gunman," Maria said. "He would've killed Johnny."

"And he almost succeeded," Grant said. He took off his coat, handed it to Maria and then rolled up his sleeves. "His bullet is still in Mr. O'Neil's shoulder, and it's deep. His femur is damaged where it meets the pelvic bone, and it will heal, but I'm afraid he'll walk with a limp for the rest of his life."

"Doc, tell me, not her," Johnny said. "I'm barely conscious and I'm in a heap of pain, but I can still hear you."

"Miss Perez, I need to operate, but I'll give him ether and I ask your help to administer the anesthetic."

"Of course, Doctor."

"Here, is this going to hurt?" Johnny said, looking worried.

Grant smiled. "There's a ninety percent chance you'll feel nothing."

"What about the other ten percent?"

"Ah, in that case it will hurt like hell," Dr. Grant said.

Chapter 40

Like a warrior, Rusty Chang was buried on the range under a large bur oak, his Greener beside him.

To Johnny O'Neil's surprise, Sheriff Beason attended along with undertaker Clem Milk and his assistants, who dug the grave and suppled a finely made pine coffin.

Even more surprising, Milk and another man, under Maria Perez's mother hen supervision, carried Sean to the graveside, located on a rise some fifty yards from the back of the cabin. Sean was ashen, weak, and still very ill, but he'd insisted on seeing Rusty laid to rest.

For Johnny, walking was out of the question, and Dr. Grant forbade him to get out of his bed. But he watched the burial from his bedroom window, and Maria supplied him with a rosary to say his prayers for the dead.

"Damn it, O'Neil, you should be in bed," Beason said. "You look awful. How is the champ?"

"More awful-er than me," Sean said, his voice a weak whisper.

"A brave man, the champ," Beason said.

"Yes, he is, and so was Rusty."

"Indeed, he was, a benighted heathen but a credit to

his race," Beason said. "Lower the coffin, boys, handsomely now. Lay him to rest."

After the grave was filled, Sean said to Milk, "I want a stone for Rusty."

"Marble?"

"Yes, marble."

Milk produced a notebook from his frock coat and said, "Words?"

It took a tremendous effort for Sean to talk, weakness and grief taking their toll. "Just say, 'Rusty Chang. A brave man and loyal friend.'" *

"It's all the epitaph any man needs," Beason said.

Sean and Johnny O'Neil, sitting up in their beds, were not ideal patients, and they ran Maria Perez ragged with their demands. A week after the horrific showdown with Nora Kincaid, the war over steaks was typical.

"What are we having for lunch?" Johnny said.

"I haven't decided yet," Maria said.

"Blacken me a steak, maybe a couple," Johnny said.

"And that goes for me, too," Sean said. His voice was stronger, and he was on the mend, his strong work-hardened body recovering quickly.

Although in considerable pain, neither he nor Johnny had resorted to Doctor Grant's morphine. Both had seen too many wounded war veterans who were addicted to the needle.

"You're not ready for beefsteaks, neither of you," Maria said.

---

*Rusty's headstone stood until the early 1960s but has since vanished. The bur oak is still there.

"Yes, we are," Johnny said.

"No, you're not," Maria said. "You're invalids and Doctor Grant said you must have a light but nourishing diet."

"I'm hungry," Johnny said.

"Then I'll fix you something."

"Lady, I could eat a whole longhorn steer, hide, horn, hooves, and beller," Johnny said.

"I'll ditto that," Sean said.

"My, we are starting to feel better," Maria said. "Appetite is a good sign."

"So, what are we having?" Sean said.

"Edna McPhee sent us two dozen eggs from her own hens. You'll have a nice soft-boiled egg."

The promised menu was greeted by a stunned silence. Then Johnny yelled, "Hey, Sean, she's trying to starve us."

"Seems like," Sean said. "I've never, in my life, eaten a soft-boiled egg."

"Then you don't know what you've missed, do you?"

"I want a steak," Johnny said, sounding just a little petulant.

"If you two quit complaining, I'll allow you a little bacon and a biscuit with tonight's egg," Maria said.

Silence.

"Good boys," Maria said.

After lunch, while Sean was asleep, Maria fluffed Johnny's pillow and then sat on the edge of his cot. "What will you do when you're well again?" she said. "Return to Boston to your business?"

Johnny struggled to sit up, but she firmly pushed him back. "Lie there and relax and later you can take a nap."

"You're making an invalid out of me," he said. Then, "Yes, Maria, I'll return to Boston but only to sell my tavern. This ranch is Sean's life, his dream. I figure I owe it to him and myself to stay here and make it work."

"But you know nothing of ranching."

"I'll learn. And I'll learn even faster with a good woman to help me."

The girl rose. "I'll leave as soon as I can get someone here to look after you."

"No, woman," Johnny said, "You'll stay."

"I can't be that woman, Johnny. Maybe I once was, but now I'm spoiled goods."

"But I want you to be that woman," Johnny said. "My woman."

"There could never be love. How could you ever love me?"

Johnny stretched out and took Maria's small hand in his huge paw. "There can be love, I know there can. In fact, I think I love you already."

"And I think I love you already."

"And I think we can be happy together."

"And I think you could be right," Maria said.

Keep reading for a special excerpt!

**WILLIAM W. JOHNSTONE
and J.A. JOHNSTONE**

**SONS OF THUNDER
A Slash and Pecos Western**

**Slash and Pecos match wits with the wiliest
opponent they've ever had—a wickedly smart
woman who can't be caught—in their wildest
western adventure yet . . .**

It sounds like an easy job: track down the lady friend
of notorious outlaw Duke Winter and bring her in for
questioning. There's just one problem: Slash and Pecos
have never met a woman like Miss Fannie Diamond,
a glamorous showgirl who's prettier than a French
poodle, slicker than a Dodge City gambler, and more
slippery than a Mojave rattlesnake. She knows that
Slash and Pecos are coming for her and has no intention
of being caught—not without one hell of a fight . . .

By the time the duo arrive at the Rocky Mountain mining
camp where Miss Diamond is performing, the devilishly
clever gal has already arranged a welcome wagon for
them: some hired thugs who knock Slash and Pecos silly.
Still, the show must go on—so the pair decide to snatch
Miss Diamond off the stage in the middle of a
performance. It doesn't take long for Slash and Pecos to
learn that there's no business like show business—and no
showgirl like Miss Fannie Diamond. Sometimes, the
female of the species is deadlier than the male . . .

***Look for SONS OF THUNDER,
on sale in September 2022!***

Chapter 1

Thunder rumbled like angry gods bowling with boulders. Witches' fingers of lightning poked across the firmament, intermittently lighting up this rain-tortured Rocky Mountain canyon, which had been turned by the late-summer monsoon storm into howling bedlam.

Between lightning bolts, the Colorado night was as black as the bottom of a deep well save for the buffeting gray curtain of wind-lashed rain that seemed to have no letup in it whatever.

Hunkered low inside his oilskin rain slicker and seated in the driver's box of the stout Pittsburg freight wagon, holding the sodden harness ribbons tight in his gloved hands, James "Slash" Braddock turned to his long-boned partner seated beside him and shouted, "Good Lord, Pecos. I do believe we have a good chance of drowning out here, sittin' in our consarned wagon no less!"

He looked down at the ankle-deep rainwater churning on the floor of the driver's box. It had soaked his boots and socks and damn near frozen his feet.

"If the river keeps rising," returned Melvin "Pecos Kid" Baker, pausing as another peal of near-deafening thunder hammered down around them, "we might be swimmin' for it, Slash!" He turned his head to regard the Poudre River where it churned and pounded loudly in its rocky bed off the trail's right side. "It looks to me like it's starting to swell out of its banks!"

"We have to find shelter soon!"

"That old ghost town of Manhattan should be dead ahead. Last time we passed through there, a saloon was still in operation, remember?"

"I do! And I also remember, if my memory hasn't gotten even cloudier than I think it has here on the downhill side of my allotment, the fella that ran the place was a big Swede everybody called 'the Dutchman,' who served a thick dark ale and cooked a mean T-bone steak!"

"And he piled up a whole passel of greasy fried potatoes around it, too! Cooked to a crispy brown, just the way I like it!"

"Oh, Lordy, you're killin' me!"

"I'll be hanged if I ain't killin' myself!"

"I hope Manhattan is as close as you think it is!"

"Hey! Look there!" Pecos straightened in his seat and thrust out his right arm to aim his pointing index finger over the two stout, rain-silvered mules hitched to the wagon. "I think I see a light!"

Slash gazed straight ahead, around the steady stream of rain sluicing down from the crease in the crown of his black Stetson. Sure enough, a pinprick of soft amber light shone in the gauzy darkness.

"Well, well, looks like you had it right!" Slash said.

Pecos grinned and pressed a finger to his temple. "Yours might be gettin' murky, but my thinker box is workin' just fine, Slash!"

"I suppose you think that means you oughta be doin' the thinkin' for both of us." Slash chuckled and wagged his head as he shook the reins over the lumbering mules' backs. "Lordy, I shudder at the thought!"

"I'm too cold an' wet to kick your scrawny behind, so I'll let that one go!"

Slash laughed.

The mules quickened their pace despite the sodden trail, which had become a shallow stream churning with muddy water that shone amber when the lightning flashed. They climbed the gradual grade on top of which the ghost town of Manhattan sat in a wide horseshoe bend of the river.

A loud crashing boom sounded, cutting through the stormy din, making mules and men jerk with starts. Slash and Pecos turned to see a lightning bolt strike a thumb of rock on the far side of the river. A lone pine rose like a sentinel from the top of the rock. It glowed brightly, as did the entire thumb, against the darkness of the mountain wall, sizzling loudly.

The pine exploded, and the thumb broke loose from the stone wall from which it jutted and tumbled down against the wall with several more explosive roars. Burning tree and sizzling rock tumbled away in the stormy darkness.

The scorched-stone aroma of brimstone peppered the air.

"Yikes!" Pecos said.

"Yeah!" Slash agreed, again flicking the reins over the mules' backs. "Come on, you mangy broomtails. Pick it up less'n you wanna get roasted alive out here!"

Mules, wagon, and men flattened out at the top of the

rise; and the two rows of mostly vacant and eerily dark business buildings of old Manhattan, a rollicking gold camp just a few short years ago, pushed up around the wagon. The only build ing with lights in its windows shone dead ahead, on the street's left side. That would be the Dutchman's place.

"Should be an old barn up here, on the right," Pecos said.

Slash swung the mules over to the large log barn standing tall and dark and doorless on the right side of the street, between a boarded-up bordello with a tumbledown front stoop and a boarded-up barbershop, its once colorful pole having faded to gray. Slash hazed the mules on into the barn, and as the wagon followed them in, the rain stopped lashing him and his partner, though the storm, hammering the old building and echoing around inside the cave-like interior.

The smell of moldy hay and ancient ammonia touched the two men's nostrils.

The mules brayed uncertainly.

The two men, former outlaws turned freighters—when they weren't working as unofficial federal lawmen for the devilish scalawag Chief Marshal Luther T. "Bleed-'Em-So" Bledsoe, that was—clambered stiffly down from the wagon. In their late fifties, neither man was as young as he used to be, and they felt the weight of their years— especially during cold, rainy spells like the one they were enduring this night in the Front Range, west of their hometown of Camp Collins, in northern Colorado.

They'd delivered a load of supplies to a gold mine at the west end of Poudre Canyon, and they'd expected to be home by now. The storm had slowed them down considerably.

As the two men unhitched and tended the mules, first rubbing them down and then feeding and watering them, Slash couldn't help thinking of his lovely bride, the former Jaycee Breckenridge, who was waiting for him back in their second-floor suite of the saloon/gambling parlor/brothel that Jay owned in Fort Collins.

"What're you grinnin' about?"

Slash turned to his partner, who was opening a stall door at the rear of the barn. "Huh?"

"What're you grinnin' about?"

Slash led the second mule toward where Pecos was leading the first mule into the stall, the clomping of the mules' hooves on the hard-packed earthen floor all but drowned by the rain, wind, and thunder battering the old barn, making the roof leak in places and the timbers creak.

"I didn't know I was grinnin'."

"Like a jackass with a snoot full of cockleburs. Never mind. I know what you were grinnin' about. Or, should I say, *who* you were grinnin' about," Pecos amended, then gave a wry snort as he stepped out of the stall. "Don't worry. You'll see her soon enough."

"Who?" Slash said, playing dumb, as he led the second mule into the large stall, then set down a bucket of parched corn for the second mule, just as Pecos had done for the first mule.

"Your're newly betrothed, fer cryin' in the queen's ale! You don't have to be embarrassed about bein' eager to see your wife, you know, Slash. There ain't no shame in it." Pecos placed his hand on his longtime partner's shoulder and leaned toward him, as though to impart a closely held secret. "There ain't no shame in missin' your woman. Especially when that woman happens to be one Miss Jaycee Breckenridge!"

"Ah, hell," Slash said, sheepishly brushing a fist across his chin. "It was that obvious, huh?"

"It was that obvious. Let me repeat—there ain't no shame in it."

"I know there ain't no shame in it, you big lummox!" Slash said, removing his hat and batting the excess water from it against his leg. The truth was, however, that despite having been married to Jay for a good six months now and having learned to open up more about his feelings, he still found himself falling back into his age-old natural habit of being reluctant to show those feelings to his male pards.

Or his male pard, as the case was. About the only friend the middle-aged former outlaw still had on this side of the sod was the Pecos River Kid himself. In fact, Pecos might have been the only true friend Slash had ever had, Slash being more than a tad on the contrary and solitary side. It still surprised Pecos that his friend, who was shorter and darker than Pecos's gray-blond six feet four, was finally married, since the only women he'd ever kept company with before Jay had come along were percentage gals.

Whores.

Pecos grinned slyly. "What were you thinkin' about?"

"Huh?" Slash said, indignant.

"Come on. What were you thinkin' about that made you grin that big horse fritter-eatin' grin?"

"Hah!" Slash said as the two men walked back toward the barn's front opening and the gray curtain of rain and flashing light just beyond it. "Wouldn't you like to know!"

Pecos chuckled. "I suppose she's gonna be worried when we don't show up tonight."

He and Slash stopped to regard the storm, neither one overly eager to brave it again, even though they hoped they'd find a surrounding of good hot food inside the saloon, if the Dutchman hadn't closed up on account of the storm. The wavering lamplight in the windows told them he hadn't. The Dutchman, an ex-prospector, lived on the building's second story.

"I reckon she will, but it's probably raining in Camp Collins, too, so she'll likely know why we're delayed." Slash winced, adjusted the set of his hat. "She'll still be worried, though. I don't much like worryin' the gal," he found himself openly admitting. "It's the one thing about marriage . . . in fact, it's the only thing about marriage . . . I've so far found dis agreeable."

"Must be nice, though," Pecos said with a wistful sigh. "Havin' somebody back home worryin' about you."

"You know what you need to do, don't you?" Slash said. "You need to get down on your hands and knees and ask ol' Bleed-'Em-So's queenly secretary to hitch her star to your wa gon. Then you'll have a worrier of your own at home, pinin' for ya an' singin' sad songs when you're away."

Pecos had recently become right friendly with the jade-eyed, golden-haired Nordic beauty Abigail Langdon, though they'd both so far kept that fact from the owly chief marshal himself. Bledsoe had hired Slash and Pecos to do his dirty work—the assignments he didn't feel comfortable saddling his bona fide deputy marshals with, mostly because said assignments were off the books for being in part or in totality *illegal*. Rather, he'd coerced them into working for him, under threat of being hung or sent to prison for their past sundry indiscretions.

But their working for him didn't mean he approved of either former cutthroat.

As a deputy U.S. marshal once himself, Bledsoe had chased the pair and their former gang, the Snake River Marauders, from Canada to Mexico and back again several times without running any of them to ground. He had also taken a bullet from Slash several years back. It had been an inadvertent bullet, a ricochet, but the blue whistler had confined the nasty old gent to a push chair, just the same.

When and if Slash and Pecos went down in a hail of hot lead during the implementation of one of the chief marshal's dangerous assignments, the colicky old federal would shed no tears at their funerals.

"If Bledsoe ever found about me an' Abigail—and if we tied the knot, he would—he'd shoot us both," Pecos said. "Me? I deserve a bullet. Hell, a bullet's too good for me. But I wouldn't want that fate to befall dear Abigail." Pecos gave his big head a sad wag. "Nah, we'll just have to keep meetin' in secret until she finds someone younger and more upstandin'."

"Well, that shouldn't be too hard." Slash grinned.

"You're damn lucky I'm too cold and wet and hungry to whup your ass."

"You'd have to catch me first, ya big lummox.

Speakin' of hunger, come on, partner," Slash said, pulling his hat down tight and lifting the collar of his rain slicker. "Let's go say hi to the Dutchman!"

The two former bank and train robbers ran into the rainy street.

Chapter 2

Slash and Pecos entered the Dutchman's saloon in the nick of time, for even though it was only nine o'clock, the big, blond, long-limbed, and bony Scandinavian had written off any further business this stormy night and was about to blow the lamps out and head upstairs to his living quarters.

He was all smiles to see some company and badly needed business, however, for it had been a quiet several days. After giving the two freighters the key to a room they would share upstairs, where he had five to rent, he hustled back into the kitchen to stoke his stove and fry up a couple of big T-bones and a cast-iron skillet of his signature potatoes, which he cultivated himself in an irrigated garden behind the saloon.

Slash and Pecos chose a table close to the fully stoked and pleasantly ticking potbelly stove, draped their rain slickers over their chair backs, and sat down to nurse the two frothy dark ales the Dutchman had drawn for them.

"Ah, shelter from the storm!" Pecos intoned, lifting his mug to suck some of the froth from the rim of his mug.

"Nice quiet one, just how I like it," Slash said. "The

older I get, partner, the more peace and quiet I like. Less'n, of course, I'm snuggled under the bedcovers with that good-lookin' gal of mine. Then forget the peace *and* the quiet!"

"Sure, sure, rub it in," Pecos groused before taking another sip from his dimpled schooner.

"Sorry about that," Slash said with mock chagrin.

"No, you're not."

"No, you're right. I'm not," Slash said and chuckled. He loved nothing more than to torment his partner out of sheer deviltry.

He sank back in his chair, enjoying the heat emanating from the stove and soaking deep into his cold bones, loosening the age-tender muscles. Now that he was inside and out of it, sitting by a warm fire, he even enjoyed listening to the drumming and whooshing of the storm, the dribbling of the rain down the sashed windows, and watching the intermittent flashes of the lightning.

Peace and quiet, at last. Good beer. Even better food on the way. And a couple of warm beds waiting for him and Pecos upstairs.

Yessir, Slash remarked silently to himself, *you just can't beat it*.

Presently, the drumming of horses rose from the street, as did the shouting of several men. Neither Slash nor Pecos could make out what the men were saying, but the newcomers' tones told them they were pleasantly surprised to have found a still open sanctuary in this otherwise boarded-up, cold, and uninviting ghost town.

"There goes our peace and quiet," Slash said before taking another sip of his beer.

"Oh, well," Pecos said, hauling out his makings to roll

a quirley, "the Dutchman will be pleased as punch for the business."

"I reckon."

When the Dutchman brought two smoking and loudly sputtering platters out from the kitchen, and Pecos informed him of the added business he was likely to get when the newcomers had stabled their mounts, the big, blond, red-faced man rubbed his big, fleshy paws together greedily.

"*Jah*, it is a good night, after all!" He clapped his hands together as he ambled around behind the big mahogany bar with an ornate backbar complete with leaded glass mirror. "*Jah! Jah!* Now we're talking!"

He rubbed his big hands on his apron and adjusted a couple of the glasses arranged in a pyramid on the bar before him. Meanwhile, Slash and Pecos tucked cloth napkins into their shirt collars and hunkered over their platters, eating hungrily. They were both a little over halfway through their steaks and potatoes when shouting sounded from outside again—men exclaiming in jovial tones, as though in celebration.

A woman's cry was added to the din.

Then another.

Slash and Pecos looked up from their meals and exchanged curious frowns.

"Hmm," the Dutchman said, waiting behind the bar and now frowning toward the door, as well.

Boots thumped on the stoop.

"Last one inside's a rotten egg!" a man shouted just outside the door.

The door opened abruptly, fairly flying open, as a man entered with a young woman draped over his right shoulder. She wore a sodden dark blue dress, which clung to her legs like a second skin. She was kicking those legs desperately, struggling inside the grasp of the man who carried her on his shoulder as though she were a fifty-pound sack of oats. The dress's hem was pulled up to reveal soaked pantaloons, also clinging to the young woman's slender legs.

The man was grinning beneath the brim of his high-crowned black hat, from which rain dripped liberally. He was a short, broad-chested man in his middle twenties, with a red mustache and side-whiskers and twin Colts holstered on his hips, beneath a pale linen duster as wet as the dress of the girl on his shoulder.

Another, taller man followed him into the saloon, with yet another young woman draped over his own right shoulder. Both girls—yeah, that was what they were, girls of maybe sixteen or seventeen, Slash judged—complained loudly and kicked their legs and futilely slammed their clenched fists against the backs of the men carrying them. The men only whooped and laughed.

The smaller, red-mustached gent glanced at the Swede standing behind the bar and said, "Hope you got beds upstairs, partner, 'cause that's where we're headed!"

The taller man whooped loudly and followed the small man and his own unwilling cargo toward the narrow staircase rising at the room's rear.

"Stop!" bellowed the plump blonde in a lemon-yellow dress who was draped over the taller man's shoulder. "Put me down! Oh, please put me down this instant. You're *hurting* me!"

As the men and the two complaining girls passed Slash and Pecos's table, the two cutthroats-turned-freighters shared expressions of mute exasperation. Slash, seated facing the front of the room, started to rise from his chair and protest the girls' ill-treatment but froze halfway up from his chair when he saw several more men enter the saloon, all wearing either soaked canvas dusters or rain-beaded oilskin slickers.

They kept coming in, talking and laughing and swatting their hats against their legs, dislodging moisture, until a total of eight men had entered, including the two now mounting the stairs behind Slash. What had stayed Slash's rise from his chair was not only the number of men entering the Swede's watering hole, but also the fact that three of the newcomers were carrying Winchester carbines. The others were armed, as well. Slash could see a few holstered guns and even a couple of sheathed knives inside unbuttoned dusters, or he could see the telltale bulge of said armaments behind buttoned dusters and slickers.

These fellas were armed for bear!

Not possessing a suicide bent, Slash sank back into his chair as the other men favored him and Pecos with passing glances. The last newcomer to enter slammed the door on the continuing storm and followed the others to the bar.

"Gotta be fifty thousand dollars, fellas," announced one of the six heading for the bar, patting a swollen pouch of the saddlebags draped over his shoulder. "Fifty thousand dollars if there's a dime!"

"Sure enough," said another. "I couldn't believe my eyes when we blew the lock off that strongbox and opened the lid. Holy thunder! What a mother lode of greenbacks and coins!" The speaker slapped the shoulder of the portly, shaggy-headed, bearded man bellying up to the bar beside him. They turned to the Swede, who was eyeing them with an uncertain smile on his broad mouth, and, slapping the bar, loudly ordered whiskey and beer.

Slash and Pecos shared another look. This time a *knowing* look. Pecos still held a thick bite of steak and a couple of crispy potatoes impaled with a fork halfway between his plate and his mouth, having frozen in that position when he'd first heard the girls yell.

It was obvious to both former train and bank robbers that the newcomers were outlaws who'd recently taken down a stage, plundered the strongbox, and kidnapped the two young women—a pair of unlucky passengers aboard the coach when the tough nuts had struck. Now those unlucky girls were upstairs with two of the outlaws, with the rest no doubt soon to follow, and the girls' luck was likely heading even farther south.

The obvious question was voiced by Pecos, albeit in a register that couldn't be heard above the celebratory outlaws' jovial din over their run of good luck: "What're we gonna do about this, Slash?"

Slash winced as he cut into his meat with a serrated knife, trying to at least make a casual show of continuing his meal. "I'm open to suggestions." He cut his eyes to the men at the bar, who, with the exception of two standing sideways to it, had their backs to him and Pecos. "The roughtails ain't payin' us any attention at all."

Pecos swung his head for a quick look. "That's 'cause they're young and we're old. They ain't afraid of us."

Slash glanced sidelong at the celebrating firebrands, one of whom had poured the loot out onto the bar and was loudly counting it with the help of one of his pards.

"No damn respect," the former robber said through an angry snarl. "Proba bly think we been freightin' all our lives." He gave a caustic laugh. "If they only knew!"

Pecos jutted his jaw and hardened his eyes at his partner. "Slash, will you keep your damn voice down? If they knew who we were, they'd likely have opened up on us by now, filled us so full of lead we'd rattle when we walked."

"A little respect—that's all I ask!"

"What are we gonna do about those two poor girls up there?" Pecos raised his eyes to the ceiling, from which emanated, beneath the din coming from the six at the bar, the other two outlaws' raised voices and the girls' cries, as well as a good bit of stomping around.

Slash forked potatoes into his mouth and chewed, sliding his furtive gaze between Pecos and the six men at the bar. While he continued to eat, he was no longer hungry, and the food no longer tasted good. "Well, there's eight of them. Two of us."

Pecos stiffly forked more food into his mouth. "Tall odds."

"Maybe too tall."

"You thinkin' if we stick our noses in, you're liable to make Jay a widow after only a half a year's worth of marriage?"

"That might be soon enough for her, after spendin' six months with me . . ."

"You can say that again!"

"But six months ain't long enough for me with her . . ."

"Slash, I do believe you've grown a heart."

"That bein' said, we can't sit here and listen to what

them two girls is goin' through upstairs without at least tryin' to do somethin'."

"Which brings us back to what?"

"True enough." Slash switched his gaze to the bar again and inwardly flinched when he saw that one of the six tough nuts was looking straight at him. Slash feigned a smile and nodded at the man, whose expression grew wistful. He opened his mouth and ran a thumb pensively along his jawline, then, scowling curiously, turned back to the bar.

Slash turned back to Pecos and cursed.

"What is it?"

"One of 'em looked right at me. Like maybe he recognized me."

Pecos shuttled his own gaze to the bar. "Which one?"

"The oldest one of the bunch. The one who carried in the saddlebags."

Pecos studied the man of topic in the backbar mirror, then turned back to Slash. "Ah, hell, you know who that is?"

"Who?"

"Scratch Lawson. We had a run-in with him about ten years ago, when he was still wet behind the ears but meaner'n a stick-teased rattlesnake."

Slash took another quick glance at the man in the mirror. He was of medium height, with curly pewter hair tufting out from beneath his battered, funnel-brimmed cream Stetson. He was long-faced, cow-eyed, and wore several days of pewter stubble on his narrow jaws. His sodden duster bulged where two pistols were holstered on his hips.

"Ah, hell!" Slash said.

"Yeah."

"Our gang got crossways with his gang down in Mexico, when we robbed that *rurale* supply depot. Turns out his bunch, led by Loot Wiley from Galveston, had targeted it, too.We got to it first, and they came after us."

"We killed two of theirs, and they wounded one of ours."

"Bo Gleeson . . . Yeah, I remember."

"I reckon if we're gonna do somethin', we'd best get down to it," Pecos said. "Before Lawson puts names to our faces."

Too late.

The outlaw of topic, Scratch Lawson, suddenly slapped the bar and whipped around to face Slash and Pecos, yelling, "*Slash Braddock and the Pecos River Kid*!"

He grinned and slid both flaps of his wet duster back behind the bone handles of his matched Smith & Wessons.